THE WORLD STILL MELTING

ALSO BY

ROBLEY WILSON

Novels

SPLENDID OMENS

THE VICTIM'S DAUGHTER

Short Fiction

THE PLEASURES OF MANHOOD

LIVING ALONE

DANCING FOR MEN

TERRIBLE KISSES

THE BOOK OF LOST FATHERS

Poetry

KINGDOMS OF THE ORDINARY

A PLEASURE TREE

EVERYTHING PAID FOR

ROBLEY WILSON

THE
WORLD
STILL
MELTING

THOMAS DUNNE BOOKS/ST. MARTIN'S PRESS
NEW YORK

This is a work of fiction. All the characters, organizations, and events portrayed in this book are fictitious or are used fictitiously. Although aspects of the story told in this novel were inspired in some respects by actual events, those events have been completely fictionalized and this book is not intended to portray, and should not be read as portraying, actual events.

THOMAS DUNNE BOOKS.
An imprint of St. Martin's Press.

THE WORLD STILL MELTING. Copyright © 2005 by Blue Garage Co. All rights reserved. Printed in the United States of America. No part of this book may be used or reproduced in any manner whatsoever without written permission except in the case of brief quotations embodied in critical articles or reviews. For information, address St. Martin's Press, 175 Fifth Avenue, New York, N.Y. 10010.

Portions of this novel have appeared earlier, under the titles "Payment in Kind" (*Sewanee Review,* Winter 1985; reprinted in *New American Short Stories: The Writers Select Their Own Favorites* [New American Library, 1987], and in *Terrible Kisses* [Simon & Schuster, 1989]) and "The World Still Melting" (*New England Review,* Fall 1992). The poem on pages 233 to 234 first appeared, as "For a Spring Burial," in *Out of This World: Poems from the Iowa Heartland* (Iowa State University Press, 1980).

I'm indebted to several University of Northern Iowa students, especially Mary Peterson, J. Harley McIlrath, and Elizabeth Wheeler, for their personal and often ironic insights into Iowa farm life.

www.stmartins.com

Book design by Jennifer Ann Daddio

Library of Congress Cataloging-in-Publication Data

Wilson, Robley.
    The world still melting / Robley Wilson.—1st ed.
        p. cm.
    ISBN 0-312-33679-9
    EAN 978-0312-33679-0
    1. Triangles (Interpersonal relations)—Fiction. 2. Married people—Fiction. 3. Rural families—Fiction. 4. Family farms—Fiction. 5. Middle West—Fiction. 6. Farm life—Fiction. I. Title.

PS3573.I4665W67 2005
813'.54—dc22   2004056109

First Edition: February 2005

10   9   8   7   6   5   4   3   2   1

In memory of Richard Rackstraw

PART ONE

ARLENE

1

The tall cottonwood, just east of the long driveway that led out to the county road, was Arlene Tobler's index to the Iowa seasons. It once had been a pair of trees sprung up too close together. Over the years the two trunks had merged, then branched and branched again, higher up. Now the cottonwood was a single enormous tree opened into the shape of a lyre—or so it looked to her from the kitchen window of the farmhouse. The tree had become for her a natural instrument the Iowa winds played as the year revolved.

And it was an official landmark, prominent on the county maps; she knew because Paul had seen the wall chart in the Black Hawk County sheriff's office in Waterloo, and there was the Tobler tree, he told her, five miles northwest of West Fork, in Hagen Township, on the graveled back road to New Hartford, marked on the map by a black cross in a circle of red. Did *they* call it "the Tobler tree," she had wanted to know, the men at the sheriff's department? *They ought to,* Paul had said, *my family planted it.* Seventy feet, eighty feet; she wasn't able to estimate the height of it, and it towered over her perceptions in the same fashion, with the same visual force, as the muggy-summer clouds piled high and black in the western sky before a lightning storm.

When Sarah and Peter were in their teens, they had gathered friends and playmates and begun to build a tree house in the shadowed space where the cottonwood trunks leaned away from each other and crotched, some fifteen feet off the ground. At that height, the floor of the house was to have been an eight-foot-by-six-foot rectangle, the two-by-four frame of it nailed securely at its four corners, and one-by-six boards laid across. Arlene could still see what was left of the house—one joist after all these years fastened to two of the tree's verticals, another secured at one end but fallen at the other, the cross-planking lost and rotted and overgrown in the tall grass and wildflowers and scrub cedar under the tree.

The house was never finished, though the enthusiasm it was started with should have been sufficient to drive it to completion. The girls had lost interest first. They weren't strong enough to lift the lumber up so the boys could fix it in place, and why couldn't they do the nailing while the boys fetched and panted and got splinters? No, the boys said, do it our way. Then, when the girls had drifted away, only Peter stayed on the project—for reasons of his own, and for only a few more days. The other boys got tired of the work and climbed down and raced each other over to the Hansens' barn to put halters on the mares and ride bareback into town to buy soft ice cream at the Dairy Queen.

So much for enterprise. The Tobler children were long since gone off to their own lives, Sarah to children of her own, Peter into his strange sort of exile, and only the wreckage of the tree house remained. But the cottonwood flourished. It was like a clock for the year. In late spring the fluff of its seeds drifted in the bright air like ash, settling in the lee of the toolshed to make a fold of narrow gray blanket against the blocks of the foundation. By the time the great tree had begun to scatter its cotton—and if the spring had not been so wet that it kept Paul's tractor out of the fields—the corn was already planted, already beginning to show the delicate green haze of its new shoots as far as Arlene's eye could reach. In the fullness of summer, the cottonwood leaves shimmered against the hot winds like silver light on water, and the noise of them seemed endless—like tides, like a rushing through palpable time. In autumn those same leaves filled the edges of the driveway, piled up in the corners of the back porch as if they were nests built by wild things, flew past the kitchen windows like flocks of grackles or swallows changing direction as abruptly as chance.

When the tree was bare, when winter had settled in, Arlene would marvel that she was never prepared for it—the harshest season in her life with Paul, the time of being frugal with the electric (though what was there to do if she were not allowed enough light to read by?), of fretting for the year to come, of sitting in silence in the chilled house while the man she married for love pored by the hour over catalogs, or totted columns of profit and loss, or sat by lantern light at a kitchen table covered with newspapers to repair a carburetor or a diesel pump or some small mechanical enigma picked up at an auction earlier in the year because "I could maybe make something of that." Dark mornings she stood at the kitchen sink, the black of the horizon turning slowly to a lavender light, and listened to the crows. Whatever weakness of winter sun emerged, there were the crows, high up in the long, stark branches of the cottonwood—like leaves themselves, only black, not silver—sometimes dozens of them, screaming their relentless *because, because.*

Because I chose it, Arlene would say to herself, meaning the farming, and the schoolteaching vocation she had given up for a man—as if the crows cared enough to be posing questions.

This was August, and Arlene still had the habit of getting up at first light, dressing quietly in the bathroom so she would not wake Paul, and going out to the kitchen to make coffee. Sometimes she used supermarket coffee, and once in a while, if the morning seemed in some indefinable way "special," she would take from the cupboard under the sink the small Braun grinder Sarah had given her two Christmases ago and fill it with Colombian beans she bought at a specialty shop in Waterloo. The beans were small and dark and slippery; they reminded her a little of the Mexican jumping beans her father had bought for her to hold when she was a child, when she had been distressed to learn that the beans jumped because the warmth of her palms roused a tiny worm—some sort of borer—inside.

While the coffee steeped and dripped through, she went out to the front porch to assess the day. This summer, morning after morning, the days had been identical: a lip of yellow-orange along the eastern horizon, over which the light streamed into a bowl of sky that looked leaden but would turn out to be a pale, high blue; the air still, seeming, when she breathed, already to carry nearly enough of the weight of heat to smother her; ragged veils of fog hanging in the shallows of the fields that opened away from the farmhouse and across the county road to the creek, and beyond the creek as far as the eye could reach. And the mornings were not quite silent. The chorus of crickets was constant, there was almost always a solitary robin chirping in one of the cedars and a chatter of cardinals in the cottonwood; from the main highway a mile to the east she could hear the hollow roar of trailer trucks. Somewhere she had read that in silence, absolute silence, you could hear a high-pitched sound that was your own nervous system, and a deep, boiling sound that was the circulation of your blood. If that were true, then the crickets might be her nerves, and the far-off trucks her blood. She didn't know about the robin or the cardinals; something of the spirit, perhaps, that the scientists always left out.

By the time Paul came into the kitchen—at six or seven, depending on what he planned to do with his day—the coffee would be half gone, and he would find her sitting at the table, cup in hand, staring idly out the screen door. He said nothing—he had become a man of rare words; in all these years she still could not claim to know him—but took a mug from the drain board and poured an inch of coffee from the flask. If his first sip told him it was a store brand, he filled the mug and sat opposite her—not like a man making himself comfortable with his wife, but on the edge of the chair, tensed to go about some unannounced business. If the coffee was the Colombian, he muttered something just below her hearing and emptied the stuff into the sink. Either way, his next move was outside, to the weather station he had put together beyond the shed: rain and wind gauges, tools for measuring temperatures and pressures and moistures—instruments acquired as a hobby, but consulted this year with a regularity bordering on the fanatic. No rain had fallen for six weeks, the heat rose into the nineties or hundreds, day after sweltering day; humidities were high, the barometric pressure high, the winds sluggish. There were not even thunderstorms. After ten minutes with his gauges Paul would come in, scowling. "Better close up the house," he said. Never more words than those, and her heart ached for him.

This morning she watched him come back from the ritual of reading the weather and realized, as if for the first time, how truly old he had gotten—or tired, or whatever it was that happened to a man in thirty-odd years of a working life he had never intended. She had known the first time she met him that he was a lover of books like herself, a person of sensibility whose life would be wasted on machineries and crops. It was Karl Tobler's death, before Paul had finished at Iowa State, that made him a farmer—as if he had no choice, as if the land that had been in the family for generations required his love and loyalty and labor.

Now that labor seemed to have drained away much of the measured energy that used to carry him from one chore to another, one outbuilding to another, one dream to another. He walked with his head down, his shoulders slouched, one hand tucked into a pocket of his overalls and the other rubbing absently at the back of his neck. When he came up the porch steps and through the screen door, his sigh was audible, a distress signal.

"Better close up the house."

She had heard the forecast on the television news last night: no relief, no rain, highs close to a hundred degrees. In the southern part of the state the government was letting the farmers turn livestock onto their set-aside land early, and some counties were already eligible for disaster loans. She could not recall another such summer.

Paul stood in the middle of the kitchen. He looked as if he were trying to remember something, as if he had been on his way to a place, a task, and was disturbed to find himself in an unexpected setting. Then he turned toward the sink, took a tumbler down from the cupboard, and filled it with tap water. He studied the water before he drank it. *Dear God,* she thought, *now is he fretting about the well?*

"What is it?" she said.

He drained the glass before he responded, and when he did look at her he compressed his lips in what she took to be an ironic smile.

"I was thinking how my old man could have taken a look at the sky, and at the weather vane on the old barn," he said, "and known just as much about the damned weather as I do by reading all those dials."

"Oh, dear," she said. "Is this going to be the speech against progress?"

"Something like that."

"Take a few minutes and have coffee with me," she said. "You can spare me that."

He pulled out his chair and brushed the orange cat—the indoor cat she had named Grimalkin, "Grimmie" for short—off the seat.

"I'll sit," he said, "but I'll pass on the coffee." He studied her. "What's on the docket this morning?"

"I'm going to can tomatoes—such as they are. Then I'm going into town with Nancy Riker."

Paul heard this information without reacting. Arlene knew what he thought of Harvey Riker's wife: he got along with Harve, but he thought Nance was ditzy and wondered how Arlene could be her friend. To Paul's credit, he had never made much of this, and now his thoughts were already somewhere else, his eyes reading the linoleum patterns off the floor. She drank her coffee; it was lukewarm and slightly bitter.

"I think I'm going to go into that west forty," Paul said. "I walked through it yesterday. Looks to me like it might make twenty percent, but no more."

"You going to chop it for silage?"

He nodded. "Burt Stone can feed it to his damned cattle," He hauled himself to his feet. "While you're in town, get me a six-pack of something."

Most of the morning she spent dealing with the tomatoes. The drought hadn't done them any good; there were plenty of them, but they were small and hard, not anything she would have wanted to serve in a salad. It was hot work; by ten o'clock the thermometer outside the kitchen window had reached 89—and that was in shade.

She was interrupted only once—by a woman in a gold Cadillac, who rolled into the yard in a cloud of white dust and came to the back door to talk to her about Jehovah's Witnesses. In the middle of the serious question of Salvation, Arlene cut the woman short.

"It's a personal matter, isn't it?" she said. "And I've got tomatoes waiting."

The woman went away, leaving behind her a copy of *The Watchtower*. It was only when the Cadillac turned out of the yard that Arlene noticed a man slouched in the passenger seat.

Perhaps the woman's husband, or father; he wore a Panama hat. She thought how she hadn't seen a Panama hat in years and years.

A thick cloud of dust followed the car down the road. All over Iowa these gravel roads were like boundaries, defining the size and shape of the farm fields. Every mile a road to market, east–west, north–south, and heaven help the ignoramus who wanted to build a diagonal. West forty—that's where Paul was chopping down a cornfield that might in an ordinary year have delivered one hundred and seventy bushels an acre, but now wouldn't touch thirty-five because of the weather.

Probably she ought to have said to the Jehovah's Witness lady that she didn't believe in God anyway—that she had used to believe, but in the years of living on this farm with Paul and his insistence on "luck" she had come to see how everything was up to her and to him, how between them each spring they made something appear from nothing just like any magic, any religious power, and how they controlled the earth and manipulated growing things and almost but not quite used the weather to best advantage. She ought to have told her that the roads and fences were what imposed order onto chaos. She ought to have said that eternity was only an endless succession of growing seasons, and if that wasn't argument enough she could have talked about Sarah and about Peter's wildness and about the third child, who never got named. That might have been the last glimmer of her faith; yes, probably it was. And then she ought to have explained to the Jehovah's Witness lady about sweat and machinery and bank loans. What did God know about all that?

She waited until after twelve-thirty to have lunch, hoping Paul would join her even while she knew he wouldn't. She sat at the table in the kitchen, a glass of iced tea and a bowl of bran flakes with milk in front of her, listening to the simmer of the tomatoes on the stove. How much she had gotten used to being alone;

now that Sarah and Peter were gone, her life seemed almost reclusive, her marriage like the ritual passage of a man and woman on tracks that paralleled but rarely crossed.

Yet this was to have been the year for her and Paul to rediscover each other. When the Agriculture people announced in the spring that farmers could set aside as much as eighty percent of their land and be paid with surplus grains already stored, it had seemed to Arlene that for the first time ever her husband would find time heavy on his hands. All the wives shared that belief.

Arlene remembered an evening in this very kitchen, in early March, when Paul and Burton Stone and Jess Eriksen and Harvey Riker had sat playing a card game called pepper and talked about PIK—Payment-in-Kind—while she and Nance Riker sewed in the side parlor. Jess's Carol had died just two months before, of cancer, on a night when the temperature had plummeted to twenty-seven below and nobody's car would start and Jess couldn't be at her hospital bedside when she gave up the ghost. This was his first socializing since the funeral.

"It's nice to see Jess out again," Arlene had said, "but it's too bad he won't have Carol to share all this new leisure everybody's talking about."

"He's lost weight," Nance said.

"Is that it? I know when I first saw him, I thought, 'My God, the man looks ten years older.'"

"I miss Carol," Nance said. "She was the den mother."

"She was," Arlene agreed.

In the kitchen, the men had been discussing the merits and liabilities of the set-aside rules.

"It'll be like going back to the prairies," Burton was saying. "Like the Iowa I knew when I was a kid."

"The hell," Paul said. "The Iowa you knew as a kid was leather jackets and switchblades. What's all this 'prairies' crap?"

Burton grinned. He was the youngest of them—*and the luckiest,* Paul sometimes said—barely forty years old, not married. He had come home from Vietnam to raise cattle on his father's land, had bought an adjoining farm, had just built himself a wonderful new house.

"Burton's too nice to be a bachelor," Nance whispered to Arlene.

That meant Nance wanted to be with the men. "I need coffee, too," Arlene said.

"You know what I mean," Burton said as the two women came into the kitchen.

"Sure do," Nance's Harvey said. "There'll be nothing grown on half my acres this year."

"Not going to plant cover?"

"Weeds cover." He filled his glass from a new bottle of beer; the foam spilled down the sides and puddled on the table top. "If I had horses, I'd plant brome or timothy—maybe alfalfa. But I don't." He lifted the glass and with the side of his palm brushed the spilled beer onto the floor. Arlene winced, but pretended not to see. Harvey was drunk; you made allowances for friends.

"You could do worse than get into the horse business," Jess Eriksen said. "That parimutuel bill's gone through. There'll be racetracks all over."

"You could raise greyhounds," Paul said. "They're legalizing dog tracks, too."

"They make it legal to race Herefords," Burton said, "I'll be sitting pretty."

"Paul here ought to open a bicycle shop," Harve said. "Now the county supervisors have given the old railroad right-of-way to the bike people, there'd be lots of business real close by."

Paul made a show of looking at his cards one by one. "Play the damned game," he said, refusing to be baited. He looked up at Arlene and Nancy. "Why don't you girls get back in the game?"

"No, thank you," Nance said. Arlene had noticed then that she couldn't seem to take her eyes off Burton Stone.

Much later that same night, when the pepper was finished and the men had scraped frost off the windshields of their pickups and gone home through the crisp night, Arlene had lain beside Paul in bed and thought about the spring planting, how it would be affected by the government's payment-in-kind program.

"How come you gals didn't care to play cards tonight?" he wanted to know.

"You didn't seem in the mood for women," she said. "Nance and I felt shut out. I did, anyway."

"Wasn't intended." Paul shifted away from her in bed, rolled onto his stomach and hauled the pillow against his face.

"The way all of you were talking, it sounded as if none of you is happy being a farmer."

"That's just talk," Paul said. "Just joking around."

"And was that really you, saying Iowa was leather jackets and switchblades when Burton was growing up?"

"Let it pass," Paul said, and Arlene knew she had overstepped, harping on the knife word.

"I suppose it might be all right," she said. "Not planting so many acres. Letting things go a little way back to nature."

"Don't get all romantic," Paul said. "It's just for this year, probably; nobody's inviting the Indians back to chase buffalo."

"Maybe we could do more things together, you and I."

"Maybe," he said. "We'll see what comes along this summer." He'd pulled the covers up to his chin. "You going to sit up and read?"

"I was thinking about it," Arlene said, wondering if she was in the mood for Jane Austen.

Paul grunted. Then he said, "Is something going on between Nance Riker and Burton?"

Arlene had felt a shiver along her spine. "I don't know," she said. "Why?"

"The way the two of them look at each other," he said.

"Sometimes I think Nance isn't very happy with Harvey." That was as much as she was going to say to Paul about what might be going on with her best friend. She got her book off the nightstand, found her place, and started to read. *All these daughters to marry off,* she thought. *We were lucky to have only Sarah.*

"Just goes to show," Paul said. "Money can't buy it. Harve made a real killing ten years back when he sold half the farm to that developer from the Cities. Now his wife's mooning over a younger man, and I do believe Harve's doing more drinking than is good for him."

"Nance doesn't complain," Arlene had said, "but it can't be easy for her."

She turned a page. She knew some things about the Rikers, but it was a topic she didn't want to pursue in bed.

Paul raised himself on one elbow. "You really think I was smart to sign up for this PIK program?"

"Aren't you comfortable with it?"

"I might get that way." He lay back. "I might set aside that northeast corner where I need to put in tile; I'd probably have the time—and Harve might want to do the tiling on his side."

"You should talk to him about it," she had said. Of course he would find a way to avoid leisure; that was Paul, and always had been.

He had chuckled then. "That Kraut s.o.b.," he said, "giving me grief about that damned bicycle trail. He knows how I feel. He knows the railroad people promised the farmers to give back the right-of-way if they ever closed down the line."

Then he fell asleep.

She found it amazing that Paul was always able to sleep, no matter what was bothering him, no matter what he felt passionate or frustrated about. The bike trail business was typical. He railed against it, spent hours reviewing actions he might take, had once called a lawyer—that fall, when the Illinois Central spokesman first made the announcement about giving the railroad's abandoned right-of-way to the county parks commission—even though Harvey Riker had warned him that the lawyer would charge him more than a dollar a minute for his advice. Sometimes the trail seemed to have become an obsession with him; some days he ate it and drank it and worried it from morning until night. Yet here he was, dead to the world, snoring the snore that once had kept Arlene awake, but now was the lullaby she could not have slept without. No matter his waking wars; at night he was at peace with himself. Or perhaps his argument with the Illinois Central went on in dreams.

She knew, from talking with Nance, that at home Harvey Riker shared Paul's dissatisfaction with the railroad people. For Harve, land was money; for Paul, land—the having of it—was important for its own sake. The Riker and Tobler farms were adjacent, and both bordered the I.C. tracks to the south. When the two men were together the trail was a perpetual topic, according to Nance, though she admitted she couldn't always hear what they were saying as they drank coffee or a cold beer in her kitchen. She thought they were making plans, Nance said to Arlene, but she couldn't imagine what the plans might be. She was sure they also put their heads together when they were at the Happy Chef in Cedar Falls. Arlene wondered if they wrote letters—poison-pen letters—to the railroad people.

"I doubt it," Nancy had said. "Harvey's a lot of things, but he's no letter writer." Then her eyes would seem to glaze over, and Arlene knew she was thinking of all the things Harvey *was,* and how none of those things could hold a candle to the virtues she thought she'd found in Burton Stone.

Since that night, Paul had said less and less about the bike trail—as if whatever he thought of it, there was nothing useful to be done. This summer the trail had become a fact, and its formal dedication was only a couple of weeks away. Arlene was relieved that the deed was done, that Paul could put his mind to his life and his work—but it had already turned out to be a false hope that between the drought and the setting aside of additional acreage the two of them would have more time to themselves.

Arlene rinsed her lunch dishes and left them in the sink. Some of the jar lids had already popped; the rest would have to talk to themselves without her. It was time to pick up Nance; Paul could make himself a sandwich when he felt like it.

The Shed was a small, white-clapboard place on the outskirts of town. It was a man's restaurant—local farmers, truckers passing through—but the two women stopped in for coffee on the way home from the shopping mall. At the largest of the chrome and Formica tables, men in overalls were talking and joking. The men's conversation was not steady; long periods of silence intervened, so that what was said made a pattern of loudness and silence—a rhythm appropriate to custom and long friendships.

Neither Nancy nor Arlene had bought much. Arlene had rummaged through the remnants in a fabric shop until she found a length of cotton she might make into a summer shirt for Paul, and she had stopped off at the Hy-Vee to buy his six-pack of Old Milwaukee. Nancy had bought nothing—had seemed to fall further and further into depression as she followed Arlene past the rows of stores in the mall. She was a year or two younger, a small, solemn-eyed woman whose black hair was shot through with gray and whose skin was so pale as to seem translucent. Now she sat across from Arlene, digging through her purse until she found a cigarette package with two cigarettes left. She offered one to Arlene.

"No," Arlene said. "Thank you." She had not smoked in nearly ten years; she didn't propose to start again.

"I don't know why that shopping mall upsets me," Nancy said. She lit the cigarette, then immediately set it to smolder in the ashtray.

"At least it was air-conditioned."

"I think it's something to do with all those children—those teenyboppers, or whatever they call them now. How can they bear to—to just wander like that?"

"I suppose it's that they're young," Arlene said. Nance had something on her mind, though it was not clear what it was.

Something to do with Burton, or Harvey, or both; Arlene could only wait. Half she was curious; half she dreaded whatever confidence Nance would finally share with her.

The coffee arrived. Arlene poured a little sugar into her spoon and stirred it into the cup.

"Do you think they look forward to anything?"

"Those youngsters? I certainly hope so." She smiled at Nancy. *Am I reassuring?* she thought, *or am I just turning into a Pollyanna?* "Doesn't everybody?"

"I wonder. Sometimes, evenings when I want to be by myself, I drive the highway into Waterloo, and I see those thirteen-and fourteen-year-old girls standing at the corners, leaning against the traffic-light poles. I swear—I almost know how they feel. Waiting for something. Not really knowing if they'll recognize it when it arrives."

"I think it's always a boy with a car," Arlene said.

"And what scares me," Nancy said, "is maybe they're more like us than we give them credit for."

"No," Arlene said. "For us it was a boy with a tractor."

"Isn't that the truth?" Nance stubbed out the unsmoked cigarette. "Do you ever try to imagine what life would be like if you hadn't married a farmer?"

"No. Not since the first two or three years."

"I do," Nancy said. "Dear God, I do."

Arlene waited, but Nancy only looked down at the coffee cup cradled in her palms and shook her head.

"I've thought about being married to a different kind of farmer," Arlene said. "I've thought, 'What if we kept hogs?' "

She saw the shiver in Nancy's shoulders, hoping the movement meant laughter.

"Oh, Arlene." Nancy raised her head. The barest trace of tears glistened at the corners of her eyes, but she was giggling. "Hogs, Arlene. The smell, the dirt, the awful noises they make. And they eat people."

"Hog heaven," Arlene said.

"Living high off the hogs," Nancy said. She got a handkerchief out of her purse and dabbed at her eyes. "Hog city." She subsided. "I'm sorry," she said. "You're such a funny person when you want to be."

"And sometimes I do want to be," Arlene said. She glanced around the cafe. The men were still self-absorbed; the waitress was at the cash register, sorting through meal checks. "You have to be able to laugh at yourself—it's such a crazy way to live."

"This is the worst yet."

"I know." Of course she didn't, but she assumed it had something to do with marriage. "You can't think life is all strawberries and cream with Paul and me."

"I don't even get a civil sentence out of Harvey. I lie awake these hot nights and I think I'd rather be anywhere else, doing anything else. Anything."

"Years and years ago, when Sarah and Peter were both nutty about riding, I did use to think Paul and I could have made a good thing out of raising horses. The war in Vietnam was still on. Sarah had that wonderful quarter horse Paul picked up at the sale barn in Waverly, and Peter talked us into buying him that huge gelding, Lopez, that was part quarter and part thoroughbred. Sixteen and a half hands. I thought we'd have to carry a stepladder so Peter could get up on him." She smiled, remembering. The very thought of horses made her sentimental, because . . . Because it was long before the terrible business between Peter and the Jensen boy. "Peter was ten or eleven, I can't think which."

"Sarah stayed with horses a long time," Nancy said.

"She had a year of college left when she finally decided she couldn't keep up with the work of it, couldn't really give Cloud the care and the exercise."

"I'd forgotten what she called it."

"Red Cloud. He was a chestnut gelding." She picked up the check and looked at the numbers. "Sometimes I really wish we'd gone into the horse business. The weather wouldn't affect us quite so much—I mean, it would affect feed prices, but it couldn't wipe us out."

"There's other things," Nancy said. "Like in Texas a few years back. Equine something. You recall they used to have that margarine commercial on the television, about not trying to fool Mother Nature? That's what's wrong with marrying a farmer, and it doesn't matter if you raise corn or beans or pigs or horses. You can't fool Mother Nature, but it's okay for Mother Nature to fool you."

"Why not let me buy the coffee?" Arlene said.

"I think it's my turn," Nance said.

"Next time," Arlene insisted.

She laid a pair of dollar bills on top of the green slip of paper. She watched Nance take out the last cigarette and crumple the package beside her coffee mug.

"I dread going home," Nancy said. "There's nothing there I can laugh at," and as she gathered up check and bills, Arlene could see the shimmer of real tears in her friend's eyes.

W hen she had left the money at the cash register, and the two of them were in the pickup, Nancy reached out her arms to give Arlene a sweaty hug.

"You're so good for me," she told Arlene. "You're the nicest person I know."

"Oh—Nance," Arlene said. She felt awkward, being held this way, wanting to hug back but not exactly knowing how to do it—and not knowing the real reason for this sudden affection. She stroked Nancy's hair; it felt coarse, like a tattered scouring pad. She gave Nance a light kiss on the cheek. In the confined cab, the younger woman's perfume seemed too sweet. "I'm just a good listener, I guess."

Nancy sat back and turned the rearview mirror down to look at her face.

"God," she said. "Harvey'll say, 'Peeling onions again?' That's the only reason women cry, in his world. Or maybe when they're in labor—but he wouldn't know about that, and neither would I." She dabbed at her cheeks with something out of her purse—some kind of makeup base in a round black compact.

"He doesn't seem to know much," Arlene said.

Nancy faced her. One side of her face still showed tear traces.

"Sometimes I wonder if I could get along without him," she said. "I really wonder. Maybe I can, and maybe all these years the reason I've thought I can't is just that I'm used to him. Just a habit is all he is."

Arlene felt her stomach turn, a pocket of fear blossom in her chest. If she started the truck, put it in gear, would Nancy stop saying whatever it was she seemed determined to say? Maybe—although the desire not to share Nance's secrets was no less strong than the curiosity to *know*. She turned the key, pulled the shift lever into first, let the pickup groan out of the parking lot toward the highway. Nancy was patching the streaks under her other eye.

"I've been seeing Burton," Nancy said, not looking away from the mirror.

Arlene couldn't think of anything to respond with. *I knew you'd say that.*

"I know. He's young for me—that's what's going through your head. I'm a good dozen years older than him. More, maybe."

"Is it serious?"

Nancy put away the makeup and rested her hands on her purse. "God," she said. "Everything's serious in this world."

"I mean to say, how serious is it? Do you want to leave Harvey?" *This is none of my business,* Arlene thought. *I should listen, but I shouldn't prompt.* "You don't have to answer."

The pickup idled at the edge of the highway. Now the traffic from both directions had thinned out, and she looked at Nancy, as if to say: Should we go?

"Yes," Nancy said. She made a frustrated gesture with her hands. "Go ahead. Drive. There's not much to tell."

"If you *should* tell," Arlene said, wanting to give Nance the opportunity to reconsider, to let herself change the subject.

"I don't know if I want to leave Harvey," Nance said. "I know I have every reason—his temper, the times he's hit me or pushed me, the things he calls me—but I don't know what he'd do if I left."

"Would you live with Burton?"

"I think so. We've talked about it some."

"Do you love him?"

"I guess," Nance said. She leaned one elbow against the windowsill. "Oh, Leenie. It isn't like it was some torrid affair out of a Harlequin book—just a couple of times, two or three. At his place, usually. It started—by accident, I guess you'd have to say. I'd stopped by because he asked me—this was a long time ago, when we were all over at your place for cards last winter— He'd asked me for that casserole recipe. You remember? The one with the asparagus and the cheese and macaroni all the men liked so much. He said—you probably heard him—that he wondered if a bachelor could cook up something like that, and I'd told him I didn't think recipes knew if they were being used by men or women, hitched or unhitched. He'd thought that was funny— what a nice smile he has, don't he? Anyway, I stopped by to give him the recipe."

"And that's when it started?"

"Not exactly then. He met me at the back door, him and that black Lab of his—I thought that old dog was going to take my leg off, but Burton just spoke to him once and he simmered right down, went off and laid down somewhere—and I could see he was in a strange mood. He seemed serious—too serious for Burton Stone, anyway. Then he told me he'd been up in the attic, that he'd been thinking about cleaning it out, getting rid of a lot of old stuff that had been stuck up there when his father died— and that's better than ten years ago. What happened was, he'd found a lot of old photographs of his parents, and of him and his sister—she was a couple of years older than Burton—when they was kids. Well, you know, it had sort of made him moody. I remember I put my arm around him and hugged him a little—God, who'd have thought all my hugging would finally get me in Dutch?—told him I understood how he felt."

"Nothing wrong with giving sympathy," Arlene said. She watched the road, directing most of her attention to her driving. Maybe Nancy was exaggerating this thing. Sympathy was all right; caring was all right. *We're all neighbors, old friends.*

"He'd also found an old recipe box, he told me. His mother's, he guessed, though it might have been the property of an aunt of his that used to live in the house with them. Anyway, he'd found an apple cobbler recipe, and there were still some apples in the shed from last season—Cortlands—and he thought he'd try his hand at making cobbler. 'Don't nobody ever say I'm not a brave man,' he said. 'Who would dare?' I said. Well, the next thing I knew I was saying I'd come to lunch the next day and try his cobbler."

She looked at Arlene, leaning as if to catch her eye without distracting her from the highway.

"Aren't I all innocence?" Nancy said. "I'm married twenty-six years to the same man, I look old enough—damned near—to be Burton Stone's mother, all the two of us are doing is swapping recipes like a couple of old biddies at the Suds & Duds. There's nothing to tell Harvey; he goes into town to have his lunch at the Happy Chef six days out of seven. What's he care?"

"Harvey and Paul are birds of a feather," Arlene said, knowing that Paul followed almost the same ritual, showing up two or three days a week, noon sharp, at the Happy Chef. And ate the same meal: steak and eggs and hash browns, coffee and carrot cake. "They're both creatures of habit."

"Anyway, when I got there next day, Burton was just closing the oven door on the cobbler, and apologizing that he had to leave me for a couple of minutes while he went out to the shed for cream—that's where he keeps this old refrigerator that used to be his daddy's. So I walked out with him; it was that first balmy day in the middle of May, and you know how when the weather makes its mind up to really give us summer, it's like catnip to an old fool like me."

"Paul always says Iowa's got just the two seasons: winter and summer."

"I was feeling frisky," Nance said. "Jokey. You can tell Burton's not used to being around women, and I know—thinking about it afterward—he had his mind on his sister, who was probably the woman he was closest to in his whole life."

"Is she not alive?"

"Died when he was in Vietnam, in a car wreck. He told me about it later on."

"That's too bad," Arlene said.

"One thing led to another," Nance said. "We were in the shed, that shut-in air so hot and close and, you know, smelly with manure and Burton's cows and that wonderful man-sweat I don't believe I'll ever outgrow being bothered by."

Nance let out a long sigh; the pickup engine drummed, the tires whined on the pavement. Now they were at the end of the Riker driveway, and Arlene kept her eye on the rear-view mirror as she made the left turn onto gravel. "Anyway, he kissed me. Or I kissed him. I don't know which it was; probably both."

"Probably," Arlene echoed, picturing the scene, wishing she had a little less imagination.

"Then we walked back to the house and sat in his parlor on the sofa. We were all over each other—almost before I knew what was happening, or why it was happening. I can't tell you how crazy I felt. Then I got scared." She covered her face for a moment, remembering. "He wanted me to come upstairs with him. I said no—that time. But since then—"

"I don't think you ought to be telling me all this," Arlene said. Any other day when they went to the mall in Waterloo, they sang Girl Scout songs on the way home; they didn't exchange true confessions. She stopped the truck. Nancy opened the door and stepped down to the bare yard.

"You can't imagine what he's like," she said. "What a sweetheart he is."

"Whatever happened to the cobbler?" Arlene said.

Nancy laughed, standing beside the truck, ready to close the door between them.

"We never had it," she said. "He forgot all about it being in the oven, and by the time we smelled it, it was burned so bad he had to throw it out."

Driving home, Arlene saw a teenage girl on horseback. The sight conjured everything that made her daydream: her children, her expectations for the years ahead and the complacencies of years long past. She saw Kentucky, the expanse of bluegrass dotted with graceful, powerful animals. She remembered Peter astride Lopez, Sarah on Cloud, the two of them riding side-by-side up the long driveway. She ached at the memory of a young Paul, baling hay off the ten acres they set aside in those horse-owning times for alfalfa one year, brome the next, and there came to her all in an instant one night when Paul had come into the house exhausted, face and neck sunburnt and covered with chaff, the sweat dripping off him, drenching his undershirt—how he had lifted her, carried her upstairs and kicked the bedroom door shut behind him. The heat of him, she remembered; the ardor of his loving her in that summer room, almost as if he were a newlywed and he and Arlene just beginning to teach each other love.

The girl was in a hollow on the other side of a gravel crossroad, mostly hidden by the crown of it. All Arlene could see of her was from the shoulders up—and not always that much, sometimes just her head, because of the movement of the animal under her. It looked as if the girl was going at a canter, and for a few moments Arlene slowed the car to admire the way the girl carried herself, her chin high, her long brown hair streaming out behind her. She could have been the twin of young Sarah. Arlene wondered if the horse looked anything like Cloud.

Then the rider rose out of the ditch onto the shoulder of the road, and there wasn't any horse under her after all—only an all-terrain vehicle, three-wheeled, rubber-tired, painted a vivid red that glowed in the light of the sun low on the horizon, and made Arlene squint as if the image hurt her eyes. She knew how Paul would have reacted to this scene; she could hear herself saying for the thousandth time: *Oh, dear Paul. Is this the speech against progress?*

2

Just in the hours since she and Nance had been at the mall, a portable sign had appeared in front of Jess Eriksen's produce stand:

SORRY

CLOSED FOR THE SEASON

THANK YOU

GARDEN DRIED UP

The stand was shuttered tight; the fields beyond the Eriksen house and barn and toolshed were either brown or bare. She should tell Paul. He would shrug, look off into that space where he could not be followed.

She drove off the blacktop onto the county road. Inside the fences the fields of corn were brown, straggly, practically worthless. Only the ditches showed anything healthy, and even the green weeds were faded under a thick coating of dust. Nance's misery was commonplace; they all felt it: What sort of life was it, that you could be fifty-five years old, a good mother, a patient wife, a strong worker, yet you had no more money, or leisure, or happiness than the day you chose the risk of marriage? Even Arlene's own mail-box mocked her—its support made from an old ploughshare painted bright red, and the box in the shape of a barn with TOBLER printed on its sides as if her husband's name were no different than a billboard for Mail Pouch tobacco. How could you blame Nancy if she wanted a little excitement?

She stopped at the box to gather in the mail. A pleasure horse magazine she had never had the heart to cancel, even after the children left home. A letter from her mother in South Dakota, addressed in the failing hand that sent a chill of fear through her—if she let herself think about it. Paul's *Farm Journal*. She laid everything on the seat beside her.

Driving up the narrow lane to the house, she found the farm-yard crowded with young people on bicycles—perhaps a dozen of them, all on the flimsy "English" bikes of her childhood: nar-row handlebars, hand brakes and skinny tires, the curious loop of chain at the rear axle, the high, pointed saddle seats that always looked too uncomfortable to be sat on. Some of the bikers wore white helmets that perched on top of their heads and strapped under their chins to make them look like hockey players or TV roller skaters. Boys or girls, they wore cutoffs that showed their lanky, tanned thighs, and sneakers without socks or colorful bik-ing shoes with knee stockings; some of them had on t-shirts with slogans: "Scrambled eggs and beer—not just for breakfast any-more" or "Bikers are better lovers." The girls had blond hair streaked from too much sunlight, or long, dark hair that flowed down to their narrow waists, or short, boyish cuts that caught in damp curls against their foreheads. Most of the men had mus-taches or beards; they looked like brothers from one enormous family. Paul was in the midst of them, shouting, and Arlene's heart sank. This had happened before, in March, when the bikers first brought around their petition asking support for the bike trail along the old Illinois Central right-of-way. Paul refused to sign, and long after the railroad had given the land to the county he was more furious than ever—had tried to form a committee with other farmers, but gave up when Jess Eriksen accused him of wanting to lead "a goddamn bunch of vigilantes." Only Harvey Riker had been on Paul's side.

She parked the pickup in the shade of the barn and approached the group.

"I've got a living to make," she heard Paul say. "You think it makes me happy to see good farmland wasted?"

"It's already done," one of the bikers said. "The county's already made it a bike trail. All we're asking is for you to meet us halfway—respect our right to use it and help us protect it."

Now Arlene could see they were not all young people. They were various ages—late teens to late thirties—and they were serious-faced, intent.

"A strip of land like that might make the difference between profit and loss for me someday," Paul said. "Next spring I've got to plant fence line to fence line. If this year doesn't put me in the poorhouse."

A bearded man nearby turned his front wheel toward Arlene and winked. "Farmers," he said. "I've never met one yet that wasn't losing his shirt. They only keep farming because it's so much fun."

She wondered whether or not to be angry with him. "I'm his wife," she said. "You have to understand that he's telling the truth. That land was his—at least it was his great-grandfather's—long before the railroad needed it."

"This is only about the bridge," the bearded man said, "the I.C. bridge over the West Fork. Some farmers out in Winthrop set fire to a bridge just like it, really wasted it. We're talking to all the farmers around here, asking them to keep an eye out for that kind of thing."

"My husband's not one of your fans," Arlene said.

"We're not asking him to love us. Just live and let live."

Arlene smiled at him, liking him. "That seems simple enough."

She went on into the house, put the mail on the table and

the six-pack into the refrigerator. The air in the kitchen was humid with canning heat. A solitary fly buzzed against one of the windows. "Wasted," the young man had said of the bridge in Winthrop, and she wondered if he had been in Vietnam, one of the lucky ones, like Burton, who'd come back unhurt. She went upstairs and changed into a pair of blue shorts she would never have considered wearing outside the house and came back down to the kitchen. Paul was standing inside the door, looking out. The bicyclists were just turning onto the county road, bent over their handlebars like jockeys, a glitter of sun dancing off their machines.

"What do you think of that?" Paul said.

"I think it was polite of them to talk to you."

"You know what's going to happen," he said. "Kids littering the place with trash from McDonald's, soda cans, candy wrappers. Wrecking the fences."

"They aren't all kids," she said. "Some of them are nearly as old as you or me."

"Second childhood," Paul said. "Then we'll have beer cans along with the soda cans, and condoms instead of candy wrappers."

He went to the refrigerator, took out one of the cans of beer she had just put in.

"That'll be warm," she said.

He opened it anyway. "What's a strip of dirt mean to somebody who can spend three, four hundred dollars on one of those fancy bicycles?" he said.

"Oh, Paul—" But words to argue with him wouldn't come— as if she couldn't betray him even when she wished to.

"I know," he said. He sat heavily and laid his cap on the table. "It isn't like me to bitch all the time."

"It's the drought," she said.

"It's everything. I chopped that field this morning and just got madder and madder. I thought, five or six weeks from now we'll get a damned foot of rain, and it'll be too late."

He took a drink from the warm can and made a face.

"What I know is, I need land one whole hell of a lot more than a bunch of overgrown babies on two-wheelers."

"You'll have the PIK money," she said.

"And that's a joke." He gave her a look that was nearly scornful. "I didn't have the brains to set aside that much, and anyway, it's the big company farms that'll rake in most of the PIK money, and the grain dealers that'll get rich, handling corn from five years ago all over again."

He set the beer can aside.

"It's the principle of the thing," he said. "The President of the United States gave this land to my great-great-grandfather—the only decent thing the government in Washington ever did for the Tobler family. No one ought to ask me to give it up—not any of it."

"It's such a tiny bit."

"I don't care if it's no bigger than a goddamned postage stamp." He put on the cap and yanked its bill down over his eyes. "I'm going into town where the beer's cold," he said.

But the bike trail doesn't matter, she wanted to say, watching him climb into the cab of the pickup, hearing him grind the gears in frustration. It was the weather and the government both, and Paul knew he couldn't beat either one of them.

For the rest of the day she tried to keep busy. She hauled the sealed Mason jars down to the basement and shelved them alongside the green beans she had done the summer before. She thought about the young man who was probably a Vietnam veteran, and how fortunate it was that Peter had been too young for that war, too young for more crazy violence in his life. She did the laundry, though she might have put it off another day or two, and got out the mending basket to do some odds and ends she'd been saving for cooler weather. Once she looked up from sewing a shirt button to see that the light had changed sharply. Clouds, she imagined. In the excitement of thinking there might be rain, she went outside for a moment to look westward, but it was simply dust in the air.

It was not like Paul to solve his problems by drowning them. To have a few drinks—that was all right, but he hated to be drunk, to feel he had given up control. What he liked—and it mostly amused her—was to clown with her, to giggle, make bad jokes, pat her lewdly on the buttocks. She'd wake up in the middle of the night and the bedroom would smell sweet, like apples fermenting, and she'd remember his careless passion. But lately . . . no, she could not say what had changed. Something that frightened her, a desperation, a willfulness. *Dear heaven, if I can't put my mind on something pleasant, I'll start inventing trouble when there's already plenty to go around.*

One distant summer, when the children were still young and at home, still interested enough in horses to feed and groom them as well as ride them, Arlene took them to Kentucky, to the marvelous green expanse of the countryside around Lexington, to visit the horse farms. Paul had not gone—couldn't get away, he said; the land needed him.

The second day she drove to Calumet Farm, still full of the pleasure of Walnut Hall the day before, where Sarah and Peter had driven a foreman crazy with questions. Walnut Hall didn't breed racehorses; the children—Sarah especially—had begged for Calumet, but when the three of them arrived at the Calumet gate they were stopped by a sign: NO VISITORS. Peter took the matter calmly, acidly: "If they think they're too good for us, then that's just fine with me." Sarah cried. Arlene was disappointed. Beyond the forbidden entrance they could see white buildings trimmed in red, with red-roofed cupolas. "So near and yet so far," she'd said to Peter.

In Lexington she tried to make up for the morning's failure by taking the children to a fancy restaurant, but there was no forgetting. Sarah was impossible, Peter merely petulant. After the dismal lunch she went to a public telephone and looked up the Calumet number in the book.

"I'm terribly sorry," said the woman who answered the phone. "Calumet Farm is open for persons in the horse business—not for tourists."

"I'm here with my two children," Arlene said. "We drove all the way from Iowa. As it happens, we own a quarter horse named Cloud and a part-thoroughbred named Lopez. Does that put us in the horse business?"

There had been a lovely silence.

"You all come on ahead," the woman said. "Park at the main office and I'll find one of the men to show you around."

Then they had been allowed everywhere except the breeding barns—the stables, the tack rooms, the meadows surrounding. In Arlene's memory the fences were an astonishing white, the trim of the buildings a dark, perfect red, the bluegrass deep and green. She and the children had reached through the rails to stroke the blazes of chestnut-colored yearlings with names engraved on brass plates riveted to their halter straps: Sunglint, Morning Sun—names she had never forgotten. Even grown up and scattered, Sarah and Peter remembered Citation, a Triple Crown winner—an enormous bay stallion, nearly twenty-five, shambling alongside his groom like a solemn old man lost in his memories. Not many years after, when she read of Citation's death, Arlene had wanted to cry, had left the room so Paul wouldn't question her.

That wonderful summer. Traveling without Paul, coping with the two children, gaining them entry to a forbidden place. It had been the proudest and happiest family event of all her married life. Nothing could steal that from her—not bad weather or poor crops, not Peter's ordeal a year later, not the deceit of businessmen or the sins of neighbors and friends.

She woke up in the black of night, alone in the bed. Paul's side had not been slept in; neither his warmth nor his reassuring man's smell was on the bedclothes. She imagined him sitting in the D-Town Tap, drinking beer and quarreling with the others—farmers, some of them, but laid-off factory workers too, and truckers between hauls—a small army of men whose occupations had lost their value or vanished entirely. Sensible family men getting drunk.

She looked at the alarm clock, on the nightstand on Paul's side of the bed. Its greenish-yellow hands showed nearly four o'clock. The Tap closed at two. If he'd gone off to play pepper with his usual cronies, he would never have stayed out so late. He wasn't the sort to sit in a pickup on a back road and drink beer with a buddy—hadn't done such a thing since college, since coming home from Korea.

She got out of bed and went to the bathroom. In the harsh glare of the overhead light she closed her eyes and touched the lids with her fingers. Her hands were hot on her cheeks; the nightgown clung to her back and sides. It used to be that you could depend on the nights to cool down, and you closed the doors so you and your husband could say silly words to each other in whispers that wouldn't alert the inquisitive children—to what? To the secret that you cared more for each other than for weather and work?

She tidied herself, turned out the light, went through the hallway and gingerly down the front staircase. This year everything was weather. The sun, dry days, a crying need for rain. The dust would be far worse when the farmers in Kansas and Nebraska did their fall plowing. Then in late September and October she would notice the whole western sky dark orange—like the eerie approach of a tornado—and for days the tawny dust would be thick on everything: cars and trucks and machinery, windowsills and porch railings. When it rained—and finally it would pour, Paul was right—if you caught the rain in a bucket or pan it would be murky with Plains dirt. All those concerns lay between Paul and herself. Those and more: practical matters like credit at the Farm Fleet, credit for parts needed to overhaul the machinery in time for spring plowing and planting. And what to plant, how much to plant, what would the government—the crazy-dumb Congress—do next? Arlene understood without being able to tell Paul—in Paul's language—that what absorbed and frightened him likewise frightened her.

Dear Paul.

She felt her way down the front hall, unlatched the screen door and stepped onto the porch. A slight, warm breeze brushed across her face and bare arms, and sighed in the branches of the nearest ash. Too early for the robins. The night was almost black; there was no moon, but off to the east she saw the glow of light that was Waterloo, and due south from where she stood was a throbbing of light she could not at first make sense of. It seemed to be—it was—where the old I.C. right-of-way met the West Fork near Dysart. *Dear Paul.* She wanted the light to be— Anything safe. A campfire, a bonfire tended by some of the teachers-college students having a kegger to celebrate the beginning of classes. False dawn.

Now, back in bed, she could not drift back into sleep. She tried to imagine what Nancy Riker was doing—whether like herself she was lying awake, fretful for what Harvey might be doing, where he was drinking (and how much), and was he getting himself into trouble. But something was going on in Nancy's life that made her different from Arlene. Now that Arlene was sure it involved young Burton Stone, she still couldn't quite imagine the boundaries, the limitations of that "going on." Infidelity. It was a crime—or a sin—she believed herself incapable of committing against Paul, just as she believed Paul incapable of betraying her.

Was that true? Was she as sure of Paul as of herself? They had in fact taught each other. Both of them, in college, naïve as children, finding each other out—their pleasures, their hesitations, their amazed explorations and startling sexual hungers. They had begun by touching, first accidentally, then deliberately. They kissed, seriously and for the first time, one night as he was putting her on the bus to Ankeny. When spring came, Paul bought an ancient Ford coupe, and with warmer weather they began parking on secluded gravel roads, far away from town, where they could sit in the rumble seat and see the stars. They necked, talked in whispers. They had begun wanting each other.

One night she invited Paul up to her room. They read poetry to each other—Paul was in Oral Interpretation, so he declaimed, rather than read—and after "To His Coy Mistress" the two of them undressed each other, half scared, half desperate, and went to bed together, reveling in their nakedness and kissing hotly, but stopping short of intercourse. A week later Paul proposed to her.

Paul could never have turned from her to another; he would have been too embarrassed, too afraid of getting lost on the unfamiliar ground of another woman's body. He was a man wedded to basics; there were hardly any frills in his life. Consider the matter of coffee, Arlene reminded herself. When she ground beans and used fancy Colombian or Sumatran blends, Paul turned up his nose. They were unfamiliar—their aromas, their excess demand on his notion of the "proper," the familiar. It was supermarket coffee he was accustomed to and therefore preferred, and it was the familiar cans she saved for him when the coffee was used up, knowing he would fill each of them with assortments of screws and nails, paintbrushes and rusty hooks, nuts and bolts, washers—all those Folger's and Maxwell House coffee cans in a row in the shed, like a wall of stained glass in a church. The time she had bought the mocha-flavored beans and brewed the expensive after-dinner coffee, its aroma as sweet as candy, Paul had left the kitchen. For almost an hour he had sat on the porch, arms folded, his gaze set across the fields to the rising moon. It was as if by her pretension to a higher taste she had insulted and demeaned him. Dear Paul; nothing could have been further from her mind, and when he came inside, sheepish because he didn't know how to explain his behavior, or how to apologize for it, she tried to make light of him—but gently, not mocking or unkind.

Nancy would have mocked, for she had a different sort of marriage. It was no less austere—as if no farmer could spare the time for a proper expression of love toward his woman—but it was a far colder marriage than Arlene's. It was a childless union; *that* mattered, and she knew the failure was Nancy's. The failure, but not the fault—for how could you blame a woman for the flaws of her body? Yet Arlene imagined that in some concealed part of his mind Harvey Riker blamed his wife for depriving him of sons, of strong backs and quick hands to help him in the fields, of heirs to whom he could leave land and money when the time came.

And Harvey was so different from Paul, it amazed Arlene that they were friends. Perhaps it was only that they both had German ancestors, and some intangible bound them, alien in a world of Danes. She never envied Nance. Harvey was sour, harsh. There was in his temperament an imperative that was positively Prussian; if Nance fell short, he punished. Well, that was it, wasn't it? It was no surprise if Burton Stone's gentleness and warmth attracted Nancy as it would never have been able to attract Arlene. What a sweet relief it might be to turn away from a love as cold, as unforgiving as Harvey's. Dear Paul. She could never have been—could never be—untrue to him.

She turned the lamp back on and opened the book she was reading—*Pride and Prejudice,* a book she had not picked up since her college days—thinking of the troubles women seemed always to have with the men in their lives—and vice-versa. The image of the light on the horizon insisted itself between her reveries and her reading. Certainly she knew the old railroad bridge was burning, and her own man was too simple and direct not to have done it—probably with Harvey, the two of them drunk and angry after the Tap closed up. And how easy it would have been, how thorough. She had seen fenceposts, kindled by spring fires set in the roadside ditches, that burned for days, slowly and to the heart, and she imagined the timbers of the bridge—black with creosote, dry with age—smoldering long after the fire department volunteers had done all they knew how to do. She could imagine the seeds of flame growing in the scars carved by axes and chisels when the bridge was built, and the charred wood steaming when the first too-late rains touched it. *Oh, the things we say we love,* she told herself—half-dozing over her book in the stifling room—*and the things we have to do to prove it.*

She got up for good at six-thirty and made coffee from the Colombian beans, standing at the sink to watch the misty light dissipate in the fields. Paul was not home; there was no telling when he would appear, whether he would be sheepish or arrogant, whether he might have Harvey Riker with him—to soften the consequences of what he had done, the way a boy brings home a friend to shame his mother out of her anger. Yet she might be mistaken, jumping to wrong conclusions. And even if she were right, the worst of that was the way Paul would expect her to take his side, see his reasons, help him explain. He would never see that he was trying to lead her to a place where she ought not to follow.

When the sheriff's car came down the gravel road from the east, kicking up the dust that would add one more layer of white to the weed leaves and stems, Arlene thought at first it was the Jehovah's Witness lady in the gold Cadillac. *They never give up,* she was thinking. Believers. Fanatics. Then she saw the bubble of light on the roof and the license plate that was green instead of blue, and last of all she recognized the county shield on the front door. She watched the car stop near the toolshed; watched the young deputy stride toward her in his morning-fresh khakis; wondered if she would tell even him what in her heart she knew about her husband's anger and frustration.

For a terrible moment as the young deputy crossed the yard toward the house, squinting into the low morning sun, it entered Arlene's mind that perhaps he was bringing bad news—Peter having set the precedent more than a dozen years ago—that his errand was one of condolence, and that whatever crime she had imagined Paul guilty of, it was a thing turned insignificant in the face of tragedy. An auto accident, a drunken brawl, anything that might have ended in bloodshed or death. Then, as the uniformed boy—for that is all he was, she saw clearly—started up the porch steps, her mind calmed itself and she told her frantic heart that, no, he was too young to be entrusted with bad news; they'd have sent an older man, someone with a lined face and a serious mouth. An old dog, not this eager puppy. Even the black holster at his hip, and the walnut-colored handle of the revolver protruding from it, were too big, too grown-up, for this child.

She stood in the doorway, already pushing the screen door open to admit him, as he came up the steps. He was hatless, but when he saw her he raised the fingers of his right hand to his brow, as if he were touching the brim of a hat, or saluting the woman in front of him.

"Mrs. Tobler?"

He did not come in—not yet—but held the door open where she had pushed it.

"Yes," she said. *So young,* she thought. *So blond and beardless and fresh-cheeked.*

"Good morning, ma'am. I'm deputy Gish."

"Good morning, Mr. Gish." *Why do I know that name?*

"And I wonder if I could speak to your husband—to Mr. Tobler."

"He isn't here," she said. She stepped back from the doorway. "I don't mean to be rude. Do please come inside."

Now he followed her into the kitchen, taking a small blue notebook out of the shirt pocket over his heart, finding a stubby yellow pencil in the breast pocket on the other side.

"Already at work, is he?" the deputy said.

"No," she said. "The truth is, he hasn't been home all night."

The deputy wrote in his notebook, standing in the middle of the kitchen, between words wetting the tip of the pencil with his tongue.

"Is that unusual?" he asked.

"A little." How ought she to have answered such a question?

she wondered. And how much trouble had Paul gotten himself into? "I've made fresh coffee," she said. "Would you like a cup?"

The boy smiled. He was—what? Twenty-three? Twenty-four? A few years younger than Sarah. "I wouldn't say no to a cup, ma'am. I thank you much."

"You can sit at the table if you'd like."

He pulled out Paul's chair and sat. Arlene poured coffee and set the cup before him.

"Do you need cream or sugar?"

"No, thanks."

She sat across from him, looking from the notebook to his child's face to her own hands folded on the table in front of her. He sipped the coffee, testing it.

"It's hot," she said.

"But it sure has a good aroma," he said.

"It's from beans. From South America. I grind them up myself."

He set the cup down and nodded, as if in appreciation of her work. "I'm not used to drinking such good stuff," he said.

Arlene took a deep breath. "Is something wrong?" she said. "Is Paul all right? Has he done something he shouldn't have?"

"It's possible he has done something." The deputy flipped the notebook open to a page already covered with scrawls. "There was a fire last night—or early this morning, one. Somebody burned down the Illinois Central bridge over the West Fork—"

"Burned it *down?* Completely?"

"Yes, ma'am. At least it's not safe anymore; not usable."

"My lord."

"Yes, ma'am. And there's a possibility that your husband, and a friend of his—"

"Harvey Riker."

The boy studied the notebook page. "Yes, ma'am. Riker. That the two of them might have done the deed." He looked up at her. "As they say."

"Did somebody see them do it?" It was a useless question.

Even she could *see,* in her mind's eye, the two men, just drunk enough to have set reason aside, stumbling around the wooden bridge, whispering instructions to each other, stopping to giggle and lean against the old timbers under the blind night sky.

"Not actually. But it seems they talked about doing it; they were pretty loud about it. I got a call around four A.M. to go out to the bridge, and it was burning pretty good then. I called the fire station in Cedar Falls to see what they could do, and then I scouted around the area. There was a light on in the Tap, over in Dike, so I stopped and talked to the owner."

"And he said Paul and Harve had been in."

The deputy drank his coffee. "Had been in, had drunk a whole lot of beer, had bragged how they were going to get even with the bike-trail folks by taking out the bridge. The owner said 'taking it out' was just the way they put it. It's a military expression."

Arlene sighed.

"Then apparently the two of them went on to a place called The Alibi, over in Waterloo. Drank some more. Talked big some more. Left when the place closed up at two."

"Paul hardly ever goes to Waterloo," she said. " 'Too many blacks,' is what he always says."

"You don't know where he might be now?" the deputy said.

"Have you been to the Rikers'?"

"I stopped there first; it was on my way. Mrs. Riker didn't even seem upset when I told her why I was there so early." He cocked his head at Arlene. "I can see that you're bothered by this. Mrs. Riker . . . well, it just didn't appear to faze her."

"She was probably still half asleep. She'll be bothered when she's really awake." But then she thought that probably Nance hadn't even been to bed, at least not to sleep—that probably she'd been with Burton Stone while Harvey was out drinking and destroying other people's property.

"That may be."

Arlene stood up from the table. "More coffee?"

"No, thank you."

"You're welcome to wait here for Paul." She took Deputy Gish's emptied cup, set it in the sink, and ran water into it before she thought about the well and about how she probably shouldn't be using water unnecessarily. *It isn't like me to make a habit of waste,* she thought, and then she wanted to blame the carelessness on her worry over Paul. "It's not like him to stay away long. He's got fieldwork to do."

"It's a tough year for farming," the boy said. "My old man— I never heard him bitch so much as this year—*complain,* I mean, begging your pardon. 'Dry, dry, dry,' is all he says."

"That tells it all."

She looked out the window. A light breeze was shaking the leaves of the cottonwood, making them flicker from green to silver in the early sunlight. The sky was perfectly cloudless. Through the open screen door she could hear only the uneven whisper of the wind in the big tree. And then she caught the hum of a car's engine, far away, and now she saw a plume of white dust rising along the county road toward the west, and it was Paul's pickup.

"Here's Paul," she said. "Now you can ask him all your questions."

The deputy stood on the porch as Paul got slowly down from the truck cab and walked toward the house. Tired, Arlene thought, and he's probably got a peach of a headache.

"Mr. Tobler," the boy said, "I'm Deputy Gish."

Paul shielded his eyes and looked up at him. "I know why you're here," he said.

"Yes, sir, I thought you might."

Paul mounted the steps. The deputy moved aside, then followed him into the house. Arlene turned from the sink to look at her husband. His face was pale; there was a smear of black at his left temple and a three-cornered tear in his left sleeve.

"You all right?" she said.

He shook his head, but he said, "I guess."

He went past her to the sink and ran water, just enough to wet both hands, and then he pulled off a couple of paper towels and dried his hands. The towels turned black.

"Don't I know your old man?" Paul said over his shoulder. "Fred Gish, works part-time over at the Farm Fleet?"

"That's him," the deputy said.

"I'll be damned," Paul said. "I knew you when my daughter was your baby-sitter."

There was a painful space of silence in the room. An impasse. As if this revelation had short-circuited the procedure every deputy was taught to follow in the business of arresting people. Arlene thought the boy might never speak again, but at last he did.

"I remember her," he said. "Sarah. She was the only one who'd let me stay up on Friday nights to watch the horror shows."

Paul opened the cupboard door under the sink and threw the filthy paper towels into the wastebasket there. "Well," he said, "what's the drill?"

"I have to ask you about the bridge," the deputy said. "But you don't have to answer if you don't want to. You can call a lawyer."

"No. I did it," Paul said. "That's simple enough."

"By yourself?"

Paul hesitated.

"I'm going to call on Mr. Riker after I've finished here," the boy said.

"In that case," Paul said, "I might as well say *we* did it. Harve and me—we're the culprits."

The deputy sat down again and wrote in his notebook, using the kitchen table as a desk. Paul remained standing, his back against the counter, his arms folded across his chest. Arlene saw that though he was still pale, there were spots of color in his cheeks—a flush of anger, or of frustration.

"Are you arresting me?" Paul said.

Gish went on writing.

"If you're planning to take me in, then I ought to make some phone calls. I'm in the middle of chopping one of my cornfields into silage. If I can't finish, I've got to find somebody who can."

"I haven't decided what to do," the deputy said, still writing, not looking up.

"Christ, you even sound like your father," Paul said. "Him and me, we used to go fishing, up in the Boundary Waters."

"I remember," Gish said.

"You just tell me what to do," Paul said, "and I'll do it."

The boy sighed and sat against the back of the chair, tucking the notebook back into his breast pocket. Arlene watched him, and she felt sorry for him. How difficult for him it must be, to have to make such decisions involving a friend of his father's, to be loyal to his love for his father—she assumed this love without evidence—and at the same time do his duty by the laws of the county he worked for. And then to weigh that conflict against his own young man's judgment of Paul: If he did not actually arrest him, could Paul be trusted not to run away—to *flee*, the courts would say—from prosecution? If he treated Paul kindly, would some clever defense lawyer use that kindness to get Paul off scot-free?

"Should Paul have a lawyer?" she asked the deputy.

"No lawyers," Paul said. He looked at Arlene, the look telling her to stay out of this.

"I don't think anybody wants to throw you in jail," the deputy said. "But I do have to take you back to the courthouse with me—to have a stenographer take your statement, to do a bunch of paperwork. After that, I don't see any reason not to bring you home to get your corn chopped."

"I'd appreciate that."

"The court clerk'll call you about a trial date."

"What if I just want to plead guilty?"

"Then she'll arrange a date for sentencing."

Arlene turned away and went into the living room. *Sentencing.* The word made her shiver. She stood, one hand on the back of the sofa to balance herself against her emotions, staying out of it, listening to the two men in the kitchen.

"Well, let's get it over with." *Dear Paul.*

She heard the deputy's chair scrape on the floor.

"I think we'll stop at Riker's on our way," Gish said. "Two birds with one stone, if you've no objection."

The screen door creaked open. Arlene came back to the kitchen and followed Paul toward the porch.

"Don't talk back," she said to him.

He looked at her, and for an instant, for the first time in a couple of days, the flicker of a smile touched his mouth. Then he was following the deputy down the steps. Halfway across the yard he stopped and turned back toward Arlene.

"Better close up the house," he told her. "It's supposed to be another scorcher."

She stood at the kitchen window, leaning against the sink, until she had watched the deputy's car turn left, toward town, at the end of the long driveway. As the car plunged into its funnel of pale dust, she turned her attention to the porcelain under her hands. The black from Paul's washing up was a gray shadow around the drain, and there was a broad, darker smudge on the side of the sink under the cold-water faucet. She reached for the cleanser that sat on the drain board and shook some of the coarse powder onto a yellow sponge. It was the work of a moment to rub away the thin residue of ash Paul had carried home with him, and it took another moment more to rinse the sink clean. By then the dust on the road had settled into its perpetual haze, and the deputy's car was long out of sight.

In early September, on the day Paul went before the session of the county court, Arlene got up from a nap in mid afternoon, feeling no more rested than when she had laid herself down on the big bed. The drought had not broken, and heat was all over her, like heavy clothing; there was nothing to do for it but strip out of her things and bathe in a cool tub. She slid gratefully into the water until it was up to her chin; only her head and knobby knees showed above the surface. She tried not to think of what Paul would say if he knew she had filled the tub instead of going down to the basement and using the shower. Every morning lately he had gone to the kitchen tap to get a glass of water, studying it, smelling it before he finally drank it. If the water table fell far enough, sometimes the water took on a faint rotten-egg odor; sometimes little black grains of heaven-knew-what would settle at the bottom of the tumbler. If the drought went on and on, one morning she would see the emptiness of the well in her husband's face as he considered the water glass in his hands.

Nowadays Paul seemed always to expect the worst. Sometimes Arlene thought he created his misfortunes by defining them in his mind ahead of time—as if, like some kind of pagan sorcerer, he brought a material world into existence out of nothing. Perverse magic. A courtship of bad luck. How else would you explain his present predicament? Anyone would have known that setting fire to the I.C. bridge was the kind of act that would bring the whole machinery of the county, perhaps the whole state of Iowa, down on him hard. In this day and age. And he *wanted* to be tangled in that machinery—that was the marvel of it: he wanted to be caught and sentenced. He wanted to speak his piece. In the three weeks since the deputy had taken him in to be charged, Paul had rehearsed his arguments with her. Sometimes Harvey was with him, the two men sitting in the kitchen late in the afternoons over cold beers, justifying each other.

"It's a question of integrity," Paul would say.

"Damn straight," Harvey would respond. It was like a chorus,

Arlene thought. An ancient Greek play, or the voices you heard if you stood outside the A.M.E. church in Waterloo.

"This is all about how the rights of the individual conflict with the demands of the state," Paul said, Harvey drinking and nodding across the table from him. "It's a confrontation."

And it would never have occurred to Paul, drunk or not, to break the law and then try to hide from punishment. She knew it wasn't his style. He'd told her once that when he was in basic training, just before the military sent him to Korea, he'd gotten so thirsty he'd stolen a quart can of tomato juice out of the mess tent and carried the can off into the brush, where he used his pocket knife—*men with their knives,* she thought—to punch holes in the top and drank the whole can in one sitting. The men were in the field, playing war games—*"games" indeed,* Arlene thought—and as soon as they were back at the base, Paul turned himself in to his sergeant. The sergeant thought he was crazy; refused to punish him. When the unit was allowed a three-day pass before being shipped overseas, Paul went to a grocery store, bought a can of tomato juice, and delivered it to the mess hall the next morning. *Dear Paul.* Now he was refusing even to hire a lawyer. What did he expect from this angry adventure? Whatever it might be, he refused even to let her share it with him, refused to let her come with him to witness his stubborn strength.

"Now they know where we stand," Harvey said. "The goddamned bureaucrats."

But where, Arlene thought, *where on earth would it end?*

She forced herself to get out of the water before she turned entirely into a prune, enjoying the sense of being chilly as she toweled dry, but wishing—as the water ran silently out of the tub, then growled like some wild animal over the last dregs—that she had thought of some use for the water. *I could have taken it, a bucket at a time, out to the vegetable garden,* she thought. *I needn't have wasted it so, just because I was sticky.* She vowed that next time she'd take a quick shower. And she wouldn't tell Paul of her self-indulgence today.

But dressed in clean clothes, feeling refreshed and alive again, she arrived in the kitchen with only the slightest remnant of guilt to nag at her. It was nearly four o'clock. Fifteen, twenty years ago, Sarah and Peter would have been at the kitchen table with their homework, getting the math and geography and English out of the way so they could play in the cool evening, or go to 4-H, or help their father in the fields, or—this would have been Sarah—saddling Cloud for a long ride in the direction of Hudson, arriving home in the early dusk, walking up the long drive ahead of Cloud, cooling him out. That one terrible winter, when Peter was at Independence, she'd have visited Peter, told him about home, how she and Paul and Sarah were waiting. Nowadays, four o'clock meant only that in a little while she'd have to start supper for Paul and herself, just the two of them, and begin to prepare herself to listen sympathetically to the complaints of the day.

She stood at the sink and rinsed out the coffee cups from lunch. She thought she might heat up what was left of the coffee on the stove, in spite of the oppressiveness of the kitchen. A breeze might come up as the sun went lower; she would open the windows, let the stale air out of the house. She put aside one of the muslin curtains to look down the driveway, not because she expected to see her grown-up children materialize as the youngsters they'd once been—she didn't have Paul's knack for making something from nothing—but because it was habit, a moment of survey: how does the land lie at this moment?

This time, a man was walking up the driveway toward her. Tall, in jeans and a short-sleeved plaid shirt, a green cap with its bill pulled down low on his forehead. Sharp-toed boots. Now she saw it was Burton Stone. As he came into the farmyard, he took off the cap and wiped with the back of his hand at sweat along his hairline. Putting the cap back on, he saw Arlene watching him. He smiled, waved, strode toward the porch. *What a good-looking boy,* Arlene thought. A strong face with a full lower lip and wise eyes. Big, useful hands. Those shoulders of his. No wonder Nancy was crazy about him. She dried her hands on the dish towel and went to open the door.

"Burton," she said. She let him into the kitchen. "What a surprise on a hot day."

"Sorry to barge in on your afternoon. My truck broke down. Busted a radiator hose on me."

"Oh, dear."

"I thought Paul might have a piece of hose I could make do with. Something with a little weave to it. And maybe lend me a screwdriver."

"I'm sure you're welcome to look," she said. She stood uncertainly, facing the man. Burton was still in the doorway, light surrounding him, his cap in his hands. "For goodness' sake," Arlene said. "Have a chair. I'll get you a Coca-Cola or something."

He pulled out one of the chairs and sat; he crossed his legs and hung the cap on his knee. "I'd settle for a glass of water," he said. "I guess I ought to make this into partly a social call, it's been so long since I've seen you two."

"A lot's been happening." She filled a glass with water and set it in front of him. "As you know."

"What's the latest?" Burton said. "What are the actual charges?"

"Take your pick. There's malicious mischief. There's willful destruction of county property. There's vandalism. There's conspiracy. I don't know what else."

"That would seem sufficient."

She sat at the table across from him. "Harvey Riker's attorney wants him to plead guilty to malicious mischief. He thinks they'll give him a light sentence, maybe a fine and probation. He thinks they'd be willing to drop the other charges."

"He going to do it?"

Arlene looked hard at Burton. For a moment she thought she might smile, but she compressed her lips into a line, erasing all traces of irony before she spoke.

"You'd probably like to see Harvey in jail for a while," she said.

It was Burton who grinned. "I probably would," he said.

"Anyway, I don't know what he's going to do."

"What's Paul's lawyer say?"

"What lawyer?"

"He doesn't have one?"

Arlene opened her hands, as if to dramatize helplessness. "Can you imagine? 'Eighty dollars an hour!' he said to me. 'I'll be goddamned if there's a man on this earth who's worth eighty dollars an hour.'"

Burton drained his glass. "Well," he said, "that's old Paul."

"Not *so* old," she said. "He just acts that way."

"So what's he going to plead? No contest?"

"He's made up his mind to plead guilty on all counts."

Burton shook his head, almost as if he were expressing admiration for Paul's decision, then he looked serious and said, "I've got to get at that hose." He stood, put on his cap.

"There's bound to be hose in the shed," Arlene said, "where he keeps the tractor. Look on that west wall; he's got all sorts of stuff hanging there."

"I think I need about a 5/8-inch diameter. That's pretty common."

"I wouldn't know."

"Tools there too?"

She went to open the kitchen drawer. "If it's just a screwdriver you need, here. Bring it back when you're done. It belongs to me, not Paul."

He took the screwdriver. "I'll take good care of it."

"You need something to cut the hose with?"

Burton winked at her. "I've got my trusty switchblade," he said.

———

She watched him cross the yard to the tractor shed and pull open the side door, pushing one of the gray barn cats aside gently but firmly with the side of his boot. He was in the shed for only a few minutes, and when he emerged he was carrying a loop of brick-red hose that looked to be something a little less than two feet in length. He closed the shed door behind him, glanced toward the kitchen window and held up his free hand in an "O.K." gesture. He stopped long enough to find her yellow watering can up against the end of the house, filled the can from the spigot and lugged it down the length of the driveway, little bursts of dust following his footsteps. His truck was a couple of hundred yards east—she could just see the hood of it raised above the stricken tops of the corn plants—which meant he had been coming back from town, not from the Riker place.

Where was I? she asked herself, and then she remembered and decided she would indeed heat up the breakfast coffee, indulge herself, sit for a while and wait patiently for Paul to come home and announce the outcome of his day in court. When the coffee was heated up in the small saucepan, she poured it into a clean cup. It was bitter on her tongue; she added sugar, though it was rare for her to drink anything but black coffee. Had Burton been nervous about asking for help? Knowing that Nance must have talked about him, perhaps feeling as if Arlene's knowledge somehow undressed him? Lord knew, he seemed cool enough. *But it's no business of mine.*

The Des Moines paper was scattered across two kitchen chairs where Paul had left it that morning, the pale orange sports section uppermost. Arlene found the editorial pages and spread them open in front of her. The lead editorial dealt with the drought, as if the paper's opinion about it could somehow lessen its impact; the letters to the editor today were mostly about handgun registration, the ones who were opposed to it sounding curiously alike in their philosophy, their fear that only criminals would own guns; she didn't understand the political cartoon, which showed the state's young Republican governor sitting in a highchair on the steps of the capitol building.

It was a relief when she heard Burton's truck outside, and she went to the window almost with eagerness. She watched him put the watering can back where he'd found it, careful to set it upright because it wasn't empty—or so she surmised. She met him at the kitchen door, took the screwdriver from him, and dropped it back into the narrow drawer by the sink.

"I'm much obliged," he said.

"I'm pleased to help."

"But it's sure hot out there. I didn't tell you: when I drove past the bank this afternoon, it said one-oh-two."

"My lord."

Burton winked and saluted her. "I thought I was looking at the time," he said.

She stood watching through the screen door as he went down the porch steps, the shirt across his broad back drenched with his sweat. *A very nice boy,* she thought. So sure of himself. So easy in the world.

"Burton," she said, surprised at how loud she said it.

He stopped, halfway across the yard.

"You be good to Nancy," she said. "She deserves it."

Burton hesitated, as if he wanted to say something back to her, but no words came. Then he tipped his cap and climbed into the truck.

Just after four-thirty, Paul telephoned to say that the judge had given him a choice between a five-hundred-dollar fine or sixty days in the county jail.

"I pled guilty to everything," Paul said. "Five separate charges."

"There's the vacation money," Arlene reminded him. "You never let me spend it. We've got more than enough to pay the fine."

"No," he said, "I told him I'd take the jail time. I gave a little speech. Some of the people in the courtroom gave me a round of applause."

"What about the harvest?"

"Such as it is." Paul said it with a false laugh, and a tone of sarcasm she wasn't used to. "They offered to let me wait—serve my sentence after the harvest was done. I said no, I wanted to make as much of a fuss as I could. I wanted the whole world to know how bad the railroad and the county were screwing us."

"You don't have to make the speech to me," Arlene said.

"Sorry."

"What can I do?"

"I'm going to go straight into the pokey," Paul said. "Get it over with. You might bring my shaving gear and my toothbrush over to the courthouse. Get Burton or somebody to drive you over. Give the stuff to the clerk; she'll know how to deliver it to me. I'll leave her the keys to the pickup so you can take it home with you."

"All right."

"You understand," he said, "why I had to do it this way."

"Yes," she said. "But what about Harvey?"

She could hear his oddly sharp intake of breath. "He paid," Paul said. "He said his time was too valuable not to."

"Did that surprise you?"

"It pissed me off," Paul said. "Pardon my French."

"I'll bring your gear," she said. "I'll call Burton and leave as soon as he gets here."

"And underwear," he said. "Maybe you should bring me a couple of changes of underwear."

"I will."

"One more thing," he said.

"What?"

"There was this reporter from the TV at the sentencing. She took notes while I was having my say to the judge. She was pretty friendly to me afterward and she seemed interested in the bike-trail thing. She might come out to talk to you."

"What should I say to her?"

"Just say the truth."

"All right."

"Just say the Illinois Central Railroad doesn't have any sensitivity to the difficulties faced today by the family farmer."

"Is that from the speech?"

She heard him laugh. "Yeah," he said. "I wish you could've been here. I wish now I'd let you come."

Midmorning of the next day, Arlene was buttering toast when the reporter arrived, driving a gray Chevrolet with the logo of a Waterloo TV station on its doors. She was a young woman, a little heavy, with blond hair cut short as a boy's, and she wore a white linen skirt and jacket over a daffodil-yellow blouse with ruffles at the throat. Her clothes looked small on her, Arlene thought. The woman had a video camera slung over one shoulder, and she carried a black cardboard case in her free hand. Arlene watched her make her way clumsily across the yard; she wore high-top sneakers, a footwear—in Arlene's judgment—much too casual for someone doing a serious job. Still, nowadays everybody wore them; nobody really dressed up anymore. She met the young woman at the kitchen door.

"Connie Blair," the woman said. "Hawkeye NewsWatch."

"Come inside," Arlene said. "Put all that paraphernalia down somewhere."

"You expected me?"

"My husband said you might visit."

"I do a segment called 'Constance Comments' on the evening news," Connie Blair said. She made room for the case on the kitchen table, pushing Arlene's toast plate dangerously near the edge. "Maybe you watch it?"

"I don't have much interest in the TV," Arlene said. "I usually have the radio on when I'm working around the house." She watched the reporter fuss with the equipment—the case held a silver-colored tripod and a microphone; the case itself seemed to double as some kind of battery, which she plugged into the camera. The camera, threaded onto its tripod, she aimed in the general direction of the table.

"You ought to look in," Connie said. "I do a lot of features with a woman's slant to them. Remember the wife in Parkersburg who stabbed her husband to death with the kitchen shears? She lived on a farm, like you. I interviewed her right after it happened—before they even knew she was the one that did it."

"That's awful," Arlene said. "I don't think I'd have liked that story."

"I know," the young woman said. "It was pretty gross."

"Why would you put something like that on the television? Especially if you know it's 'gross'?"

"It's strictly business. We had a seventeen market share with that one."

"Whatever that means," Arlene said. She wondered what Connie Blair had told Paul, why he thought this young woman could be good for him. Perhaps she had been flirtatious with him and he had been too polite and embarrassed to say no to her.

"Would you sit there, please," the young woman instructed her, "at the end of the table."

Arlene sat. The cold toast was in front of her.

"Were you just about to have breakfast? That's good. Just pick up a piece of the toast—you know: as if I'd interrupted you in the midst." She looked into the viewfinder and aimed the camera at Arlene. "Were you going to have coffee with that?" She looked around the kitchen; in the corner cupboard she found a cup and saucer from the Toblers' best china pattern and set them in front of Arlene. "We'll pretend there's coffee in the cup," she said. "Nobody will see that it's empty."

"You certainly take charge," Arlene said.

Connie smiled. "The camera's on," she said. She held the microphone out toward Arlene; the end of it was covered with black sponge rubber. "Just be yourself and answer my questions in a natural way."

"What did you say to my husband?" Arlene asked.

"That we could publicize his fight with the railroad people. That we could stir up sympathy for him."

"And get him out of jail?"

"I didn't make him any promises."

"And get him his land back?"

"Mrs. Tobler, this is supposed to be my interview. It's supposed to be me asking *you*."

"I guess I don't see how answering questions is going to change anything," Arlene said. And she didn't; it wouldn't bring Paul home any sooner, it wouldn't improve the corn crop, she was sure it wouldn't undo the bridge burning or Paul's arrest or whatever he thought he was accomplishing in jail.

"Would you say that your husband is 'obsessed' with this bike-trail battle of his?"

"He cares about this farm."

"Has he ever broken the law before?"

"Never."

"It came out in what he said to the judge yesterday that some bikers were on your land one day this summer," Connie said. Every time she asked a question, she raised the round sponge of the microphone so it hid her mouth. "Did your husband threaten them?"

"Not that I know of."

"Is that a 'no'? He didn't threaten them?"

"I wasn't here when they arrived," Arlene said. "But Paul isn't the kind of man who makes threats."

"He doesn't threaten," Connie said. "He acts. Is that a fair statement?"

"Something like that." Arlene began to see that Constance Blair was chasing after an image of Paul as a volatile man, unpredictable, maybe reckless. What appeared on the television would be a fiction—Paul a character in this woman's little drama. "I don't think you're asking the right questions," she said.

"You don't?"

"How do you know the bikers didn't come out to this farm to threaten Paul?"

"*Did* they threaten him?"

"I don't believe so, but that isn't the point. I think you want to use words like 'threat' and 'battle' and 'break the law.' I think you don't know how to tell a story about a quiet, private, hard-working man who loves the land he's farmed all his life, and who's willing to stand up for his rights even when he knows he'll lose."

"You're proud of what he's done?"

Arlene hesitated before she answered. "I'm proud to be his wife," she said.

"Isn't that the same thing?"

Arlene stood up and carried the empty cup and saucer to the corner cupboard to put them away. "I have to telephone my children," she said. "I don't want to talk with you anymore."

"Are the children proud of their father?"

"This isn't news," Arlene said. She opened the door to the porch. "You should be ashamed even to ask such a thing."

3

Sarah came home at the end of September—Paul was still in jail in Waterloo—the cottonwood leaves letting go and swirling in the dust of the farmyard, the barn cats chasing the sultry autumn wind while Grimmie sat in the parlor window and watched the play and switched his tail impatiently until Arlene let him out.

At first Arlene didn't know who it was. The car wasn't familiar: a newish green Dodge with no front license plate. It rolled up the long drive too fast, spraying gravel under its tires. A woman was at the wheel. *Sarah,* Arlene thought. *My God, it's Sarah.* Then: *But I didn't ask her to come.*

She stepped onto the porch and held out her hand in a motion that was more acknowledgement than greeting. She formed the word *Sarah* with tongue and teeth, but no sound came. She wished it was Peter in the car, and for the first time since Paul's arrest her whole long memory of her son's life swept over her like the wind. Facing Sarah—watching her slide out of the ugly car, the familiar frown creasing her daughter's forehead, the deliberate way she avoided looking at her mother—Arlene juggled a mix of feelings. Affection, wariness, an odd sort of maternal gracelessness that must have come from distance and time and a lack of practice. She knew she would see herself in Sarah: the impatient set of the jaw, the hand gestures, even the fullness of hips. "If you turned my clock back thirty years and set us side by side," she would tell Nance one day, "you'd swear she was me."

She knew, too, they would have to talk about Peter, and the buffer years she had so carefully maintained between *now* and *then* would be like wood smoke on the wind, dissipating, all that space and time vanished as if they had never happened—and there would be Peter, her mad child. *An episode,* as the doctors had said. *Only an episode.*

Now the car door slammed shut and Sarah was coming toward her, a canvas carryall in one hand, a leather overnight bag in the other. The younger woman stopped at the foot of the steps, turned her scowl upward.

"What is Daddy thinking?" she said. "What in the hell is he trying to prove?"

Sarah had flown into Cedar Rapids on United, one stop— Denver—from LAX, an itinerary that meant she had to rent a car and drive eighty-odd miles to her parents' farm. Better that, she had decided, than sit miserably in a bouncy commuter plane from St. Louis to Waterloo with its dinky terminal, and then have to ask her mother to fetch her.

The car was a new green Dodge, a pale version of green Peter would have called "early puke," carrying a single license plate from the state of Florida. Never mind the question of what a Florida car was doing in the state of Iowa, but how much money did Florida save, she wondered, by not requiring a front tag? And what did Florida's jailbirds do with their extra time? Maybe they made bird feeders for the governor and his friends; maybe they read the classics. And as for that, what was her father doing, sitting

in a county jail because he and Harvey Riker had declared war on
the bicycle? Riker she could understand; he had always been
short-tempered and stupid—"the Hun" Peter called him—but
Daddy was never like that. How could those two possibly have
come together for arson?

Although, thinking about it as she drove north on the new
interstate, Daddy had his blindnesses. Seeing the spotty fields of
corn, the dry, brown-gold sweep of soybeans, the pyramid hog
houses of the farm near Dysart she remembered from her childhood, she could hear her father expounding on the importance
of land. Sitting at supper, Sarah and Peter and their mother heard
the passion in Paul Tobler's speech, listened on winter nights to
its resonance in the warm kitchen. *Land. Land.* Yes, she could
imagine, especially in a time of unfriendly weather, her father
going a little off the deep end. Peter had learned to shut Daddy
out; Sarah never had. When she called her brother to ask if he
would fly back to Iowa with her, the tone of his voice was as
physical as a shrug. "Moral support," she had told Peter. "What's
moral about Dad's obsession?" he'd said. "And when did he ever
understand about *support* unless it was a crop subsidy?"

But that was Peter. You had to make allowances. You had to
take a deep breath and tell yourself that his temper and temperament, what he had provoked, what he had *done* when he was in
high school, colored the rest of his life. Mother had always made
those allowances and more, as if persuading herself to believe that
what had happened *never had.*

Turning off the interstate, passing through the drab outskirts
of Waterloo where in a decade nothing had changed except to
look more rundown, driving perhaps too fast over the graveled
county roads—the rented car fishtailing at a corner—she realized
she was passing the place where all those years ago she had
watched Peter kick Corey Jensen's textbooks into the ditch.
Slowing the car, the dust catching up with her and sifting over
the windshield, she had felt a sadness, a renewed depression, as if

old events were recent, as if the half forgotten were stark and indelible.

Pulling into the driveway where the mailbox on its ploughshare support read TOBLER 427—the family name and the map number the county fire people had assigned—Sarah felt a familiar easiness. *Home.* Never mind she had not lived here in a decade, here was Mother, waiting—as if Sarah and Peter were just off the school bus, running up the slalom of driveway, mother on the porch to greet them—to say, "How was your day?"

"You didn't have to come," her mother said now. "There's nothing you can do to help. Your father's determined to grin and bear it."

"I doubt he's grinning," Sarah said. She carried her bags into the kitchen. "How are *you,* is what I wondered."

"I'm fine. I visit your father every day." Arlene brushed at a wisp of hair—how gray she'd gotten!—and drew one of the chairs back from the table. "Put those bags down and have some coffee with me. Tell me how you are."

Sarah sat. So it was to be like this—courteous, a little formal, a dance of will-you, won't-you, please and thank you. She watched coffee fill her white mug and top off her mother's, spooned too much sugar into hers, stirred self-consciously and cast about in her mind for words that might sound reasonably natural in this reunion scene.

"How is Philip?" Arlene said.

Sarah shook her head. "You don't really want to hear about Philip," she said.

"Then tell me about the girls. I care about them."

"Mindy loves kindergarten. Vivian hates day care." She sipped the coffee, which was too sweet. "Philip, by the way, thinks I shouldn't even have come to Iowa."

"Not surprising," her mother said. "I agree with him."

"I didn't like the idea of you being alone while Daddy stood on his principles—or whatever it is he's standing on. I know you'd prefer Peter to be here instead of me."

"I don't think that's true."

"And I imagine you're reminded of Peter every time you go to the jail to see Daddy."

"Peter was never in jail," Arlene said. "He just spent a little while at Independence."

"Same difference," Sarah said.

"I did try to call him," Arlene said. "I got a recording, a woman's voice that said his number was no longer in service—so I assume he's moved again."

"He's just given up his apartment because they're sending him to China. Some kind of agricultural mission."

Her mother folded her hands and sat straighter. "He might let somebody know what he's up to."

Sarah smiled. "When did Peter ever let you and Daddy know what he was up to?"

"Rarely," Arlene said.

"Anyway, I talked to him," Sarah said. "He thinks Daddy is obsessed."

"Harvey Riker is obsessed," Arlene said. "Your father got roped in."

"But Harvey paid a fine and went home. Dad didn't. I don't call that being 'roped in.'"

"Don't be critical of your father," Arlene said. "He only does what he thinks is right."

"Except when he sets fire to somebody else's property," Sarah said. "What's right about that?"

"Don't be so quick to condemn." Her mother got up and went to the open door. "There's Grimmie," she said, "sitting beside that broken board on the shed, waiting for something to poke its head out."

"Cats are weird," Sarah said. "Especially Grimmie." She joined Arlene at the window, put her arm around her mother's waist. "Let's not quarrel about our men. We both love them. The difference is that you still look at Peter and Daddy through those famous rose-colored glasses."

"I always will," Arlene said.

Sarah could understand her mother not wanting to talk about Peter's "episode"—could certainly, as a mother herself, comprehend the anguish Arlene must feel, even after so many years. As for herself, the memory of what Peter had done remained vivid *because I was there.* And sometimes it was too vivid, its colors— red, orange, green—like a television picture whose settings had gone haywire. Not that she dwelt on it; for most of her adult life the events of her twelfth year were like discarded toys, shoved to the back of the mind's closet where memory's light seldom penetrated. When she did remember, it was some unexpected trigger that pushed the winter clothing aside and revealed the dusty past—perhaps the dazzle of the carving knife as Phil poised to slice the Easter ham, or the morning sun glittering off the windshield of a school bus, or, like today, the chill of passing the place where murder had almost happened.

It surprised her that she recognized it, that place. If someone had asked her to draw a picture, she would have produced an abstraction, a version so unspecific as to be worthless as historical document: a meadow's edge, a fence line, September corn taller than a grown-up. And the sky. The sky she remembered as gray— a violet-hued gray because, yes, a storm was building from the west and there was already a rolling of thunder like a far-off freight on a trestle. She'd have drawn a truthful sky, but no more than that.

My God, Sarah had thought, *am I going to relive it? Am I going to be the witness all over again?* The weathered fence post where Peter had carved Corey Jensen's initials, then drawn a deep cut across the letters with Corey's own knife. *"Crossing you out, Corey."* She could hear Peter's voice, the sneer in it so unlike him—a sound nearly animal. And the barbed fencing—now rusted blood-brown and sagging under the weight of more than fifteen years—her brother had pushed the younger boy against while he held the blade to Corey's chest, Corey afraid to speak but breathing like someone who'd run a long, long way. She remembered Corey on tiptoe, maybe wishing he could raise himself into flight, into escape, and Peter's taller form a sudden eerie shadow of darkness cast by distant lightning.

None of it, not the smallest part of all of it, made sense, even to this day. Beforehand, on the bus taking them home from school, it was Corey inviting attention, opening and closing the new switchblade his father had bought him for his sixteenth birthday. *Unlucky birthday,* Sarah thought now, and that's what it was: nothing but bad luck. They all had knives, those farm boys—pocket knives, knives for whittling, knives for sticking in the earth and throwing against the sides of barns, knives for quartering apples—but never switchblades. Switchblades were movie knives, television knives, big-city gang knives for self-defense and adolescent vengeance. No need for such a knife in the Iowa countryside; no call for a city weapon in a rural world.

But *that*—she saw it now, looking back down the long pathway to the year she turned twelve—that had been the fascination, that was what riled Peter, who sometimes carried an ordinary Scout knife in the buttoned-over pocket of his left boot, who'd never especially liked Corey or Corey's snooty family with their fancy Mercedes car, who couldn't resist taking the switchblade away and taunting its rightful owner for being a showoff. It was funny at first, then Corey'd got mad and swung at Peter and their friends took sides and shouted and egged both boys on while the girls held their collective breath.

Then the bus stopped. The driver, old Mr. Lubker, whose wife was the art teacher, came back to see what the fuss was, and when he found out, he put Peter and Corey off the bus, right there in the middle of nowhere, almost a mile from their proper stop. Sarah had gotten off too, out of loyalty to Peter, and the bus had released its brakes in a whoosh of air and driven off, leaving the three of them in its dust.

"I hope you're satisfied," Corey had said. "Now give me back my knife."

"Fuck you," Peter said, and Sarah felt her face go hot for hearing a word Peter had never used in front of her. Of course she knew what the word meant, but the understanding in the Tobler family was that it was a word not to be spoken.

"Come on, Petey. It's mine."

"Not any more," Peter said. He had jumped the roadside ditch and now he made a figure eight in the air with the handle of the knife. "I'm confiscating it."

"Then you're a thief," Corey said. "And you'll get punished for it." He slid down into the ditch and climbed up beside Peter.

"And who's going to do the punishing?" her brother said. *No, he'd sneered the words.* "Whorey Corey? Little Jenny Jensen?"

"Sticks and stones," Corey said.

"You self-righteous little shit." And then Peter had shoved Corey—one hand, the hand without the knife, catching him on the chest, making him stumble.

"Hey." Corey dropped his books and clenched his fists.

"Hay is for horses," Peter said, and pushed again. "Grass is for cows."

"Give me back my goddamned knife," Corey said. Sarah could see the tears brimming in his eyes. "I'll tell."

Peter held the knife out toward its owner, then snatched it back when Corey reached for it. "If it's a *goddamned* knife," Peter said, "you'd better not touch it. Maybe you'll go to hell."

"Give it back."

Corey took a wild swing at Peter, and that was when Peter lost his temper. He raised the knife above his head and pressed the button that released the blade. Against the violet-gray sky the thin steel shot out like a flicker of lightning. He brought the knife down to waist level and turned its point at Corey's heart.

Corey took a step backward. "Don't be stupid," he said.

Peter moved forward. "I'm not stupid," he said, "and I'm not afraid to use this goddamned knife."

Now the younger boy had come up against the barbed fence wires; the tears that had been threatening were wet on his face.

"Stop it, Petey. It isn't funny." Corey was scared; Sarah could hear the frantic edge in his voice.

"Who's trying to be funny?" Peter had moved closer, so close that the tip of the knife blade almost touched Corey's shirt. "I want this knife. I think if you don't let me keep it, I'll probably kill you with it."

"Peter." The sound of her own voice had surprised her, because it didn't seemed to be hers. It was thin and it broke on the first syllable of her brother's name. "Peter, don't"

"Nothing's going to happen," Peter said. "Corey's giving me his knife 'cause he knows it's not worth dying for." He held the blade an unwavering half inch from Corey's chest. "Isn't that right?"

"Peter," Sarah said.

She didn't know how everything would have ended if Corey had just stood still and let her talk Peter out of whatever it was he thought of doing, but Corey didn't give her a chance.

"It's mine!" Corey yelled, and he grabbed at Peter's wrist. Peter took a half step back—she remembered she'd thought he wasn't going to hurt Corey after all—and then he lunged forward. The knife blade went into Corey's chest up to its hilt, and when Peter pulled it back, blood—vivid red—followed.

Corey's eyes were huge. "Oh, God," he said. He looked down at the blood on his shirt front and covered it with both his hands. "Jesus God," he said. "Look!" Then he dropped to his knees.

"I told you, didn't I?" Peter said. "I told you what would happen."

Corey looked up at Sarah. "He's crazy," he whispered, and he fell over on his side. His eyes closed.

"Peter Karl Tobler," she'd said, their grandfather's name adding weight to her horror. "Oh, Peter, what have you done?"

Peter stood back from the fallen boy. He knelt and wiped the blade on the grass at his feet, then turned to the fence post and worked Corey's initials into the wood with the point of the knife.

"Crossing you out, Corey," he said grimly. "Like you never were."

"Oh, Peter," was all Sarah could say.

"He asked for it," Peter said.

He stood up and flung the knife across the fence, twenty yards deep into the dry gold and brown of the cornfield. Then he walked around and pushed at Corey, using his hands and, finally, his feet. The boy's body hung for an instant, then rolled down into the ditch beside the road. He kicked Corey's books after him.

"Let's go," he said.

She'd followed him up onto the shoulder, trotted alongside him to keep up with his strides toward home.

"Why did you do that?" she said. "Why leave him in the ditch?"

"He's dead, isn't he?"

"What will you tell Daddy?"

He'd stopped and glared at her. "Nothing," he said. "And nothing is what you'll say, too, because there's nothing to tell. We all got off the bus, and Corey went his way and we went ours. And that's all that happened. When they find him dead, that's an awful, awful thing, but it's news to us."

Corey Jensen wasn't dead. It would have been better for everyone—except Corey, of course—if he had been. She and Peter could have stuck to their stories, and who would have been able to prove murder against a teenager, if the only witness kept her mouth shut?

But Arlene had been worried. "I saw the school bus go by without stopping," she told the children, "so I wondered if you'd been kept after school. And why. You know I hate it when you misbehave."

"Just because you used to be a teacher," Peter had said.

"No. Because I'm the mother of two smart children, and I don't expect them to be discipline problems."

And Peter had slid his books onto the kitchen table and kissed his mother on the cheek. "Never fear, Mother dear," was what he'd said.

"It was so nice today, I wanted to walk," Sarah said.

"And I wouldn't let her go alone, so I walked with her."

"My hero," Sarah had said, putting into the words as much sarcasm as she could muster. That was how sisters talked to older brothers.

Paul had come in from the barn and they'd all sat down to supper. Then the phone rang, and all hell broke loose.

Corey was lucky. The blade missed his heart by barely an inch. He didn't lie in the ditch bleeding to death as he probably should have, but managed to crawl out of it to the edge of the road where Todd Clausson, the rural mailman, found him and raced him to the Catholic hospital in Waterloo. Naturally he told everything, named names, and when Peter and Sarah were confronted—Corey's father, the Toblers, two men from the sheriff's department, all standing in the Tobler kitchen and Corey's statement sitting on the kitchen table like a centerpiece—what could they have said?

At least it wasn't murder, and because of his age Peter wasn't brought to any sort of trial. But those were the Independence days, the daily visits she and her mother made to the Mental Health Institute while Peter sat in a private room on a locked ward for "observation" and a lot of tests. "They want to know what makes me tick," Peter told them the first day, "and if I don't tick, why don't I?"

Daddy never went with them to the MHI. It was as if by staying away he could make his son's madness—if that was what it was—cease to exist. Sometimes Sarah herself didn't actually see Peter: those days when the doctor suggested only Mother should visit, and Sarah waited alone in a cold corridor under institutional globed lamps that looked like a perfect row of white balloons. After Peter came home, Paul refused to acknowledge his son, the tension in the small farmhouse building and building until there was nothing for it but to send Peter away. "It's not a military school, exactly," Peter wrote her from Indiana, "but it might as well be. No one is allowed to think, or to have opinions, or to speak unless spoken to."

That, exactly, was what Daddy had intended.

The Jensens moved away. Sarah never heard what became of Corey, but she hoped he grew up into a normal and happy life. It was understood that no one in the Tobler family was to speak of Corey, or what Peter had done to him, or of the brief, sad time when Peter Tobler had been a patient in Independence.

I never understood what got into Peter," Arlene said. "He was never like that—never mean, never physical or rowdy like so many boys nowadays."

"I blame the detasseling," Sarah said.

They were sitting in the kitchen the next day, waiting for Nance to make her morning visit—a visit Sarah didn't look forward to. Arlene was pondering what she'd said. "How does that make sense?"

"You know. All those teenage kids away from their parents all day. No adult supervision."

"But the leaders were grownups, weren't they?"

"Two on each bus, if you count the driver. All they cared about was getting the work done and getting home. They weren't teaching etiquette."

"And you detasseled," Arlene said. "Everybody in Iowa detassels; it's how high school kids make summer money."

"I just did it for a couple of weeks," Sarah said. "You remember: I got heatstroke and had to come home and go to bed. I was sick for a week."

"I do remember. You looked like a beet."

"But that was time enough—riding out to Pioneer Hybrids on that decrepit school bus, all those rough kids from East Waterloo, black kids and white, boys *and* girls, all of them with the dirtiest mouths you ever heard."

"I guess that doesn't surprise me," Arlene said. "Or shock me."

"And then in the fields . . ." Sarah filled her coffee cup at the stove. "Pulling those damned tassels and getting yelled at if you missed a row. Everybody swore all the time. I learned my entire four-letter vocabulary in just those few days."

"I wondered," Arlene said.

"And sex," Sarah said. "Kids hiding in the fields we'd already finished with, actually screwing under that beastly hot sun. And coming home on the bus. . . ." She trailed off.

"What about that?"

"I blame those bus trips for the change in Petey. I think the black kids challenged him, made him dare to be as coarse as they were. You remember? That was the year his grades started dropping, the year after his one summer of detasseling."

"Why didn't you say something at the time?"

"Oh, Mother. Daddy never paid any attention to what I had to say. I don't think he ever will."

Arlene sighed. "Well," she said, "it's all water under the bridge, isn't it."

But Sarah was thinking of the bus ride home, her last day detasseling, the same day she faltered and fell in a tall field east of Hudson, another girl—she was from Orange Township School, Sarah still remembered—finally noticing, running to ask *What's the matter?* and fetching the leader. The leader was a college boy from Ames; he thought she was faking. The Orange Township girl finally had to start hitting him with her fists—weeping, shrieking—before he could be made to realize the emergency.

"Paul always says I should erase it from my memory," Arlene said.

"Mother," Sarah said.

Her mother looked around. A woman was standing at the screen door, hand shading her eyes, looking in.

"Nancy." Arlene got up and ushered her into the kitchen. "You remember Nancy Riker," her mother said. "Harvey's wife."

"Yes. Certainly." Polite as she could be, Sarah marveled at Nancy Riker's drabness. She was what? In her fifties, and looked as if she'd been born old.

"Sarah," the Riker woman said, "don't you look blooming." She poured herself coffee and sat at the table across from Arlene. "You were talking about Peter," she said. "I heard you."

"I was only telling Sarah how seeing one of my children makes me think of both of them." No thought of the baby who'd died, Sarah noticed. That memory *had* been erased.

"The two of you could almost be twins," Nancy said. "Mother and daughter look-alikes."

"Except for my gray," Arlene said.

Sarah sipped. Nancy Riker had no children. Was that choice, she wondered, or accident, or incapability? Though who would want to give kids to Harvey? No sensible person. Yet Nancy seemed envious of Mother.

"Will you two be upset if I smoke?" Sarah wanted to know. "I can go out on the porch if you'd rather."

"All right by me," Nancy Riker said.

"I guess I can put up with your bad habits," Arlene said. "I'm probably responsible for them."

"I'll have one with you," said Nancy.

Sarah lit a filtered cigarette with the silver lighter Phil had given her last Christmas. She sent a first cloud of smoke upward and reached across the table to light Nancy's Marlboro. "Are you visiting Daddy today?"

Arlene was bringing a heavy glass ashtray down from the top shelf of one of the cupboards beside the sink. She set it on the table between the smokers. "I go over to the jail every day," she said. "I hope you'll come with me this time."

"No," Sarah said. "I told you before: what I think of his stupid martyrdom—not to mention what got him there in the first place. I couldn't be very kind to him."

Arlene shot a glance at Nancy that said: *You see?* "Suit yourself," she told Sarah.

"I came to see *you,*" Sarah said, "to keep you company while Daddy played his games."

She had planned to stay only a week, but in the end she stayed nearly three, calling Phil and the girls once or twice a week, hearing the impatience in Phil's voice each time he asked when she'd be home. "Anyone would think you couldn't live without me," she said to him, perhaps a little peevishly, "but you hardly ever act like that when I'm around."

She was settled, more or less, in her old room at the head of the stairs, sharing the bathroom with her mother. The bathroom counter was soon covered with the black boxes and bottle caps of her Chanel colognes and powders and lotions; her skirts and dresses hung from the shower-curtain hooks. She knew it was an up-and-down experience for her mother, that in a curious way she was rejoining the family, not as a daughter but as an equal, vying for space, pushing. For every happy occasion when the two of them were recalling halcyon days, like times when Sarah brought home from school her home-ec experiments—always some exotic dish, overspiced or undercooked, that Daddy could not eat and her mother didn't dare *not* eat—there would be days of argument. They argued her father, they argued Peter, they argued Nancy Riker, whose presence seemed to Sarah constant and numbing. They argued her marriage to Phil, and how she didn't realize how fortunate she was to have a loving husband and lovely children.

One day, finally, she agreed to go to Waterloo with her mother, but when they arrived at the jail, she begged off and sat in the parking lot while Arlene visited. On the drive home, they fought again.

"We truly don't understand each other," Arlene complained. "You don't have the faintest idea how terrible this is for me—Paul in jail, how lonely I am at night, you reminding me of when I was a young woman like you. Peter's trouble. Bringing it all back. You don't even try to understand your father; you can't begin to see why he won't spend the money to stay out of jail."

"And you don't know the first thing about my life," Sarah said. "Or my husband's. Or my children's."

"I think you still don't know what you want out of life. You never did."

"And maybe I never will." She took out a cigarette. "And you forget: Daddy never did like Phil. 'Accountants never kiss first,' is what he said to me once." She lit the cigarette. "I hated that. It was too true; even now, Phil is the passive one. But I was still upset."

"Phil makes a good living," Arlene said. "You have a roof over your head—"

"And three meals a day. Yes, Mother."

"A lot of people don't."

She rolled the window halfway down and threw the scarcely smoked cigarette out. "And even Daddy's got that in the county jail. You think that's sufficient?"

Yet she had no idea what she would say if her mother probed her dissatisfaction—how much she would confess, how far she would reveal her miseries. Would she admit she was sorry she had given up the library job? Tell how she hated Philip's home office—his clients traipsing through her living room? Betray the secret of their bad sex? Or complain that the demands of two small girls were turning her mind to pudding?

Sarah wondered when she had first decided not to confide in Arlene: *long ago,* was the answer, *and for good.*

O n her last morning in Iowa, Sarah sat in the kitchen with her mother, the two of them drinking coffee and sharing a single doughnut. The car was loaded; she had called to confirm that her flight was on schedule and was allowing herself a conservative three hours to get to the Cedar Rapids airport. Arlene turned her half-empty cup in its saucer, looking into it as if she were reading the future—or perhaps it was the past she was seeing, for that was the turn this last conversation was taking.

"Do you remember our trip to Kentucky?"

"Oh, yes. Was it Calumet Farm where we saw that Triple-Crown winner? Citation?"

"Yes." Arlene sighed. "He's a long time dead."

"God, he was old then," Sarah said. "That's one thing I re-member from that trip." She got up and brought the Chemex to the table to refill both their cups, then put it back on the stove. "Dad wasn't with us, was he?"

"He'd begged off. It was just you and Peter and me."

"I remember we went to that society horse show. It was at a racetrack there. Do you remember it?"

"Vaguely," Arlene said.

It was clear in Sarah's mind: a racetrack, a brightly lighted in-field, crowds all around, everybody seeming better dressed than the Toblers. It was before Peter's trouble.

"We were sitting in the grandstand, and they'd already started the show—they'd judged the first class, maybe the first two—and all at once this big white Mercedes car came onto the infield. It came in really fast, and pulled alongside three or four other cars that were already parked. I remember thinking, *Wow, what an entrance!* Then this man and woman got out—he was in a tux and she wore this long sparkly gown—and they walked across the infield and across the track to a box below us in the grandstand." *Showing off*.

"Yes, now I do remember."

"I thought: God, I want to make an entrance like that someday. And then I thought of Daddy, and I got this image in my head of him tearing onto the infield at a classy show like that one, sitting up on his old John Deere tractor, waving to the horsey set. And then the two of us, Daddy and me, jumping down from the tractor in our dirty denim in front of all those society people."

"And me applauding, I suppose."

Sarah shook her head. "It was funny when I imagined it," she said.

"I don't think it's funny," her mother said.

Arlene was waving from the porch as Sarah drove away. Both women had hugged and kissed, said their good-byes as if Sarah's visit had not ended on a note of tension. She had tried to break it by noticing the weather. "Look at those clouds," she had said. "It'll rain for sure. That will make Daddy happy."

"Too late," Arlene said. "The damage is done."

By the time she reached the other side of Waterloo, the rain had commenced, driven by a wind that carried as much dirt as water, and an hour later, as she drove through Cedar Rapids, the downpour was so heavy she had to pull into a bank parking lot to wait until the windshield wipers could keep up with the filthy rain.

Three weeks later, with Paul still in jail and ten days left on his sentence, Arlene stood at the kitchen window waiting for the water on the stove to boil for coffee. In the darkness of the autumn morning—wasn't this the weekend to turn back the clocks?—she could see the cornpicker's two bright lamps moving down the long rows between the county road and the creek, and the parking lights of the empty truck waiting to carry shelled corn to storage. The men—Paul's friends—had arrived before five, and by six o'clock the thermometer read 65 degrees; a blustery wind from the southeast buffeted the farmhouse and swayed the nearly leafless branches of the cottonwood and sighed under the eaves. Even though it was late in October, the weather was warm, but at least the drought had truly broken and the rains had come; now, after two dry days, the men were anxious to get into the fields. There was no thought of waiting for Paul to be released, to see to his land by himself.

Jess Eriksen was driving the picker. Burton Stone was in the truck. One of Burton's hired help, a Jim somebody, drove a second truck she could just now see entering the field at the east end. Even though the crop was poor as poor, you couldn't let the corn just rot, Burton had said; you couldn't let a bad year be worse. She knew he was right. She knew it bothered the men to have waited as long as they had. Hadn't the sudden wet kept them out of their own fields much of the month? And how did you know the weather wouldn't take it into its head to send rain again, trying to make up for the summer drought all at once? Earth sense. The good sense that would have been Paul's, too, if he had been free.

She poured the boiling water through the coffee filter. Now that the light was growing she could see where the field was already picked, the shattered cornstalks almost yellow in contrast to the pale brown of the standing rows beyond. Where was Grimmie, she wondered—her annual fretfulness that he would be too slow out of the way of the machinery, too absorbed in the flights of frantic field mice to realize his own risk. And then— the darker fretfulness she believed she would never get used to— *What's to become of us? Never mind the silly cat. What's to become of Arlene and Paul Tobler, overextended at the bank, undersubscribed to the*

new government programs, still in debt at the Farm Fleet and the imple-
ment dealership, in the worst crop year of our lives? But it could be worse,
she told herself. *We could have no friends.*

She had finished her first cup of coffee when Harve Riker's
pickup pulled into the yard. Nance opened the passenger-side
door and stepped down to the ground, handbag over her shoulder. When she slammed the door shut, the truck backed around
and sped off down the driveway toward the fields on the other
side of the road.

Nance came up the steps and into the kitchen.

"Harvey's hopping mad," she said. "He says it's my fault he's
late." She pulled out a chair and sat heavily. "He slept through
the alarm, and the darned clock is next to *his* bed."

"Have some coffee," Arlene said.

"Thanks." She opened the bag and pulled out a wad of cloth
that Arlene recognized as an afghan Nance had been working on
forever. "Everything in my life is such a mess lately."

"Are you all right?" When Harvey was upset, you looked for
him to take it out on Nance, and so it was only natural that Arlene should ask such a question, should look to see if Nance had
been crying, if she was bruised, if her clothes had been torn
somewhere.

"I think so. I don't know." She dug out her crochet hook and
a ball of heavy black thread; she bunched the afghan under her
hands nervously.

"What's happened?"

"I think Harvey knows," Nance said. "He saw me with Burton, and I believe he's figured it out."

Arlene shivered.

"God, Arlene—What's going to become of us? What's going
to happen to *me*?"

"How could he have caught you? You've been so careful."

"No." Nancy shook her head. "We were foolish. *I* was foolish.

If it had been up to Burton, nobody'd ever have known. It was about three weeks ago, just before that first heavy rain that broke the dry spell. I told Harvey I was coming over here, to see you, to have coffee and do some sewing you and I had both been saving up for a rainy day. I knew if he telephoned, you'd think of something to say to him. You'd know what was happening."

"I expect I would have," Arlene said. *Part of the conspiracy.* That made her as guilty as Nancy or Burt. *How'd you get yourself tangled up in all this?* Paul had said when she first told him. *You know better. Good Christ, it can't lead to anything but trouble for that dumb Nancy, and the trouble's going to rub off on you, too.*

"But instead I was with Burton all afternoon. Oh, God, Arlene. You can't know—you can't remember—what it's like to be loved hard, to be held so dear as Burton holds me. How easy it is to let time go and not care. How all you want to do in the whole world is close your eyes and feel cherished."

She put out her hands and covered Arlene's. *My Lord,* Arlene thought, *she's crying; what a pair the two of us make, weeping over men.*

"Harve was doing errands in town. He was taking the pickup in for a new muffler, buying some motor oil on sale at the Wal-Mart, stuff like that. It didn't even occur to me that he'd come over to your place looking for me."

"But he didn't," Arlene said.

"No, I know—except that he headed for your place on his way back from town, and that took him past Burton's."

"Oh, dear," Arlene said. *Oh, foolish Nancy.*

"And I'd been smart enough to pull the old Datsun behind the shed, but not far enough so it couldn't be seen from the direction of town. You know. I thought, well, if he does come past Stone's, he'll come from the direction of our place."

"So he saw the car."

"He saw the car. And he stopped, of course."

"I hope you and Burton were decent." She tried to imagine Nancy's panic—the excuses she must have picked over, deciding which was the best one to try on her husband.

"We'd just come down to the kitchen. We were sitting at the table, talking, laughing, when here was Harvey's shadow in the doorway. 'What's the joke?' he said. God, Arlene. 'What's the joke?'"

"What did you say?"

"That I was doing an errand for you-all. That Paul had borrowed something from Burton, and that when I left your place he'd asked me to drop it off if I didn't mind going out of my way. God, Arlene, I was so rattled. Harvey asked what it was—what had Paul borrowed—and I was tongue-tied. I couldn't think. Burton finally saved me. He said it was his floor jack, and that explained why I was parked up behind the shed—so he didn't have to lug that heavy jack so far to put it away."

Arlene shook her head. "Paul and Harvey may not be so close as they used to be," she said. "But they've been friends since the year One. They were thick as thieves over the bridge. You know that. They talked. They drank together almost every night."

"I know."

"You weren't thinking," Arlene said.

"That's what Burton said. He said I should always have an alibi already in my mind—that I should keep it simple, not full of stuff people could ask questions about. Like why would you expect me to go out of my way, instead of asking Burton to come pick up his jack. Or why would he have to borrow things from Burton, when he'd been keeping up a farm for thirty years."

"You're too honest," Arlene said. "You don't have any talent for deceit."

"Oh, Leenie, what will I do? I can't give him up. We're good together. He does things Harvey's never done—not even when we were first married. It's like he's got a knack, a gift. A gift for loving." She dropped her voice. "He makes me come; Harvey could hardly ever make that happen. I don't know how he does it." She looked sheepish, lowered her eyes to the afghan she clutched in her lap. "Well," she said, "of course I know how he does it, but I'm too embarrassed to say—even to my best friend."

"My goodness," Arlene said.

"I don't sleep with Harvey anymore," Nance said. "I haven't slept with him since the first time I went to bed with Burton."

"How do you explain that?"

"I don't know how to explain it—so I don't say anything." She poked the crochet needle into the ball of thread and set it aside. "I just don't let him do it to me."

O n the first Monday in November, Arlene drove to Waterloo and parked the pickup on the street outside the Black Hawk County courthouse. It was raining again; she sat in the truck waiting for Paul to be released, watching the raindrops gather on the windshield and stream in narrow rivulets down to the sill. On the other side of the glass the world was sodden and gray, the trees that lined the street leafless, the asphalt surface of the roadway pocked with dimpled puddles. The truck's windshield was broken, cracked by a rock that a car driving too fast on gravel had flung up as it passed her; that had happened only a couple of weeks ago, and the crack had grown longer day by day until now it nearly bisected the windshield and divided her vision. Paul would have put tape over it, would have known some way for the crack to be stopped before it got worse.

He had instructed her carefully. "Don't come into the building," he said when he telephoned her. "Wait for me on the Mulberry Street side of the courthouse at ten."

At fifteen minutes after the hour he had not appeared. Arlene waited; almost she wished she had cigarettes, remembering that when she was younger, a cigarette was nearly always an accessory to waiting—that it acted as a curious sort of ground, dissipating impatience, keeping her calm. To distract herself now, she watched the activity on the other side of the street, at the city hall: policemen came and went, American flags prominent on their sleeves, as if patriotism resided in the wearing of uniforms and the carrying of revolvers; sometimes youngsters—

teenagers—trailed after them, ready to take road tests to earn their drivers' licenses; a variety of men and women seemed to have business with the city, hurrying under umbrellas or half-folded newspapers through the rain. On the courthouse side of Mulberry, cars pulled into the parking lot and drove out of sight behind the building. A meter maid appeared on the street ahead, and Arlene slipped out of the truck to push a nickel into the parking meter.

Then here was Paul.

"Ten seconds sooner," she said to him, "and we could have saved a nickel."

He laughed, embraced her, kissed her. In his free hand he carried the red-striped utility bag she had first seen in 1954, when he spent Saturday mornings at the Iowa State gymnasium.

"I figure I just finished saving us five hundred bucks," he said. "I make that ten thousand nickels." Then his face got serious. "You all right?"

"I am now," she said.

Paul opened the passenger-side door and gestured for her to get in. "I'll drive," he said.

"You remember how?"

He put his hand on her bottom as she climbed in, a touch so nearly forgotten that it seemed unfamiliar to her and unexpectedly exciting. "I've missed you," he said.

He was trying to be the old Paul—the Paul before the bike-trail business, the man whose concentration was on the land and the crop and the tradition handed down from the 1850s. She could see that. She could only hope for the best, and thinking of that she said, "Are you rehabilitated? Isn't that what they call it?"

He smiled as he started up the truck. "I was a model prisoner, Warden. I think you should parole me."

"Done," she said.

"How'd you break my windshield?" He put his fingers against the tiny round bevel that marked the place where the crack had begun.

"A rock flung up at me—the day after they finished picking."

"Looks like it might have been something from a pellet gun. Or a BB shot." He rested a fingertip in the cup made by the bevel. "You sure somebody didn't take a pot shot at you?"

"It was a rock," she said. "I remember when it happened, and where. It wasn't anybody making a political statement."

Paul nodded, compressed his lips into a thin line. "Anything ever come of that TV lady?" he said.

"No. I guess she didn't think much of my answers, but then, I didn't care much for her questions."

"So she never put you on the television," he said.

"If she did," Arlene said, "I missed seeing it."

"Probably too busy with your reading."

She could see he was trying to make a joke, and that pleased her. "They did a good job with the harvest," she said. "Burton and Jess and quite a crew of men."

"Kraut Riker?" he asked. "Did he help?"

"He did. One morning he was late; blamed Nancy for letting him oversleep."

"He's a blame-shifter," Paul said. "Always was, always will be."

"You'll forgive him," Arlene said.

He sighed. "Christ, I suppose I will."

"You just wanted him in jail so the two of you could play double solitaire."

Paul laughed. "Maybe that's why I've stayed married to you for all these years. You put me in the right perspective."

Back home, he was less comfortable. His fields were bare—some people from town had already walked through without so much as a by-your-leave, looking for the stray ears to take home for door and mantle decorations, and one morning Arlene had seen a family of deer—a doe and two fawns no bigger than dogs—browsing along a fence line. Burton would turn his cattle out to forage the rest of the fields. The weather had turned gray and bitter cold. The cottonwood was bare all at once, and when Arlene looked out to see what she thought were a few last leaves, they turned out to be a flock of crows—fastened to the highest branches, swaying over the loneliness of her life like raucous judges. Paul sat moodily in the kitchen, drinking his kind of coffee, studying the figures from the co-op elevator Jess had left for him.

"Seventy-five bushels per," he said. "Year before last we averaged a hundred seventy, and last year almost that."

"Is this the worst ever?" Arlene asked.

"It sure is," he said. "It's a goddamned killer of a year."

That night he made love to her; his hands, soft from the weeks of doing nothing, were restless all over her and his mouth was hungry on hers. She thought she had no identity, no self to give up to him, but only a loneliness he drove out of her and an emptiness he flooded.

"Two months," she whispered. "Another kind of drought ended."

"Ended for as long as we both of us shall live," he said. She thought he had never made so sentimental a declaration. He seemed almost the boy who'd courted her a thousand years ago, and his attentiveness to her almost enough to carry her safely through the winter ahead.

$$—$$

4

$$—$$

O n the second Friday in February the longest cold snap of the Iowa winter ended abruptly and blessedly. Much later in the year—when her life had gotten calm again, when her days had settled themselves into a manageable routine—Arlene would remember that the sudden moderation had seemed like a broken spell. By the middle of that morning, when she came to the kitchen to make coffee and put down food for the orange cat, the mercury in the thermometer outside the kitchen window had already reached into the high twenties. A dense fog hung over the farmyard; she could not find even the outline of the tall cottonwood, and the three wires that fed utilities to the house emerged as if from the clouds, magical, cased in silver sheaths of ice. The dulled light had become palpable, coating whatever it touched. Branches would probably give way. The power-company crews would be out in force.

Arlene was relieved. The prolonged cold had unnerved her. For two weeks she had waked in the middle of the night and gone from bathroom to laundry room to kitchen, turning on the faucets—a strong trickle—so the water from the well would move through the pipes, not freeze and burst them; she had folded old bath towels and shoved them up against doorsills as tightly as she could to intercept drafts; she had made sure the curtains were drawn and the drapes pulled together, especially on the north and west sides of the house.

Now, busy at the stove, she heard Paul come up onto the porch, stamp his feet, force open the door into the kitchen. He came inside, his mackinaw unbuttoned, and bent across the sink to see the numbers on the thermometer. "Weather like this," he said, "Harve might even get that old pickup of his to start."

"You got up early," Arlene said.

"Wanted to pull that diesel pump before the cold sets in again. I'd have said it was you that got up late."

"I was reading my book till all hours."

"You can take the teacher out of the schoolhouse," he said. He lifted his blue coffee mug out of the dish drainer and sat at the oak table, turning the empty mug between his palms as if they needed warming. "That's some fog," he said. "Hope it lifts before dark."

Tonight it was the Toblers' turn to host the gang for cards— and beers, the usual banter and complaint among the men, the predictable gossip from Nance. Thank heaven they didn't have to come out at twenty below; that was good. But now they might have to drive blind, and that was bad. Balance, Paul might have said. *Sometimes luck evens out.*

"I suppose Nancy and Burton are both going to be here," he said.

"I don't see a way around it."

"I wish you weren't any part of that."

"I didn't think I was." She poured coffee into the blue mug.

"You know what I'm saying. She tells you all about it—what the two of them do, where they do it." He lifted the coffee to his mouth, testing its temperature, but set the cup down without drinking. "How long does she think she can tomcat around be- hind Harvey's back?"

"That's the real point," Arlene said. "I don't believe she *does* think." And of course Harvey knew; everybody knew. How could the two of them not hear the whispers, not see the know-all grins?

But Paul was right; Arlene herself had long ago been drawn in, had been made a discreet partner in the adultery. But was that a bad thing? Didn't she in her heart of hearts approve, knowing Harvey Riker for the difficult, abusive man he was, tightfisted with his money except when he was buying whiskey at the Osco or beers at the D-Town Tap? Poor Nance was entitled to something better, even if it was a something stolen.

She remembered the day Burton's truck had broken down, and her last words to him after he'd fixed his radiator hose and refilled the radiator—*You be good to Nancy. She deserves it.*

And he *had* been good to her; Nance bore witness to that whenever the two women were together, but oh, dear God, how burdened Arlene was by what she knew of this difficult sexual business. *Business,* Paul would grumble; she would always hear the word in his ironic tone of voice. *Goddamned monkey business.*

The evening began as always, with a game of pepper, all six of them at the kitchen table, beer cans popping like punctuation, the cards getting damp. Arlene would rather have played bridge, but that hadn't happened since Carol's death nearly a year ago, when it was Jess and Carol Eriksen, and Nance with Arlene. That was before the Hovelands sold their farm and moved to Phoenix; sometimes Emma Hoveland sat in for Jess so the girls could have bridge and the boys could have their pepper or their poker. Jess had taken his wife's death especially hard; it was cancer, of course, and after he'd gotten past the grief he'd been profoundly angry—at doctors and hospitals and even at whatever god it was that he had faith in. Arlene could understand that; it was how she had felt when the baby died, and again when Peter went haywire. Now Jess was more like his old self, but he had also acquired a habit of enthusiasm so pronounced it rang false to Arlene—as if he were trying to generate within himself an energy that wasn't truly native to him. He seemed puppyish, a foolish stance she thought inconsistent with the personality of an older man.

When the game switched to poker—at Harvey Riker's insistence—Arlene excused herself and went to the parlor, where she took up the book she had begun reading when the mercury first plunged to twenty-eight below. Her winter project was re-reading *Middlemarch,* where she saw so much of herself in Dorothea Brooke that she had already grown impatient with the way Casaubon treated her. Nance was the foolish Rosamond, though she lacked Rosamond's manners. The male characters were less familiar; Arlene could not fit anyone she knew into the mold of Eliot's men, unless she tried to force Burton Stone into Lydgate. Burton was surely more dashing than Paul, or Harve, or Jess, but he wasn't polished the way Eliot's hero was.

She had just begun Book Four, called "Three Love Problems," when Nance joined her, taking out of the bag she had brought with her the afghan Arlene knew for a fact she had been working at for more than two years. Nance was still crocheting squares for it; only a couple of dozen of them had actually been sewn together. For a while the two women sat silently, each absorbed in her own pastime, and yet Arlene sensed that Nance was distracted, and Nance's distraction interfered with the story in her hands.

"Everything all right in the kitchen?" Arlene said.

"Same old stuff," Nance said. "Jess whining about the bets being too steep, Harvey drinking his beer too fast, your Paul sitting like the Sphinx."

"I suppose I ought to put the coffee on," Arlene said.

"Probably," Nance said. "What book are you reading?"

"*Middlemarch.* I haven't read it since college."

"Who's it by?" Nance reached over to tip the cover up. " 'George Eliot,' " she read. "Is he good?"

"Wonderful."

"I wish I was a reader," Nance said. "Maybe if I read books I wouldn't fret so much about myself."

"New trouble at home?"

"Oh, no. Just the same old stuff." She laid her crocheting in her lap, and for a moment set her teeth over her lower lip. "Ever since Harvey found me at Burt's, he watches me."

"Watches you how?"

"Just watches me. Never looks away from me when we're in the same room. God, I can *feel* his eyes on me even when my back's turned to him."

"Well," Arlene said. *You can't blame him,* she wanted to say.

"He makes me feel dirty," Nance said.

She resumed her crocheting. Arlene studied her friend—the angle of her head, the stray silver hairs catching the lamplight and showing vividly against the youthful black, the profile with its sharp nose and thin mouth and the chin a little too weak. Nance had been pretty when she was a girl, never beautiful or handsome.

"And now this thing with the doctor," Nance said. She kept her head bowed, attentive to the needles moving in her hands.

"What thing?" Arlene said.

"I went in a week ago—to the women's clinic at Covenant. I had tests." The needles stopped. The men were laughing in the kitchen; a beer can popped and hissed. "The usual things we both do every year or so," Nance said.

"And?"

"The doctor—Weissman? you know which one he is?"

"The fat one with the rimless glasses." Arlene remembered him; he smelled of something sweet—breath mints or shaving soap.

"He called me Tuesday morning. The Pap smear. He called it 'suspect.' Whatever that means. He had me go back yesterday, to do it all over again."

"What did he say?"

"He said he didn't want me to be alarmed. That was the word: 'alarmed.' He said sometimes the lab made errors. He said they might have gotten a false reading."

"They might have," Arlene agreed. How could she not? "You read about lots of carelessness in hospitals and laboratories."

"I know they might," Nance said. "I'm really trying not to be alarmed."

"That's good."

"But that's how my sister died. I mean that's how it started—with a bad Pap test. She was dead inside of two years."

"That was a long time ago," Arlene said. "They know a lot more now about treatment."

"But not cure," Nance said. "And it's not like Annette died a hundred years ago. It's only been eleven. And look at poor Carol; that's just over a year back."

"Have you been sick? Have you found anything else—any symptoms?"

"No. I've never felt better." She showed a wry smile. "My life's a mess, but I feel wonderful."

"Then they've caught it in time, even if it *is* something."

"God willing."

"Does Harvey know?"

"About the tests? No."

"Maybe you ought to tell him," Arlene said.

"I don't tell Harvey anything about anything."

"What about Burton? Have you told him?"

Nance bent to her crocheting. "What would be the use of spoiling a good thing?" she said. She started to cry, silently, her lips working. "What earthly use?"

From the kitchen, Arlene could hear small flare-ups among the men over their poker. When she knew it was hopeless to try to finish her chapter, she set *Middlemarch* aside.

"Will you be O.K.?" she said to Nance.

Nance wiped at her cheeks and nodded.

Persuaded that it was all right to leave Nance alone, Arlene went to make a pot of coffee for the men. The center of the oak table was a litter of wooden matches—the Diamond matches that usually sat in the red, white, and blue box at the back of the stove. Beer cans perched around the edge of the table; Paul was dealing, holding his arms high so as not to knock over the cans under his elbows.

"I started overhauling that injection pump today," he was saying. "Figured I'd better get to it while the weather was bearable."

"Supposed to get another cold wave next weekend," Jess said.

"You remember Steve Walsh?" Burton said. "Used to farm over in Butler County before he sold out to some guy wanted to put in another feedlot?"

"What about him?" Jess said. "I knew him. He went to work in Waterloo, at Chamberlain's."

"That's him. He told me once he was unloading a pile of scrap Chamberlain had bought from the tractor works, and damned if he didn't find a brand new injection pump, supposed to go on one of the big new John Deeres."

"Probably damaged," Jess said.

"Nope. Steve said it was perfect—still in waxed paper inside a cardboard carton. He said it shone, all brass and cast iron, like a piece of jewelry."

"Those puppies are expensive," Paul said. "Four or five thousand dollars, I bet."

"Somebody at Deere's trying to steal it," Harvey Riker said. "Stole the fucker, hid it in pile of scrap, planning to come back and get it after his shift was up."

"That's possible," Burton said.

"Had the scrap sold out from under him before he could get back to it."

"Poetic justice," Burton said.

"Stupidity," Harvey said. "Plain fucking stupidity."

"What'd Steve do with the pump?" Jess wanted to know.

"I don't know. Took it back to Deere's, I guess."

Harvey snorted. "Why in hell'd he take it back? Jesus Christ, Burton," he said. "Don't you know anybody who *isn't* stupid?"

Burton looked hard at Harvey. "Well, let's see, Harve. I know you, so I guess maybe I *don't* know anybody who isn't stupid."

Jess whooped. "He gotcha, Harvey. You flat asked for it."

Harvey scowled at Jess and took a long pull from his beer can. "Don't take much to amuse you, does it, Jess," he said.

Nance had come out of the parlor—probably, Arlene thought, when she heard Burton's voice and then her husband's. Burton looked up at her, all smiles.

"Hey, Nancy," he said. "Why don't you stand behind old Harve there; give me a signal when he's trying to run a bluff."

Arlene held her breath.

"I'm not by nature a bluffer," Harve said.

"Shit," Paul said. "We going to play poker, or what?"

Nance came all the way into the kitchen to take down a coffee mug from the sideboard near the stove. Her eyes met Arlene's, then darted away.

Arlene had almost finished making coffee when she detected another shift in the tenor of the game. As she turned away from the stove, the hot water seeping musically through the black grounds, Burton was talking about his service in Vietnam.

"It changed *me,*" he was saying. "Don't you doubt that for a second. For one thing it made me a lot more serious about the land I knew I was coming home to. What we did to those poor gook farmers. . . ." He stopped and frowned at the cards in his hand. "I got a hand like a foot," he said.

"They say it'll take fifty years for the land to come back from all that herbicide we laid down," Paul said.

"Shit," Harvey Riker said. "It'll take all Eternity for those thousands of American boys to come back."

"Thank God none of our children were old enough to go,"

Arlene said. She looked at Burton, thinking what a baby he still was by comparison to the other men at the table. "And thank God *you* came back safe and sound."

"Why, thank you, Arlene."

Jess nudged Paul. "I think your Mrs. is sweet on the rancher here."

"She don't mean anything by it," Paul said. He winked at Arlene. "She's got enough man on her hands at home."

"Hell, I'm harmless anyway," Burton said.

Jess chortled. "That ain't how I hear it," he said. "I used to see that pick-em-up of yours, parked out of the way on the Parkersburg cutoff all last fall. Almost every afternoon till the weather turned sour."

Arlene felt a chill. Burton reddened, even as he was smiling now over his cards.

"So are we playing poker?" Burton said.

"Don't deny it," Jess said. He poked Burton's shoulder with a finger. "You used to park on the cutoff just past the county bridge. I used to come by you on my way home from the market."

Paul rocked back in his chair and shook his head. "Jess, you been living alone so long, you can't separate the things you invent from the things you actually see."

"I know the difference, God damn it." Jess examined his cards—sulking, Arlene thought, because he knew a truth she hoped wouldn't be spoken out.

"I'll play these," Burton said.

"Thought you had a hand like a foot," Harvey said.

"I didn't say whose foot. It might be Cinderella's."

Harvey leaned forward with the deck in his right hand. "How many, Jess?"

"I'll take two."

Harvey dealt them. "Paul?"

"Do I want to bet into a pat hand?" Paul said. "I'm folding. Nothing can save this mess."

"Dealer takes one."

"Uh-oh," Jess said.

Poker fascinated Arlene—for its ritual quality, the rhythms of its language. Sometimes both she and Nance sat in with the men, but she always felt awkward at the table, fumbling with the matchsticks in front of her, trying to remember what Paul had told her about the odds against this or that combination of cards. Pepper felt more comfortable, more manageable. And bridge was civilized, downright polite. She wished Carol Eriksen hadn't died. She thought of Nance's test; was cancer contagious? something close friends and relatives gave you because they hated to leave you behind when they died?

"You sure you're not chasing after somebody, Burt?" Harve said. It seemed to be an offhand remark, all innocent, but Arlene wondered if she should whisper something to Nance. *Take Harve home. Go over and be sweet to him.*

"Me?" Burton grinned. "Those Asian women spoiled me a long time ago."

Jess snickered. "Or guv you the clap," he said.

Arlene glanced over at Nance, who was standing in front of the window that looked out onto the porch.

"Sounds like this is no place for a lady," Nance said.

"Well, you don't have to listen," her husband said. "Unless Burton's girlfriend concerns you."

"A girl who doesn't exist," Burton said.

"Who he parks with out on the Parkersburg cutoff," Harvey said. "If the weather's good. So he doesn't get caught with her in his house. Some married lady, no doubt." He was still looking, hard, at Nance.

"Who's light?" Paul said. "The pot's light."

Arlene rested her hand on Paul's shoulder, wifely, affectionately. She pinched, not hard but so he'd know to keep things calm.

"Jee-zus," Burton said. "How many Ford pickups you suppose there are in Black Hawk and Grundy and Butler counties? It ain't mine Jess thinks he saw."

"Probably some high school boys drinking beer," Arlene suggested.

"I bet that's it," Nance said.

"Next time you see that truck," Harvey said to Jess, "why don't you give the sheriff a call?"

"That's a good idea," Burton said.

"Although this time of year, Burton takes his woman someplace else," Harvey said.

"Whose bet is it?" Paul said.

"Fuck off, Tobler," Harvey said. "You aren't even in this hand."

"And watch the language," Burton said. "We agreed to keep it clean when the girls were around."

"Leave it to you to care about the girls," Harvey said.

"What's that supposed to mean?"

Harvey laid his cards down, leaned forward, pointed a finger at Burton. "Don't you goddamn play dumb."

Nance stepped toward her husband. "Honey," she said.

"Back off," he said. "Do you know you talk in your sleep?"

Later, Arlene would be obliged to tell and re-tell how Harve put up his right hand to push his wife back and away, how Burton slid his chair toward the stove and laid his own cards face down at the edge of the table, how Paul and Jess looked amazed and frightened at the same time, how the accusations started.

"Are you going to lie to me?" Harvey said. "Are you going to tell me you aren't carrying on with Nancy?"

"I'm just telling you that's not my pickup truck," Burton said.

"I could be wrong," Jess said. "Harve? I could be wrong about that truck."

"Never mind the truck. They meet at his place now, or he takes her to that motel in North Cedar. It's too cold for him to undress her in his truck."

"Nancy was at my place just that once. She was only doing me a favor."

"Is that what you call it?" Harve said. He stood, still leaning on the table with both hands. "You don't like my politics, but you don't mind humping my wife one God damn bit."

"Harvey. Honey." Nance tried again to reach out, to put her hands on him, to draw him away. Arlene would tell and re-tell that, too.

"For Christ's sake, Harve," Burton said, "you've been a mental case ever since the sheriff arrested you and Paul here for setting fire to the West Fork bridge."

"And I owned up to it, didn't I? I paid my goddamned fine to the county for it. You don't have the guts to own up to *your* crimes," Harvey said. "You fucking coward. What'd you do when you was in Vietnam? Rape the women and shoot the children?"

Burton stood. His fists were clenched, his face was dark. "You don't even know how to make Nancy happy," he said hoarsely. "You don't have a clue. You'd rather have a servant than honor your woman."

"Don't you throw 'honor' at me," Harvey said. "Coveting thy neighbor's wife."

Paul got up from the table. "Let's just calm down," he said. "Let's just talk this through like reasonable people."

"You're a wife stealer and a yellow coward," Harvey said.

Then the table tipped over, Arlene would say later, *and beer bottles rolled all over the place and the cards the men had been playing poker with got soaked; when I tried to pull them apart the next morning, they were all stuck together and tore. I don't think Burt and Harve actually hit each other. I think Jess grabbed Harvey, and Paul grabbed Burt, and Nancy and I just hung on to each other as tight as we could.*

Harvey pulled himself loose from Jess. He straightened his shirtsleeves and tucked his shirt deeper into the waist of his Levi's. "I wouldn't dirty my hands on this fucker," he said, and he walked to the porch door, flung it open and went out into the darkness. The damp night air poured into the room; Paul let go of Burton's arms and pushed the door closed.

"Jesus," Jess said. "That was quite an altercation."

Nance went to Burton, who put his hands at her shoulders and drew her against him. "God, I'm sorry," she said. "I don't have any idea what he knows for sure, or how he knows it. I never told him anything. I always tried to act natural around him."

It was like a tableau, Arlene would say, *all of us frozen in the kitchen light. Nance and Burton hugging, Paul bending down to lift the table upright, Jess standing in the living room doorway and breathing like a man who'd been running hard, and me—I was feeling so sorry for Nance, this argument happening tonight of all nights, and I was standing in front of the sideboard, directly opposite the door to outside. Then all of a sudden that door banged open.*

Harvey stood just inside the kitchen. He had a revolver in his right hand, and it was aimed at Burton, who pushed Nance away from him the moment the door flew back on its hinges.

"You damn well better get away from him," Harvey said to Nance.

"Jesus," Jess said.

Paul said, "For God's sake, Harve, put that thing away," and he started toward Harvey with his hands out to him.

"Paul, don't," Arlene said.

I'd seen the gun before, Arlene would tell the sheriff's people. *I'd seen it on my own kitchen table when Harve was cleaning it, and Paul was oiling his 12-gauge, and I'd heard them talk about it more than once. Harve had bought it at an auction in Waverly. He said it was a .38 caliber police special, and he kept it in the glove box of his pickup. He used it to shoot gophers and woodchucks, and crows and rabbits, and for self-defense. I never liked that gun; never liked the look of it—that dark blue barrel and cross-hatched brown grip. It scared me.*

It scared me too, Nance would say. *It scared me from the day he brought it home. I didn't want it in the house. I was the one made him keep it in the truck.*

Then the gun went off. It seemed to surprise Harvey as much as anyone. Arlene was watching his face; his eyes widened, and he looked down at the revolver as if he hadn't known he was carrying it, aiming it.

What happened after the noise of the gun firing was like a movie, a western Arlene had seen once in Waterloo, in which there was a wild gunfight, and men and horses were falling left and right like a ballet, and everything was slow motion. Now, in her own kitchen, the same kind of thing was happening. First, the Chemex flask on top of the stove exploded into hundreds of shards of glass, then the coffee spilled over onto the stove and put out the gas flame under the flask, and for a long time the kitchen was silent. Then Arlene could hear the gas hissing from the drowned unit, and she heard the sound of someone breathing—she imagined it was herself—and she could smell whatever it was that the gas company puts in the gas so you know if you've got a leak, and she could also smell something that was probably gunpowder from Harvey's revolver. Then the pilot light relit the unit in a flare of orange flame that settled back down to blue, and when Arlene looked away from the stove she saw Paul. He was sitting on the linoleum floor with his back against the oven door, and he had both hands hugged across his stomach, just below his chest. His hands were shiny and bright red.

I knew he was dead, Arlene would tell the sheriff. *I knew right then that Harve Riker had shot him dead as a woodchuck on the roadway, just for trying to be reasonable.*

When the men had finally left—the sheriff's deputy who took Harvey Riker, handcuffed, to the courthouse in Waterloo; the medical examiner, wearing Levi's and a striped pajama top under his overcoat, who pronounced Paul Tobler dead at the scene; the wide-eyed young men in white who lifted the body onto a fancy stretcher and bore the corpse away with the ambulance lights flinging red and white shadows across the world outside her windows; poor Jess Eriksen, the only one of all of them who had wept to see Paul murdered—Arlene sat for a long time in the parlor and felt the silence of the house enclose her as if she were a creature under an ocean.

Nance stayed with her, pale and quiet, as unlike her normal self as could be imagined. Partly she stayed to keep company with the new widow woman; partly it was that she could not go home to her own empty house, nor did she—even she—have the foolish courage to go to Burton's house, though when Arlene thought back on it, she was sure Nance must have ached to. Or perhaps she stayed with Arlene because she imagined she might obscure Paul's mortality with her own.

"You don't need to stay," Arlene finally told her. "I'll be all right." The sound of her own voice was amazing to her—so hollow and artificial-sounding, like hearing one of those exotic birds with the split tongues, who mimic human words without human comprehension.

All Nance would say was, "I know he didn't mean it, Leenie. I'm positive he didn't." But, having said that, she remained, arms folded, drawn together small at the end of the sofa, the unfinished afghan a heap of black and green and yellow on the cushion beside her. After a while she fell asleep, head fallen against the sofa back, mouth open in a small snoring.

Arlene unsnarled the afghan and spread what there was of it across Nance's lap. Then she went to the phone to call Sarah. She knew what she was going to say to her daughter: *Your father is dead.* She would explain the circumstances as calmly as she could, and then she would say, *Please don't come home.*

"Sweet Jesus, Mother," Sarah said over the hollow miles from California, "of course I'm coming home. I made the trip when he went to jail. I can surely be there for his funeral."

"No," Arlene said. "And mind your mouth."

"To help with the arrangements. You don't have to do everything yourself."

"There are no arrangements," she told Sarah. "Your father had a living will."

"What does that mean?"

"He signed up to donate his organs when he died. He did it a long time ago, after the baby was stillborn." She shifted the phone to her other hand and dug a handkerchief from her apron pocket to wipe at her eyes. "They've already taken him—the body—away from here. When they've done with him, they'll cremate him and send me his ashes."

"I never heard of such a thing," Sarah said.

"They call it 'harvesting,'" Arlene said.

"I still think you should let me come and be helpful."

Arlene sighed. Why wouldn't Sarah just shut up and go off someplace to mourn for her father? "If you'd like, I'll tell them to send the ashes to you."

"Mother. My God." There was a long silence, as if Sarah might be talking to someone in the room with her. Then: "All right," she said. "I won't come. Have it your way."

"You'll tell Peter?"

"Peter's still in China, but yes, I'll tell him."

"Be sure to tell him, no matter what he thinks, that his father loved him."

"I'll do my best."

"That's all anyone can ask," Arlene said, and hung up the phone.

When she went back to the living room, Nance was still snoring. Arlene sat in Paul's chair by the front window, waiting, she imagined, for the sun to appear, as if daylight might erase not merely the night, but the night's events. The doctor had made her take a tranquilizer, to settle her, to help her sleep, but her body was saying *no,* and she stayed wide awake. She wished she could be Nancy Riker, just long enough to smother her thoughts, slip for an hour or so into a sweet oblivion. Instead, she thought of Paul dead, lying on a metal table in some bright hospital room; of young doctors shopping through his body for spare parts to rebuild the living; of the peculiar use of the word 'harvesting' when the corpse was a farmer. When the sun did come, a sliver of red showing through the grove of cedars a half mile off along the creek, it changed nothing but appearances.

Later, when the day had truly begun, Arlene went out to the

porch to clear the silence from her head. The farmyard looked
torn up. Tire tracks were everywhere in the thawed earth, the
lingering evidence of the aftermath of the horror; the boxy ambulance and the white sheriff's cars, the doctor's gray sedan, Harvey's pickup and Jess's rusted station wagon—they had all carved
deep circles and arcs into the mud. And the world was still melting. As she stood, feeling Nance standing behind her in the
kitchen doorway—as if she needed to be watched, kept from going down the steps and running away to God knew where—
Arlene could hear the ice shards falling from wires and tree limbs
all around.

Afterward, Nance seemed determined to take the blame for
what had happened to Arlene and doubly determined to atone
for it. Three or four times a week she arrived at Arlene's door,
hugged Arlene and cried, sat in Arlene's kitchen and drank coffee. Sometimes she brought doughnuts with her, or pastry she
had bought at The Shed. She was beginning to drive Arlene to
distraction—as if the grief and the loneliness weren't enough,
she had this weeping woman on her hands.

"If I'd have known he was capable of that," Nance would
say, "I don't know what I'd have done."

"Been more discreet, probably," Arlene would say.

"Or given him up," meaning Burton.

"I doubt you'd have given him up," Arlene would say, for
Nance had not in fact given Burton up even after the killing.
Only now she visited the man openly, parking her car in front of
his house—the car there at all hours, like a defiance, Arlene
thought.

Other days it would be the gun Nance was guilty for.

"I could have stopped him buying it," she would say, always
telling Arlene things she already knew—from the sheriff, from
the papers, from Nance herself. "When he bid for it at the
auction in Waverly, I was with him. I could've put my foot down.

But I let him get it. I saw he was in love with it. Nobody could tell him it was useless on the farm. You couldn't shoot crows with it; it wasn't really for rabbits or woodchucks, no matter what he may have said. But he had to have it, and I let him, and *now* look."

Arlene wondered if Nance thought she could bring Paul back to life if she confessed enough. She wondered if Nance thought "redemption" was the same as "contrition"—and anyway, did Nance believe in God, so that her being sorry mattered beyond the useless words she spoke? She was a churchgoer—Arlene knew that—but whatever Nance's real religion was, or what behaviors it tolerated, they scarcely talked about. As if an hour on Sunday mattered. It had been years since Arlene had gone to church; was that why she was a widow, and Nance had love?

Finally, of course, it would have to be the honest persistence of Nance's guilt that would make Arlene forgive her. Day after day Nance stopped in—either she was on her way to Burton, or she had just left his place—to apologize, to lament, to regret. Because you couldn't say to an old friend "Leave me alone; stay away," Arlene tolerated, put up with, endured. And in the end, she imagined, either from custom or habit, she would look beyond the words to see the woman—as abused by Harvey Riker over time as Arlene had been abused by him in a split second.

And there was the cancer—whether the tests for malignancy were accurate or false still remained to be determined—which meant that Nance herself was under a death sentence whose carrying out could not be guessed. She changed doctors, but her inconclusive tests didn't change.

So it was that as the weeks went by, and the terrible winter ran its course into spring with harsher cold and deeper snow than usual, Arlene began to feel a sympathy toward Nancy Riker that in February she could not have imagined. One day—it was the end of March, a day of cold rain driven by a colder wind, the eve of the auction to dispose of everything Paul had owned except the farm itself—Arlene heard herself say:

"I wish you could give your cancer to me."

It was another way of admitting—she figured this out later—that she missed Paul so much, she wanted to be dead. Why should Nance, who had at last found some pleasure in her life, be forced to give up that pleasure, when Arlene, who had lost all future chance of pleasure, went on living?

"Don't say that, Leenie."

"I mean it," Arlene said. "What have I got without Paul?"

"You've got your memories of a long, happy marriage," Nance said. "You've got children. You've got two sweet grandchildren and probably more to come. You've got lots to look forward to."

"I don't have anyone like Burton. You've got a partnership I'll never have again."

"And besides," Nancy said, "I've probably got years and years ahead of me. What's the worst that can happen? They'll maybe take out some of my fancy plumbing—but God, I never had no use for it anyway."

"You shouldn't even talk about such things," Arlene said. As if not talking about cancer or death—or any kind of evil—made it cease to exist.

Sometimes Burton came along with Nance and sat with the two women in Arlene's kitchen, listening and talking. Always he was uneasy; Arlene noticed how there was something furtive about his presence—a slouch of the shoulders, a way of ducking his head as he looked around the kitchen. It was as if he saw or heard some afterimage, some echo either of his awful time in Vietnam at last catching up with him, or of the night Harvey Riker killed Paul. She wondered what was the shape and weight of Burton's guilt, and if he blamed himself for the confrontation that started it. It was certainly on his mind; when he talked at all, it was about Harvey and the courts—the crime and the punishment of it.

"He's got a lawyer now," Burton might report. "The court wouldn't let him *not* have one, so they appointed one. Commoner, his name is; lives in Evansdale and has a practice in Waterloo."

"Harve doesn't need him," Nance said. "He's not even going to make a defense."

"How do you know that?" Burton asked. Arlene had seen him stiffen at the notion of Nance still connected to her husband.

"I talk to him," Nance said. "He likes me to visit with him, bring him magazines and little treats. I can't very well refuse, can I?"

"I suppose not." But you could tell he "supposed" otherwise— or so Arlene thought.

Another time Burton said, "You know what will happen. There'll be a plea bargain. They'll let Harve plead guilty to a lesser charge. Manslaughter, most likely, instead of murder."

"How can they do that?" Arlene wanted to know.

"They'll say the gun went off accidentally. They'll say Harve didn't intend to pull the trigger."

But what difference did it make? Harve could plead anything he wanted, anything the county prosecutor wanted. Paul was dead, dead, dead.

When in fact Harve did enter a plea of guilty to the manslaughter charge, and when he had begun serving a seven-year sentence in Anamosa, Arlene went to Paul's grave in the cemetery behind the Lutheran church in Finchford. She had nothing to put before his marker; it was too cold for flowers to bloom, too early for trees to bud, and the snow cover lingered. She came only to give him the news.

"It's the best justice can do." She said the words softly, so softly that if someone came near they wouldn't overhear her and think she was crazy. "They've put Harve away for a while. I know he'll let Nance have her divorce, so she can live with Burton." Then, turning away from the marker as if Paul might be able to see her tears and disapprove of them, she said, "Everything's resolved." Though how could she believe in resolution when she felt at such loose ends, and the ends themselves were so frayed?

The bank waited until the middle of April before it took the farm and she had signed the bank's papers—papers whose terms put money into her hands, though it was money that would not be sufficient to make her comfortable. When the debts were squared and the funeral expenses paid, Arlene banked slightly more than twenty thousand dollars. Paul's insurance, once his loans against it were deducted, would add almost twenty thousand more. Forty thousand dollars to last the rest of her life: it would have to be an awfully short life unless she found work to do.

Now the Tobler place belonged to the bank, which would resell it, eventually, to someone who would never love the land or the house as she and Paul had—to someone not connected by blood to the land's history, ignorant of the grant from President Pierce, indifferent to the generations of Toblers who had been born, and worked, and died in this very house.

"I hate to think what might become of this place," Arlene said. "It's as if our blood is in its boards and beams."

"Has the bank said anything? Do they have a buyer?"

"They haven't said. I'd hate to see some developer come along—"

"Do you *care* who owns it?" Nance said to her. "Would you be angry if Burton did?"

They were sitting in the kitchen. It was the last week in April, and it was raining, as it had been raining off and on since the middle of March, so that farmers had been kept out of the fields by mud and were obliged to stay at home or sit in The Shed or the Happy Chef or The Embers, complaining about Nature and her caprices. A northwest wind gusted against the back rooms and made moaning around the gutters and flung the rain against the unscreened windows. Images of rain and wet were everywhere. The ditches were full, like canals alongside the highway. In the lowest parts of the rolling Iowa fields the water collected and lay dimpled with the drops of fresh rain, looking like the pictures of rice paddies in China and southeast Asia. In more fields than one tractors were abandoned, bogged down in the rich mud where a farmer's impatience had got the better of his judgment. Paul would have been patient. "It won't hurt to wait," she could hear him saying. "If I'm late planting, maybe we'll luck into a good fall; if we lose time at the front end, we can gain it at the back end."

Once Arlene had thought life might be like that: If you didn't have all the satisfaction you wished for when you were young, maybe you got it when the children were grown, when the savings account was healthy, when you reached your wise and golden years, when you retired and sold off your equities and moved to Arizona and perpetual sunshine. And if none of those things happened—well, you had each other, the way Nance would have Burton. She thought this bitterly, but it wasn't Nance's fault. She said it in her mind twice. And it wasn't Burton's.

"Burton needn't feel obliged to do that. I don't blame him," Arlene said. "If I thought Paul's dying was Burton's fault, I'd have to think it was yours, too, and you wouldn't be in my kitchen, drinking coffee out of my good china cups."

"He thinks he's ready to get away from the cattle business. Thinks he might farm, raise soybeans after all. He can't keep up with the big dealers with their feedlots. He says he wouldn't treat any animal that way, like they was part of some heartless assembly line."

"He'd have to ask at the bank."

"I hate to think what all it'll cost him to start out fresh. All the machinery. The seed, the chemicals."

"He should have come to the auction," Arlene said, although she had not attended it herself—had gone into Cedar Falls for a Saturday matinee at the College Square movie theater, and then to the Brown Bottle restaurant, where she ate dinner by herself and drank a little too much wine. When she got back to the farm after dark, she could see by the sodium yard light that the last of the tracks from the night of Paul's killing had been obliterated by the feet of the bidders. "Everything Paul ever owned sold cheap. Somebody even bought the mailbox and the old rusty ploughshare it sat on."

Nance looked down at her hands. "I imagine Burton'll stay in his own house; rent this one out. If he should buy it."

"You're going to go on seeing him," Arlene said. It was a confirmation, not a question.

Nance pursed her lips. "How can I not?" she said.

Arlene thought: *Of course I want her to stay with Burton. If she scorns him, Paul's death is even more pointless.* "I like him," Arlene said. "I like you. I want the two of you to make a go of it."

She reached to take Nance's hands in hers; Nance bowed her head, kissed Arlene's fingers. *Here we are,* Arlene told herself, *two ladies learning to be widows, my man in the ground, hers in prison.*

"I don't know why God let me be luckier than you," Nance said. "I don't know why he didn't take Harvey, and let Paul go on."

"They say He takes those He loves," Arlene said. The words were an echo from her childhood, and she wondered if she had ever believed such a thing.

"Maybe I'll live to be a hundred." Nance started to cry. "Maybe that's how He'll damn me, so I can remember Paul bleeding and dying over and over again until He thinks He's punished me enough for making it happen."

"I hope He's not that kind of God," Arlene said. She disengaged her hands from Nance's and went to get more coffee.

"He hates adultery," Nance said. "It's an awful word, but that's what it was, plain and simple."

Arlene refilled her friend's cup. Where was the Jehovah's Witness lady, driving around the countryside in her gold Cadillac with the man in the Panama hat, eager to explain the ways of God? Arlene wondered. She poured coffee into her own cup and put the flask—it was new, practically the first thing she had bought after Paul was buried—back on the burner. There was still a scar in the wall behind the stove where the sheriff's man had dug out the bullet that tore the life from her husband. Burton had promised to repair the scar, but hadn't gotten around to it.

"I'm definitely divorcing Harvey," Nance said. "I already filed."

"I thought you would."

"When I drove over to Anamosa last week, I told him. He said he wouldn't contest it."

"He couldn't very well have expected you to wait for him."

"I'm really going to marry Burton. He's asked me." She looked at Arlene, eyes wide, cheeks flushed. "Can you see me legally tied to a younger man? Will people think I'm his mother?"

"Not in this day and age." Arlene lifted her cup. "I'll drink to your future. I'm sorry I don't have any whiskey to spike the coffee with."

"What will you do now?" Nance said.

"Go home." She smiled. *Home;* it was a word whose meaning had changed completely in an instant. "To South Dakota. Poor mother's in a nursing home in Sioux Falls. I suppose I'll rent a place near there—some little town—and then we'll see what we'll see."

"How will you live?"

"I guess I can still teach school. I'll do whatever South Dakota makes me do to renew my certification after all this time. Maybe I'll go out to California to visit the children."

"You should stay there, where it's warm," Nance said.

"I'm not crazy enough for that place," Arlene said. "I'd be afraid to drive."

"Well, wherever you are, will you come back and stand up with me? Be my whatever they call it?"

"I think it's still 'matron of honor,' " Arlene said, wondering if this might be the act that would make forgiveness something more than a word, "and yes," she said, "I will. Wherever I am."

———

The first of May was her last day in the house. The rooms were bare, the furniture and rugs and appliances either sold off or donated to the Salvation Army, the china and silver and kitchen utensils packed and loaded into the pickup to be carried to wherever on earth she would be setting up housekeeping. All of Paul's clothes had been piled into cartons and carried to the Goodwill—Burton had done that for her. She could not bear to touch clothing she had seen Paul wear for all the years of their marriage, clothing she had washed and ironed and hung in the closets the two of them shared, clothing that was as empty as her own life without the man's presence to give it shape. Now she stood in the center of the parlor, where the wide boards of the floor had been scrubbed one last time for whoever would live here next, and the rain—gentler now but perversely ever present—washed against the lace-curtained windows, blurring the world outside exactly as tears did.

Jess Eriksen had just left, having come over in mid-morning with boards and a hammer and nails to crate up the few pictures she could not bring herself to leave behind—pictures that had hung in the children's rooms, mostly, and so they carried a heavier freight of memories for her than the gilt-framed still lifes and Currier & Ives engravings that decorated the downstairs walls. Jess had helped her carry the crates to the truck, had hugged her, hard, until she thought he would squeeze out all her breath. Only when she imagined he was holding on because he couldn't think of words did she break away, gasping—and then she saw it was his tears he wanted to hide.

"You're my twin," he managed to say, meaning that he was remembering Carol, and then he half ran from her, climbed into his own pickup and drove blindly away.

Twin mourners, Arlene had thought, and she raised her hand as if to wave Jess good-bye, but instead clenched the fingers and pressed the knuckles against her mouth. The drizzle of rain was cool on her face, and she felt entirely bereft; it had done her no good to be told that others felt the same.

Besides the curtains, all that was left in the parlor was the framed land grant that had brought the original farm to the To-bler family—the document given to Kurt Tobler in 1856, signed by President Franklin Pierce, college friend to poet Henry Longfellow and novelist Nathaniel Hawthorne. How did she know that? From literature classes when she was a student in col-lege; from English classes when she taught school in Ankeny. Certainly she would teach again; it was appropriate, it was a re-sumption of the life Paul had interrupted when he married her, it was a perfect symmetry. *There's the likely God,* she thought: *per-fection without sympathy.*

She had thought to leave the land grant in the house, a sou-venir for the next owner, but all at once that seemed foolish. It be-longed to the Toblers; it would be meaningless to strangers, meaningless even to Burton Stone. She took it down from its nail—the wallpaper behind it was a different, paler color—and turned it over. Brown paper was glued to the back of the frame, and when she ran a fingernail along its edges the paper broke eas-ily, making a crackling sound. She pulled away the brown paper, pried out a thickness of discolored cardboard and brought the grant itself into the light. The paper was heavy—was it actually parchment?—water-stained from some accident of the past, a bit dog-eared and dirty with mildew. She wondered how long the deed had gone unframed and which generation of Toblers had framed it to protect it. The date was March of 1856, and the orig-inal grant was for forty acres; the farm had grown to its present size by the ambition—or the simple Germanic acquisitiveness— of its owners to absorb neighbors' lands. Arlene wondered if Kurt Tobler had performed some service for the country, and if the grant was his reward. Perhaps he had served with distinction in the Mexican War. Paul might have known; now she was sorry not to have asked him more questions about his family's history.

She leaned the picture frame and its glass against the wall. The land grant and the backing materials she carried to the kitchen. The box of wooden matches was in its usual place on the stove, and she took out a few of the matches. *If we still had the woodstove,* Arlene thought, *I wouldn't have to get wet again.*

Outside in the misty air, standing by the rusted burn barrel between the shed and the barn, she held the deed and the cardboard and the ragged backing paper in one hand and struck a match with the other. She touched its flare to the paper; when the flame rose toward her hand she dropped everything into the barrel and watched the language of the grant—its terms, the name of the grantee, the president's signature—watched it all disappear into black ash. All she needed to do now was lock the porch door and drive away, and it would be as if Arlene Tobler had never, ever tasted happiness on this land, in this house, with this borrowed name.

She had barely reached Iowa Falls when the rain started, and by the time she stopped for gas in Fort Dodge, darkness had descended. There was no letup to the storm, and driving in it was like traveling through a tunnel—nothing but blackness to right and left, nothing but a colorless oval of light on the road ahead, nothing to see but the slivers of rain drumming on the window and being swept away by the wipers.

"I never will get into the fields," Paul would have said. "Drought one year, flood the next. It's positively biblical."

Arlene smiled at that. *Dear lost Paul.* How long since either one of them had set foot inside a church? The closest she herself had come to God was the day she'd turned away the Jehovah's Witness lady. That gold Cadillac, that old man in the Panama hat. Had she ever told Paul about that? How many other things had she forgotten to tell him, all the years of their time together?

Will I ever stop crying? she asked herself, and in that moment, through tears and rainstorm, she caught a glimpse of something in the road ahead. She pushed the brake pedal, hard, and pulled the wheel to the left, then straight again. It was already behind her— some animal, lying in the road. "Possum," she said out loud.

Already dead. I didn't hit it.

Her breath came back to her. All the poor dumb animals, just trying to go about the business of simply living life, and people getting in the way of it.

She was glad it wasn't a cat.

She remembered a story of Burton's, one night in her kitchen, about a soldier he'd known in Vietnam. "He drove a jeep he'd liberated from somewhere, and he'd get stoned or drunk, or both, and go driving out in the boondocks, looking for animals to run down."

"What kind of animals?" Arlene had asked.

"It didn't matter. Pigs, dogs. Big or small, he'd even go off the road to run 'em over."

Nance had been there. "That's hateful," she'd said.

"I'd see him drive into a rice paddy after some scared horse, or a flock of chickens. Then he'd get the jeep stuck up to the hubs and swear blue murder at the nearest gook farmer."

"I don't think that's funny," Arlene said. "Why would a grown man do such a thing?" It was a side of Burton she hadn't seen before: seeming to take pleasure in somebody's cruelty and craziness.

"Why would you tell a story like that?" Nance had asked.

"Maybe Harvey has better ones," he said.

I should have known right then, Arlene thought now. *I should have seen the bad feelings between them that very night, as if Harvey already knew.* And as if she could have saved Paul.

Everyone had looked at Harvey Riker. Harvey scowled at Burton.

"Nothing special," Harvey said. "I've been known to run down a ground squirrel or two with the pickup when they popped up at the side of the road. You know how they raise up on their hind legs and look sassy at you."

"And so you run over them?"

"What good are they?" Harvey had said. "Not that I hit very many. They're quick, those ground squirrels."

"Still," Nance had said, perhaps thinking that hitting even one was terrible.

It wouldn't have surprised Arlene if the pistol Harvey bought in Waverly was meant to shoot the ground squirrels—that their quickness frustrated him so. That was Harvey, a man who wanted control, even over Nature with a capital *N*. God knew what would have happened if he and Nance had brought children into the world. She shivered to think.

And that brought her back to Nance's medical mystery, the positive Pap smear that was never replicated, so that the poor woman was left in limbo: was she ill or not? did she have a future of treatments worse than the disease, or would she flourish? Poor Nance.

The weather seemed to affect her sense of time: everything happening too fast, as if the darkness and her rain-obscured vision and the unexpected appearance of a curve, an oncoming car, a road sign, all translated themselves into speed instead of surprise. But the miles passed. Here she was in Sioux City. Now she was across the Missouri. *We're not in Iowa anymore.* A sign appeared out of the storm:

CHAPPELL 20

Another half hour, and she would be in her hometown, looking for a place to stay the night, leafing through a slim phone book tomorrow morning to find a place to have breakfast. Then Mother, tucked away in her nursing home.

There was something in the road ahead.

She slowed the truck, then stopped. Her headlights had caught a raccoon—no, two. *No road kill tonight,* she thought. *Lucky animals.*

It was an image that would stay with her, like a movie, each sweep of the wipers a new frame: the two raccoons caught by the truck's headlights in the center of the road, the rain cascading down on them, their eyes bright flashes of reflected light as they turned, frozen with fear against each other. Their muzzles were like clown faces, she thought, the eyes a ridiculous black accent, not so much a mask as a mascara joke—like the makeup models wore in the fashion magazines she and Nance marveled at when they browsed in bookstores—Arlene looking for something to read, Nancy tagging along—the two of them saying to each other, "Would you dress like that? Would you put that stuff on your face? How can those comic strips pass for beauty?"

The raccoons were scared half to death, frozen in front of the pickup, fearful—*do they feel what I would feel if I were them?*—getting drenched.

She wondered—perhaps she was more tired than she thought, and fatigue had affected her common sense—if you could make pets of them, if they might be like cats with funny faces, to make you laugh when you were upset or depressed. They couldn't help but cheer a body up.

And then she remembered that when you saw a dead raccoon on the highway, you'd likely see a second or third not far off. Was it a sort of devotion, or a love not exactly like human love, that made them stay close to their dead companions until they too became *roadkill*—that terrible word—whole families destroyed by their attachment to one another?

But she had to get going; being close to Chappell was not the same as arriving in Chappell, and sure enough, the raccoons turned away and began trotting—waddling, really—down the road ahead, bumping into each other like teenagers, drifting to the shoulder, finally plunging into the overgrown ditch at the limit of the truck's headlights. It was as if they felt her impatience. They were gone; they were safe.

I know where they're going, Arlene told herself as she accelerated past the spot where the animals had disappeared. *They're on their way to be married—and I've made them late.*

My lord, she thought, *how everything reminds me of what I've left behind.*

PART TWO

NANCE

5

Married to Burton now for almost two years, Nancy had rarely given much thought to the details of farming. Sometimes as she lay awake wondering if she should get up and offer to make breakfast for her husband, the unexpected brightness of a summer morning dancing the walls of the room like the clear streams she had waded in as a child in Minnesota, she believed probably she had never understood her motives for marrying a farmer. When she was Harvey Riker's wife, she had grown accustomed early on to coming awake in an empty bed, knowing that Harvey was *somewhere,* doing *something* having to do with the crops he raised—corn one year, soybeans the next. It was like a mystery.

Burton got up at four-thirty; you heard him moving about the upstairs, coughing, clearing his throat, running water, flushing the toilet. Sometimes he sang: songs whose words were unintelligible, whose melodies broke against the other noises of his morning habits. Sometimes he talked to himself; you heard him muttering, answering himself, now and then saying a curse word as if there were an anger to be directed somewhere, at someone.

Thank heaven it wasn't at *her*—though there had been days, when she was Nancy Riker, that it was; didn't she have the marks to prove it, to witness the kind of man Harvey was? The *unkind* of man, they ought to say—that was what crossed her mind. How could she ever have married Harvey? And having done that, how could she have stayed with him for so long—until she was driven to be unfaithful, until her best friend's husband was dead? She didn't want to think about that.

Perhaps she was never meant to be a farm wife at all. Or perhaps she didn't have curiosity enough to learn her place. All she ever knew—she realized this now because it was happening all over again—was that the husband arose in the wee hours, made his noises, did his business, and then he was gone. You heard the screen door slap shut. You heard the tractor start—or once in a while it was the pickup you heard. Or you heard nothing, and later in the morning you realized the man was in the barn or the shed or out on the back porch, mending or fixing or polishing or sitting with a pad and a stub of pencil making pictures of next year's fields, adding columns of last year's figures. And then, at the end of the day, there the man was—done with his work. Ground broken or harrowed or fertilized or planted or weeded or harvested. God knew what. God knew, because it was eternal, regular as clockwork. And what good was a wife to this endless process? Was God married? No—what a ridiculous notion. Was there a wife waiting in bed while God made the world? Did a wife ask God if he wanted coffee or bacon and eggs, and did God shrug and go on about his business as if he could care less about food or drink to keep him alive? Not likely. What pastor could make a sermon out of that?

She rubbed her eyes, yawned, rolled onto Burton's side of the empty bed to consult the clock on the nightstand. The numbers were blurred; she squinted to focus them, to see that it was barely six o'clock. She closed her eyes. *I could sleep in; he wouldn't miss me.* But now she had to go to the bathroom. She could fight it, hold it, try to doze—no, she couldn't. When you were a kid,

sometimes you so hated to get up for school or chores, you lay
there, the pillow over your head, and you decided simply to pee
where you were, soak the mattress, the hell with it. You imagined
the urine hot on your thighs, the awful pleasure of the smell of
it, your parents' shock. A baby thing. But you could never *do* it,
just as she couldn't do it now. Sitting up in bed, sliding her legs
toward the edge, she groaned, yawned again. *No rest for the wicked.*
No, she thought: *weary*—that was the word. *No rest for the weary.*
She swung her feet to the floor, bowed to find her slippers. Just
at that moment something struck the window behind her—
thunk!—a dull, heavy sound. A bird, but a big one; she wondered
what.

She stood at the window and looked down, her forehead
pressed against the pane so she could see the ground as close to
the house as possible. Nothing. The grass was heavy and green
and empty; there was a black shingle that had blown from a roof
somewhere, a dandelion or two ready to shed its gray seed. No
bird. She raised her eyes; right at eye level was a tiny white puff
of feather where the bird had struck. No clue to what kind it
was. She hoped it wasn't dead. You saw a lot of birds in the sum-
mertime, robins and grackles especially, that blundered into the
blankness of glass and dropped to the ground—groggy if they
were lucky, dead of a broken neck if they weren't. She and
Arlene Tobler used to talk about luck, long before Harvey shot
Arlene's husband in their kitchen, even before Arlene's Peter
stabbed the Jensen boy. You could be lucky all the days of your
life but one, and that *one* could undo every happy thing you'd
ever accomplished.

She turned away from the light—perhaps she could see
something out the downstairs window—and went to the bathroom. The night-light was still on, the hot water faucet was dripping slowly, silently; the smell of Burton was like a warmth, a
humidity in the room. Nance turned off the lamp at the end of
the counter, then she found a match and let it flare to consume
the gassy odor her husband had left in his wake. Not that she was

offended by it. No. That was one way you knew if you loved a man: could you tolerate the smell of him—his sweat, his breath, his shit. She knew she loved Burton early on; he had smelled of cattle—pasture and manure and the rank odor of damp hide— and it was almost in the first instant of their meeting that the mingled smells of him had an impact on her that was downright sexual. "My God, how wet he makes me," she confessed to Arlene. "Aphrodisia," Arlene said, and then had to explain to Nance what the word meant.

She dropped the blackened match into the bowl and sat to relieve herself. Where had she first met Burton? She guessed it must have been at the Eriksens' on one of the card-game Saturdays. Carol and Jess, Arlene and Paul, Nancy and Harvey; they were a tradition, those nights in the various kitchens over cards— sometimes poker, sometimes pepper, sometimes bridge. He was a dozen years younger than Nance, handsome—*oh, God, was he ever*. She'd bent to him like a flower leaning toward light. Even Harve had noticed, and Harve hardly noticed anything outside matters of profit and loss and the stupidity of the government. He'd shaken her hand, Burton had. "A pleasure." Those two words; she'd wanted to make them real from the first moment. "Me, too," she'd said, dumb married woman who'd forgotten what sex and pleasure were. And then. And then. Well, here they both were.

Burton was in the kitchen. He'd made the coffee himself, and he was at the table, cup in hand, the day's *Register* open in front of him.

"Anything exciting?" she said.

"The usual horror." He took a sip of coffee and made a face at her. "You want to come into town with me?"

She pondered. "No," she said finally. "I've got to go in for groceries, but I don't have my list made."

She went to the stove and poured herself coffee from the

aluminum percolator Burton favored. The gas flame was low under it, but even as she lifted the percolator she could hear the coffee simmering inside. "You shouldn't let the coffee boil away," she said.

"Sorry," he said. He held out his cup. "Here. I'll take the last of it."

She poured it. "Mud," she told him.

"Just like the army."

He grinned at her, and her heart skipped. He made her a schoolgirl, the way he looked at her, the way he smiled—the little twist at one corner of his mouth, the pattern of small lines at the corner of his eyes.

"A bird hit the bedroom window," she said. "But I couldn't see anything on the ground underneath."

"Probably didn't hit it straight on. Glanced off it and went on its way," Burton said.

"I hope so." The ones that broke their necks she had many times picked up, held them in her hands as she carried them to the trash can in the shade of the old barn. They were still warm, usually, their heads loose, like flowers broken on their stems by a wind. They weighed next to nothing: the robins, one morning a dazzling male cardinal, the glossy grackles—the eyes of all of them filmed over and blind. But what little they weighed was dead weight; you could tell without looking at them.

"They say rain for the weekend," Burton said. He folded the paper closed and pushed it toward her. "I better get on my horse. Is this your day at the clinic?"

"Tomorrow," she said. "Will you be long?"

He stood and stretched. It always arrested her, that movement, the way almost every turn of his body took her attention and warmed her to the very pit of her stomach—the place where she'd have carried children if she'd been capable; the place that carried what the doctors still couldn't decide was a cancer or not. She had never in her life known another man so exciting as Burton Stone. She wondered she didn't get used to him, didn't take him for granted. He had swept her away at the start, and every single day since then he swept her away all over again. Was ever a man so graceful as he was? Was ever a younger man so wise in the ways he loved her?

"Couple of hours," he said. "I've got an errand at the Co-op, and I promised old Jess I'd meet him for coffee at the Happy Chef in Cedar Falls."

"I'll rinse out your cup," Nance said.

"I thought I'd swing by the Tobler house on the way back. Take a look around."

"All the more reason for me not to go with you," she said. Memories. What happened there she relived almost every time she thought of that house, that cruel kitchen. More than four years after, she shivered when she drove past the house. It made no difference that she and Burton owned it now, that Burton had bought the house and all the Tobler land from the bank. The house was stripped and empty, closed up; all they had wanted was the land when Burton decided to quit the cattle business and go like the rest of their neighbors to corn and beans. Burton went by the house periodically. Sometimes there had been vandalism— a window broken out, the front door forced, signs that somebody, kids or tramps, had slept there. Remains of cigarettes, beer cans, once a condom thrown into the sink. You couldn't stop it. The house was far back from the road at the end of a long driveway. The sheriff's department checked it often enough, but what could you do? They talked, she and Burton, about tearing the place down or setting fire to it.

But she wouldn't have wanted to destroy the house. What would Arlene think? It would be like erasing the last happy memory she had, obliterating the home where she and Paul had raised a family and known love together. Nance was not about to entertain any plan that meant the destruction of love.

Burton came over and kissed her on the forehead. She put her hands at his waist and raised her face toward him, holding him until his mouth brushed hers. She wanted to melt right there—just dissolve into him like bath water so that he could wear her as if she were his skin.

"See you," he said.

She watched him walk to the pickup and climb into it. The jeans he wore; the thin shirt, cambric, blousy at his waist—how she loved those buttocks, that strong back, the shoulders. Her hands felt all those parts of him she could not see when he made love to her one way; the parts she could see but not reach when he loved her another way. And she had to turn away from the light and grip, hard, the back of a kitchen chair until she stopped feeling giddy and weak-kneed.

Since Burton had gone to crops instead of cattle—because he said he could never imagine maintaining the cruelty of a feedlot, and that was what competition would have forced him to—most of Nance's daylight hours were solitary. There was always something to call him away from her: errands to fetch the chemicals that killed weeds and insects, weather talk and market talk with friends, regular attentions to the cropland itself, like a lover endlessly at the body of his love, caressing, stroking, penetrating until the body blossomed. And what was she to do?

In the beginning, after Harvey was convicted and put away, and even before the divorce was final—when she was already living in Burton's house, indulging herself in a breathtaking love other people had paid for—she hardly left the bed when Burton was away from her. She "lay about," as her mother would have said, scarcely ever dressed herself, relived the lovemaking of the night before until she had to touch herself for relief. Once in a while, before Arlene sold the house and moved back to South Dakota to be a schoolteacher again, Nance drove over to the Tobler house and talked: about guilt, about remorse, about being blinded by the lightning of love. She was always

home to fix supper for Burton, changing back into her housecoat with nothing underneath, ready for more of the lessons
in passion only Burton Stone had ever cared to teach her.

A few years older now, she was more calm, less fearful that
the man would tire of her and withdraw his sexual interest, but
the problem of how to spend her days persisted. Arlene was hundreds of miles away; she had no woman friend to be with over
coffee at The Shed, no one to bend her mind away from herself.
Now, at least, she dressed; now she was not so obsessed with Burton that she could not make herself leave their bed. She cleaned
the counters and did up the dishes. She swept and dusted. She
washed Burton's clothes—and who would ever witness her curious habit of holding them against her face before she let them
fall into the washer?—and ironed his shirts, those that needed it,
after they emerged from the dryer smelling only of heat and
chlorine.

And she gardened.

When she was a child she had watched her mother puttering
among the flowers in the front yard of the house in Albert Lea.
"Puttering" was her mother's word for this activity that never appeared to Nance to be organized, or even necessary. The flowers
were mostly iris and gladioli, orchidlike or multiple-blossomed,
and they pretty much took care of themselves, so far as the child
Nancy could see. But there was her mother, puttering, pinching
off dead petals, poking at the dirt with an orange trowel; probably
she believed the plants flourished because of her, that they would
wither and die if she didn't attend to them. For herself, Nance was
given annuals every spring—marigolds or pansies or petunias were
preferred—so she could putter alongside her mother. One summer, she remembered, there were yellow tulips under the front
window, and around the edges of the tulip bed were dwarf nas-
turtiums whose seeds she had planted herself. Yet no matter how
much her mother tried to involve her in the care and cultivation
of flowers, Nance could no more comprehend the attraction of
her mother's hobby than she could make sense, now, of her own

involvement with men who had chosen first Harvey's, then Burton's vocation as farmer.

Her own gardening had brought her no special insights into such matters, but of course she practiced it on a tiny scale—not like Jess Eriksen, for example, running his vegetable stand on the Finchford Road. She had a few tomato plants, some lettuce and carrots, a cucumber patch that was her particular pride. As for flowers, she had a half dozen rose bushes, blue morning glories climbing a trellis beside the front steps, a circle of bright red tulips around a birdbath shaped like a seashell. But it was something; it was work that occupied her, times when she was alone.

This morning, left alone with her thoughts, she was a long time getting dressed, cleaning up the kitchen, jotting down a few items of grocery shopping. When she finally put on her gardening gloves and went outside, the first thing she saw, next to the juniper at the corner of the house under the bedroom, was a dead robin. By the time she came back with a trowel to bury it, green flies had already begun the funeral.

When she got home from shopping it was nearly five o'clock and Burton's pickup was in the yard, parked in front of the older of the two barns—the barn they could not use because a tenant Burton's father once rented to had systematically gutted it for firewood. The loft floor had gone first, and then the horse stalls, the tack room, other workrooms built when Burton's father owned Percherons, even the barn doors. Over two winters the tenant had fed most of the barn's interior into the fireplace and the potbellied parlor stove; by the third winter he had been obliged to cut up beams and joists and other load-bearing timbers until he had made the structure unsafe. Now the old barn, unmuscled for the sake of the tenant family's warmth, leaned noticeably. You didn't dare use it for storage; you certainly wouldn't risk keeping animals in it. "One of these days the wind'll just push it over," Burton said once. "Save me the labor of tearing it down." Nance waited for that to happen, but the barn was perverse: it bowed, it leaned, it bent but would not break. Sparrows and swallows had made the barn their realm, and for a brief time an owl had established his daylight home in its eaves; right now it was home to a mourning dove family, the repetition of their cries like the sound of someone blowing across the neck of a Coke bottle.

She carried the first bag of groceries—the lightest one— into the kitchen and set it on the table, pushing aside the bowl where the rose floated, making room for the rest of the grocery bags to come.

"Burton?" she called.

"In here."

She looked into the parlor. Burton was sitting in the brocade rocker in front of the west-facing bay window. His cap was on the window seat; his feet were up, heels beside the cap, and his hands were clasped across his stomach. He tipped his head to look at her.

"What are you up to?" she said.

He grinned. "Pretty sunset."

She came over, kissed his mouth upside down. "It's nowhere near time for a sunset," she said. "Really, what are you up to?"

He put his feet on the floor and brought her into his lap. Nance relaxed against him, resting her cheek in the warm corner at his right shoulder, one arm around his neck, the other across his chest. She could feel his heart beating in the pulse at the side of his throat, could smell the familiar sweat of him as faint as flower scent, could even breathe his breath.

"I was just thinking," he said.

She closed her eyes. "About what?" Although floating here, so contented, she wouldn't have cared if he never answered her questions.

He bowed slightly to nuzzle her face. "I stopped by Tobler's."

"You said you might."

"And somebody'd broken in. Again."

"There's nothing in that house," Nance said. "I can't imag-

ine what they think they're going to find in an empty house."
What's there was awful, but you couldn't see it; *you can't rob ghosts,* she told herself.

"Just I'm getting damned sick and tired of it," Burton said. He patted her thigh and leaned against her to get up from the rocker. "Groceries in the car?"

"Yes." She slid from his lap. Summer or no summer, she felt suddenly cold outside his embrace. "I already brought in the things that need to go into the fridge."

He paused, hugged her. "So there's no hurry?"

"No hurry."

Then he swooped her up, one arm around her shoulders, the other at the backs of her knees, and swung her around, twice, like a child.

"Burton." She caught her breath. "Don't." But she didn't mean it, because she knew where this dizzying circle would end.

We could rent out the Tobler place," Nance said. She lay against him in bed, her head on his chest where she could listen to his heartbeat, her right hand gently stroking him from under his arm, down his side, to his hip and thigh. His skin was coarser than hers, less pale; the hair around his genitals was almost red, not like the hair on his head but the color of his beard when he skipped shaving for a couple of days. She never got tired of touching him, looking at him. It was as if she were memorizing him— against what separation, she could not have said.

"The last thing I want to be is a landlord," Burton said. She could feel his body tense the instant before he spoke. "A house that old, you'd spend more money than you'd take in—fixing up, replacing. And think how long it's been neglected."

"Then sell it."

"Whoever bought it would want land with it. I'm not giving up my good cropland."

"You sound like Paul Tobler," Nance said. "He used to make

speeches to Arlene, about planting every square inch of ground
he owned."

"You bet." He stroked her back and shoulders, bent his head to
kiss her between the eyes. "I can feel your goosebumps," he said.

"That's what you do to me," she said.

"You're too easy."

She drew away from him and propped herself on one elbow
to face him. "Am I?" she said. "Am I easy?"

He hugged her against him. "Only with me," he said.

"Then it's all right, isn't it?"

"It's all right," he said, "and then some."

Nance smiled, knowing he couldn't see her face. "Every once
in a while you say the right thing to me," she said.

He was silent. She could feel the muscles working across his
chest and knew he was reaching for a cigarette. He hardly ever
smoked now. He told her he had smoked while he was in the
army and for a time afterward, but then he quit cold and didn't
even miss it. She noticed that there were moments of stress or
frustration that made him want a cigarette; that seemed all right:
a pack would last him a month or more. She heard the match
strike, got a whiff of its sulphur, then heard—yes, *heard*—the cigarette smoke go into Burton's lungs under her ear. The next time
they kissed, she would taste the unaccustomed nicotine on his
breath. Not that she had any room to talk; she'd quit only after
Paul Tobler's death—as if there was a connection.

"I wish you wouldn't smoke in the bedroom," she said now.
"I don't mind in the kitchen, but it gets into the curtains up
here—the smoke smell."

He exhaled slowly. "Sorry," he said. "I guess I wasn't thinking."

"I guess you *were* thinking," she said.

"You're right. Damned house."

"The truth is: I wish you wouldn't smoke at all."

He leaned away from her and tapped ashes into the ceramic
ashtray they'd stolen from the Radisson Hotel on their honey-

moon. "I remember plenty of times seeing you sucking on the old cancer sticks." He said it not unkindly, in so matter-of-fact a way that she knew he wasn't trying to hurt her.

"Not since before we got married," she said. She sat up beside him. "Burton? What about just making it *look* as if somebody's in the house? Why not leave a light on? Hook it up to a timer, like people do when they go on vacation."

"Then I've got to reconnect the electricity and pay a utility bill every month." He stubbed the cigarette into the ashtray. "I wish to hell that old Lab of mine hadn't got himself run down in the road."

"He was never much of a watchdog."

"That's true. Still, he looked impressive."

"Maybe we could sell the house and ask the buyer to move it to a different place," she said. "You know. You see that happening sometimes, a whole house going right down the middle of the road, the police car going on ahead to stop traffic while the utility people move wires out of the way."

"No," he said, "that's too complicated, and too expensive for a house that old. Nobody'd go for it." He slipped out from under Nance's weight and sat at the edge of the bed. "I'll think of something."

"Are you getting up?" She was afraid he was. She wondered if there was something wrong with her, always wanting him to make love to her more than once.

"I'd better get those groceries put away," he said.

Her heart sank a little. "I guess I'll take a shower," she said, remembering their early days together when it had been a luxury for her *not* to shower—to keep the scent of him and the memory of his weight on her skin for as long as she dared.

She came downstairs a half hour later. Burton was at the kitchen table with a notepad and pencil, drawing some sort of diagram. A few sheets of the notepaper were already crumpled in front of him, pencil markings bold on both sides of the discarded pages. Now the sun really was setting, and the light in the room was altered by an aura of pale golden shadow.

"You'll ruin your eyes," Nance said. "In that poor light."

"Don't worry," he said.

She looked around the kitchen. "Did you bring in all the groceries?"

"Brought them in, put them away."

"That means I won't be able to find half the stuff I bought," she said. She stood behind him and kneaded the muscles at his neck, slowly, firmly, the way the orange housecat kneaded when it lay in her lap. She wanted to tease Burton out of whatever this preoccupation was, bring him back to her. "What is it you're working on?"

"Not sure," he said. "Maybe a thing that'll persuade the kids to quit breaking into that house."

"Oh?"

"I thought maybe I'd rig up a sort of booby trap. Give the next housebreaker a scare."

"Not to hurt them," Nance said.

"Scare them, I said." He looked up at her. "Some kind of trip wire, like we learned about in Nam. I can use Dad's old double-barreled 12-gauge, load it with buckshot. Or maybe rock salt."

"I don't want anybody to get shot. I had enough of that with Harvey."

Burton shook his head. "Nothing deadly," he said. "A lot of noise, maybe a few pellets to pick out. And I'll let the word get around that the Tobler house is booby-trapped. That'll damn sure guarantee no local kid will try breaking in again."

She leaned over his shoulder to study the paper he was working at. She felt funny in her stomach and chest—sensations of hot and cold, a churning of fear like the one she had experienced two years back when the doctor told her the first Pap test had come out positive. "We should talk about this," she said.

"Don't worry," he told her.

"Burton—"

"Look," he said, "I told you: don't worry. I was in Nam, wasn't I? I know what I'm doing."

That night she could not fall asleep. She had gone upstairs when it was barely twilight—"I'm climbing the wooden highway," she told Burton, using the expression he said reminded him of his mother—leaving him to clear the supper dishes and load them into the dishwasher. He hated to leave a project undone. She knew he would work at the kitchen table for as long as it took to perfect the mechanism he planned to set up in the Tobler house, and then, at long last, he would undress and crawl carefully into the bed beside her, trying so hard not to wake her that he would do just that. Even after she had drawn the flowered sheet up under her chin, it being too warm for any other covers, there was still a faint smudge of dark orange light along the southwestern horizon she could see out the bedroom window. A little she felt like a child, saying goodnight so early, and a little she felt convalescent—as if the day just finished had overwhelmed her and she needed to recover from it.

And why not? Burton's plans frightened her; the mention of his father's old shotgun she found especially upsetting. It all reminded her of Harvey at the Waverly auction, of the gun he'd simply had to own, even though he had no earthly use for it. Burton himself had said—talking about Paul's murder—that it was a mistake even to own a gun. "If you have one, the odds are you'll use it," he said. Nance remembered exactly where he said it: in Arlene Tobler's parlor, the afternoon of the memorial services for Paul, with Arlene and Jess and the Brandts and the Raymond Claussons as witness. Arlene had cried; for weeks afterward, everything set her off, but that was the first time she'd come out of the shock of it and had a good hard cry. In Nance's arms. *Dear Leenie.* Nance had felt awful and relieved at the same time. Grief and forgiveness.

Burton had sworn—she'd made him swear, before she came
to bed—that no one would be hurt by the shotgun, that he intended only to scare the next person who tried to break into the
abandoned farmhouse. "Buckshot never killed anybody," he told
her. "My dad used to drive off the wild dogs with that shotgun,
and never killed a one." Wild dogs. *Imagine.* And people still left
unwanted litters on the gravel road that ran between here and
New Hartford, though now the county was better equipped to
send a van out and pick them up before they turned feral. "What
about the rock salt?" she'd asked, and he'd only shrugged, not
looking at her. Anyway, she had to trust Burton; she had to believe him. A long time ago the Vietnam mess had changed him,
gentled him. She understood that, and knew it was one of the
things about him that had attracted her. Now, he wouldn't dream
of hurting a single living thing. If still she was fearful of the plans
he was working on so diligently, it must be her own weakness.

Weakness. She hated the possibility that her body was weak,
that it might betray her before her time. While she was still married to Harvey her Pap smear had come back positive, and though
since then she had gone back four times—to more doctors than
one, until she had finally found one she liked, trusted—and each
time the smears read negative, there was an ongoing seed of
doubt that might or might not be waiting to germinate somewhere in the sterile darkness of her womb. "It might be a cancer,"
the latest doctor, a competent woman younger than Nance, had
said, "or it might only have been a false positive." "Is that why I
never had children?" Nance had asked. The doctor shrugged.
"You told me you had an IUD when you were young," she said.
"The infertility might have something to do with that." "Nobody told me that could happen," Nance said. "We know more
now," the doctor said. "In any case, we should keep an eye on
things as you get closer to menopause. Stick to a regular schedule
of checkups."

So tomorrow Nance would return to the clinic, as she did
every six months, and she hated it—not so much for the indignity

of the examination, the probings, the unavoidable hurt, the absurdity of an examining room where the doctor had slipped pink woolen socks over the stirrups and hung overwrought Georgia O'Keeffe blossoms on the walls, but for the way it preoccupied her with herself. She thought she was not important enough for so much attention from doctors, from the God who created both women and cancer, even from herself. She dreaded lying awake the night before her visits, the nights afterward until the test results came back. She feared one of those nights she would look into herself, deeper and deeper, past her habits and lusts and mistakes and resolutions, past all the actions of her body and heart, in search of the flaw that was cancer and death, the darker flaw that was sin and a different death, and all at once she would find both, and that would make her life into *nothing*.

She got home from the clinic at a little past noon. The pickup was gone, of course, and the only sign of life in the farmyard was the presence of Grimmie, the orange housecat, sitting in the middle of the porch, waiting to be let in. "Grimmie" was short for "Grimalkin," the name of a cat in *The House of the Seven Gables*. Arlene Tobler had named it; it was in fact Arlene's cat, adopted by Nance and Burton when Arlene moved to South Dakota. Arlene was a reader, as Nance was not, which made her good at naming things. Nance remembered having read that particular novel when she was in high school—that and *Ethan Frome*—but she didn't recall the names of the authors.

Nance didn't much care for cats. Farms always had them, and when she was Nancy Riker there had always been a slew of them living in the barn and under the porch of the house. She'd have paid them no attention at all, except that when Arlene used to drop by her kids played with the Riker cats, treated them as if they were theirs. Sarah and Peter, both of them grown up now, Sarah with children of her own. One spring when a litter of kittens had gotten distemper, Sarah Tobler had persuaded her dad to take them to the vet's and poor Paul had spent sixty dollars—the cost of putting kittens to sleep on three different occasions—before he finally put his foot down. Nance had thought the child's concern was charming; it made her miss children of her own in a fashion that was close to physical.

Wasn't *that* a nice memory, especially coming on the heels of another awkward visit to the gynecologist and the prospect of six more months of not knowing if she was dying or not. She should write to Leenie, let her know she was thinking of her. Pour out her life the way she'd done before Paul's death—as if Arlene would let her, as if nothing had changed.

As for Grimalkin, he was a pampered tom—the Toblers' indoor cat, different from the run-of-the-mill barn cats—with a tom's bad habits. He had sired so many cats with markings similar to his own that nowadays Nance had to double check before she let just any orange cat into the kitchen. He ought to be fixed, but Burton was reluctant to spend the money—although heaven knew they had already spent a small fortune on Grimmie, worming him, treating abscesses from his fights with wild animals, having him sewn up when he got caught on barbed wire. That was what people meant by love–hate relationships: the way she and Burton felt about Grimmie.

"Is it you?" she said to the cat. It circled her ankles as she pushed at the front door, and then she remembered that now they were locking up the house when no one was home. Burton had begun insisting on that, the first time the Tobler place was broken into. Nance wasn't used to house keys; she wondered if she would ever get used to them. It seemed a shame to live in the country all your life, and all at once have to fret about being robbed. Even growing up in town, her folks had never locked up unless they were going to be gone for days, like on a vacation trip down to Branson.

She rummaged in her handbag and found her key, freshly cut this spring at the Farm Fleet store. Grimmie darted in ahead of her, going straight to his water dish. Nance shut the door behind her and hung the bag over the back of a kitchen chair, then something in the air stopped her short.

The whole room smelled oily, and it was obvious why. Burton had spread newspapers over the table, and on the papers lay his dad's old shotgun, the breech open, the oblong yellow box for a gun-cleaning kit resting on a grimy-looking rag. She shivered. It looked as if he'd started to clean the gun, then been interrupted by something and gone off without leaving a note. She wondered if he'd had lunch; should she get a little something to eat for herself, or should she wait until he came back from wherever? And when he did come back, do you suppose she'd be able to persuade him to do his gun-cleaning business in some more sensible location, like the side porch or one of the barns?

And now he *was* back: she heard the pickup come into the yard and the cab door bang shut. When he came into the kitchen he was carrying a box that turned out to be shotgun shells.

"I thought for sure I'd beat you home," he said, "but this is good timing." He put the shells on the table.

"That oil stuff smells dreadful," she said. "Do you have to do that in the kitchen?"

"I'm all finished," he said. "I'll put this in the truck while you make us a couple of sandwiches for lunch."

"Is that all you want? Sandwiches?"

He opened the box, slid two bright red shells into the shotgun, and closed the breech smartly. "It'll do me," he said, "and then I want you to come over to the Tobler house with me; help me set this thing up."

"Must I?" she said. "I was going to lie down for an hour or so."

"It's a two-man job," he said. He broke the gun open, took out the two shells and replaced them in their carton. "Are you feeling bad? Would you rather I called Jess Eriksen?"

"Oh," she said, "don't bother him. He's got enough to do with his vegetable stand." She took lunchmeat and lettuce and mayonnaise out of the refrigerator and carried them to the counter. "I guess it won't kill me to help you."

He watched her make the sandwiches. "What'd you find out?" he said. "At the clinic."

She shook her head. Finally he'd remembered where she'd just come from, and that was all to the good, but she was afraid if she answered him, she'd break down and cry.

"Anything definite?" He leaned the shotgun in the corner behind the table, put the boxes on the windowsill, folded the rag and laid it on top of them.

Nance looked away, attending to the sandwiches—which did not appear appetizing. She shook her head; nothing definite. Never anything definite. She heard Burton folding the newspapers and stacking them together.

"Well, what did they say?" he persisted.

"The doctor wondered if I ought maybe to go down to Iowa City—to the big university medical center there." Her voice cracked on "medical" and she cut the sandwiches in two with an angry movement of the knife. "She wondered if they might want to do a D & C, or a biopsy, or even laser surgery."

"*Laser* surgery?"

"It's a new thing. Except nobody seems to know what in the world they'd be cutting out—since nobody's been able to find anything yet."

"What about the test—that smear thing?"

"She's going to call." She put the sandwiches in front of him. "That's not much of a lunch. You want something to drink? Lemonade?"

"It isn't lemonade weather yet," he said. "Is there iced tea?"

"Yes." She poured the iced tea from the pitcher in the refrigerator and set the glass on the table beside Burton's plate. "God," she said. "Sometimes I wish they'd just cut me open like an old ripe tomato and have a good look at what's inside."

"That's a pretty thought," he said.

She stood beside him and hugged his head, hard, against her breasts. "You don't know," she said. "You can't imagine." Not that anyone's knowledge or imagining would affect one single thing that might be going on inside her.

The two of them hardly talked while Burton drove over to the abandoned Tobler house. He kept his gaze straight ahead as the truck jolted along the gravel roads; Nance leaned her forehead against the side window and watched the fields glide past, the corn early June green and knee-high as far off as she could see. Next year it would be beans, with here and there a stray, persistent cornstalk volunteering above them—from an ear the picker had missed and neither the deer nor Ray Clausson's Holsteins had found in their foraging. Then here was Jess's farm, the acres of vegetables he grew to sell at the roadside stand—this the first year in three the weather had been decent enough to let him try to earn his modest living.

And now here was the Riker farm—where she had lived all those years with Harvey. It looked well-kept, she had to admit; she couldn't remember the name of the family that was renting the place while Harvey served out the years of his manslaughter sentence, but it was obvious they cared about the land and buildings. If he was smart, Harvey would sell the place when he got out; then he'd move away—to a different state, if she had anything to say about it. Which she wouldn't, of course. But God knew he could afford it. High above the tool shed—which was freshly painted, she noticed—a redtail was circling and she wondered what it could see, far down in the greening fields, from way up there. The hawk's wings were motionless; it was riding a thermal, rising and falling with no sign of effort, the tips of its wings like fingers spread out to catch and hang onto the air currents that bore it up.

"I wonder how it feels," Burton said.

His voice startled her. "How what feels?" she said.

"That redtail. I thought you were watching him."

"I was," she said. "I was daydreaming, I guess."

"Wish you were up there? Swimming sky?"

"Maybe." *Wish I was,* she thought. *Wish I could stay there, seeing everything.*

She looked back to earth. Ahead on the left came the landmark cottonwood tree with the dilapidated tree house she remembered Peter and his friends trying to build, and then the high silhouette of the Tobler house itself. By the time the pickup was almost in line with it, the house vanished behind the cedars and scrub pine Burton had let grow untended between farmyard and road, and the house did not reappear until they were more than halfway up the slalom of driveway. The center of the drive was tall and yellow-green with witch grass, and weeds with tiny purple and yellow flowers had begun to fill the parallel wheel tracks on either side. Up close the sight of the house, shabby and curtainless, chilled her to the bone; she remembered the times she had come here to confide in Arlene, the times she had wept her frustrations in Leenie's sisterly embrace.

"All the coffee I used to drink here," she said to Burton. "On my way to your place, or coming back from it."

"I always thought Arlene knew everything about us there was to know." He shouldered open the door of the truck and slid to the ground. "No secrets between you two," and then he swung the door shut.

Nance turned her knees sideways and slid down to the ground on her side of the truck. A light breeze touched her face and caught at her hair; the farmyard was filled with a snow of cottonwood fluff, the seeds riding the air around her, whole gray-white drifts of them strung along the edges of the shed and barn and the corners of the front steps.

Burton was leaned over the tailgate, gathering up the shotgun, the shells, a brown paper bag advertising the Farm Fleet.

"Here," he said to Nance. "I'll bring in the shotgun and the toolbox. You take the small stuff." She held out her hands and Burton filled the crook of her arms with the boxes and the bag. "Don't drop it," he said.

She followed him up the steps and across the porch, waited

while he unlocked the door, then trailed after him into the kitchen that had once been Arlene's.

The room was bare, of course. Furniture and appliances had long ago been auctioned off, the curtains taken down from the windows so that the light entering the kitchen reflected with raw brightness off the linoleum; the cupboards were empty of crockery, their doors half opened so you could see the shelf paper with its dingy hem of color—red and green flowers and leaves in an imitation sampler motif. Where the gas stove had stood, the wall was a square of yellow several shades lighter than in the rest of the room, and above that was the broken plaster where the bullet from Harvey's pistol had finally stopped.

"You were always going to patch that," Nance said.

Burton looked up, saw where she was looking. "No point to it," he said. "Set that stuff down over here."

She put the bag and boxes in the center of the floor where he indicated. He already had out the electric drill, the one with the battery in the handle, and was putting a bit into its muzzle.

"Do you need me?" she said. She knew she didn't want to watch whatever it was he intended to do.

"I will after a while."

"Then I'm going to walk around a little."

She went everywhere in the house except the cellar. All the rooms were bare, the windows stark and unadorned, the floors and sills dingy with dust and cobwebs. In the upper corners spiders had spun elaborate nets of thread, though what flying insects there were in this house to capture, Nance could not have said. There were some signs of animal life: mouse droppings in several of the rooms, and odors too unpleasant to be hidden by the overall mustiness of the place. She supposed something could have come down the chimney—raccoon or squirrel or who knew what. Maybe some animal had died in the walls and was rotting away. She imagined all sorts of living creatures hiding in closets, crawl space, obscure corners, waiting for her and Burton to leave so they could emerge and resume their lives.

Hardly a trace of humans remained. You'd never have known a family—many generations of it—had lived and died under this roof, inside these rooms. When she found a hairpin in an upstairs bedroom, the discovery brought tears to Nance's eyes; when she noticed a sliver of white soap at the side of the bathroom sink, she sat on the closed stool and wept as if her heart was breaking. Downstairs, so distant as to seem like messages from another world, Burton's drill whirred in its irritatingly high voice, then stopped, then shrilled again. Once there was a spate of hammering— *wham! wham! wham!*—that made the old house tremble. Nance could not quite understand how he would do what he said he wanted, how he would set a trap for an intruder who didn't yet exist and couldn't be described. Then she heard the unmistakable sound of the shotgun being broken to receive its shells, and the harsh *clack!* of its closing.

She came down the stairway, the worn treads hollow underfoot, and stood in the door between kitchen and dining room. Burton was on his knees on the linoleum, crouched over the shotgun. The sheet of paper he'd worked over back at the house was unfolded next to him. The gun was overturned, its trigger guard up, and it rested in a sort of cradle made from three pieces of wood he'd nailed to the floor—one piece that was perpendicular to the length of the gun and prevented the stock from sliding backward, the other two parallel to the gun barrel so it could not move to either side. A fourth, a two-by-two perhaps six inches long, lay unnailed near the muzzle of the gun.

"What on earth," Nance said.

He cocked his head to look up at her. "Getting the aim right," he said. "I don't figure to kill anybody, but I'll sure give him something to think about."

The shotgun was pointed in the direction of the porch door, about a foot to the right of center.

"What makes it go off?"

"You'll see. First I get it positioned, and then I'll secure it." He crawled to the other side of the shotgun, laid his cheek against the trigger guard and sighted up the barrel toward the door. He slid the loose piece of wood under the barrel and looked up at Nance. "Get down here," he said, "and hold this steady while I nail it."

Obediently she knelt across from him and held the block of wood tight to the floor.

"Don't move it," he said. He nailed down one end of the block, the shock from the hammer traveling up her stiffened fingers all the way to her elbow. She closed her eyes.

He stood and stepped to her side of the shotgun. "Move," he said. She straightened and stood while Burton got down on all fours and re-sighted along the barrel.

"Is this something you hatched at the Happy Chef with Jess?" she said.

"No," he said. "Jess never did show up."

Nancy watched him nail the free end of the woodblock, and sight once again. "That's got it," he said, more to himself than to her.

He went over to the brown paper bag and brought out the beige-colored belt he usually wore with his good summer suit. While Nance watched in a kind of horror, he cut two eight-inch lengths from it with his pocket knife.

"Burton," she said. "That's a perfectly good belt."

"Was," he said. "Put your hands here, on the barrel, just to steady it." She did so; the metal was cold, and felt coarse under her fingers.

Burton laid one piece of the belt across the inside curve of the gunstock and nailed each end to the wood underneath. He did the same with the other strip, nailing it to the two-by-two so the barrel wouldn't move.

"You could've found some strips of leather in your dad's old tack rooms," Nance said. "Honestly, Burton, sometimes you're the limit."

"I hope I am," he said. He gave her a foolish grin, like a caught schoolboy's. He was rummaging inside the bag again, and now he brought out a spool of what looked like silver thread. "Nylon fishing line," he told Nance. "This is what makes it all work."

He unwound a length of the line; it was nearly as thin as the thread she sewed with, and looked translucent in the afternoon light that made the kitchen glow. Now she saw that Burton had already screwed a metal eyelet into the floor behind the shotgun, and it was through this eyelet that he threaded the end of the line and began tying it to one of the shotgun's two triggers.

"For God's sake, don't shoot yourself," Nance said.

"I'm not stupid," he said. "The safety's on."

"Just be careful."

He consulted the plan he'd drawn, then he stood up and walked to the outside door, unspooling the line as he went. He used his knife to cut the line. He tucked the spool into his back pocket and bent down to thread the line through a second metal eyelet screwed into the door frame at the level of the lock. Then he tied the end of the line to a third eyelet just under the doorknob.

"You see?" he said. "You see how simple? Mr. Housebreaker pushes the door open, the line tightens. Once the door's opened wide enough, it pulls the trigger."

"And somebody's dead," Nance said.

"No, no," he said. "The triggers are offset, and the lines are two different lengths; there'll be one to each trigger. The first shot will come when the door is open about six inches, when whoever it is won't even be inside the doorway. If that first blast doesn't send a message and scare him off—well, he won't get hurt unless he tries to come inside, and if he does, then he deserves it."

"You're positive it won't kill him?"

Burton grinned. "Might sting him a bit," he said, "give him some shot to dig out. But no, it won't kill him. And it'll damn well teach him not to be a thief."

Nance watched him finish his work—knotting a new line to the second trigger, unwinding it to the door and securing it. She wondered what it was about men, at least the men she was attracted to, and guns. Harvey had been undone by his; she prayed nothing would happen to Burton.

"You see?" he said. He was standing at the door and pulled it open a few inches. One of the lines went taut. "Imagine I'm outside on the porch. At this point, that first trigger gets pulled back and the gun fires. This other line—it won't put tension on the trigger until the door's wide enough open for the burglar to walk in, and then, if he's that stupid, he'll get a mess of buckshot in his legs."

"Very cute," Nancy said. "This is what you learned in Vietnam?"

"More like what I learned from Rube Goldberg, when I was a kid," Burton said. "I'm sorry I don't have the materials I'd've had in Nam."

O n the way home she tried to make her mind a blank, to think of nothing, to give all her attention instead to the land around her, green as green could be, and to the wide sky westward filling from the horizon with darkening cumulus clouds. Here was the place where one winter she had lost control of her car and slid into the ditch, and here was where Peter Tobler had almost committed murder, and here was where Murphy—the black Labrador retriever he'd named after his sergeant in Vietnam—had got hit by a cattle truck and had to be put down. *Geography below, weather above.* By dusk today there would be rain; already she could see occasional thin cracks of lightning opening up in the cloud bank, as if offering a preview of the violence behind the violet curtain of storm. Tonight she would lie awake listening to the rain; and to the thunder that followed the lightning, and tomorrow she would get up into a world of heat and humidity that would probably last for days and days. Burton would be happy; the corn would grow madly, higher and greener; Burton would begin to think of futures, prices, getting even at the bank. She would lure him into bed, lavish her love on him, allow him everything, and somewhere in the midst of his thrusting and her thrashing she would see his eyes go vacant and know that he wasn't with her—that the farm, the crop, the debts had elbowed her out of his concerns.

"I miss the old crowd," she said. The words came from nowhere, startling even herself. "I miss the card games and the beer and people laughing."

He looked at her, sidelong, a half smile on his mouth. "What brought that on?" he said.

"I don't know." She leaned her forehead against the side window. "I guess walking around in Arlene's house, seeing all those empty rooms."

"Most of the 'old crowd' is dead or gone," Burton said. "Carol's long gone, Paul's in his grave, your ex is in jail. Arlene's back teaching in South Dakota."

"I know," she said.

"You and me," he said. "We're the only survivors."

"And Jess. I know." She didn't want to pursue it. She was sorry she'd brought it up, and now she sank back into her reverie, noticing the tall weeds covered with dust by the roadside, smiling to see blackbirds with their bright orange epaulets perched at the very tip of those weeds or on fence posts or the uprights of road signs. *Territory*. That was all their lives were about: what they could control from their vantage points, the world within the reach of voice. They spread their black wings and opened their beaks to cry off trespassers, every day the same.

"Tell me something," she said.

"Sure."

"Wasn't there any other way besides a gun?"

He looked at her, just for a moment, and then turned his eyes back to the road. "I suppose," he said, "but this way sends a message."

A couple of weeks later Nance woke up too early—confused, sleep-muddled, certain she heard a tumult from the direction of the front porch but just as certain she could not have. The clock on the nightstand read barely five o'clock and Burton was already on the road, driving to Minneapolis for a meeting of the National Farmers Union. She sat up, listened. Perhaps it was something inside a dream she had heard, a storm over the difficult landscape of her mind made external by the act of waking. No, there it came again: a pounding on the kitchen door; that was it.

But at five in the morning? It made no sense.

She got out of bed, found her housecoat, and slipped it on over her nightgown as she crossed the upstairs hall to the bathroom. Then, the toilet sighing behind her, she scurried downstairs and paused for a moment at the living room window to look outside. A gold colored Dodge station wagon was parked in the yard between the house and the unusable barn; ERIKSEN PRODUCE, in block letters, was embossed on a magnetic sign attached to the driver's door of the car. It was Jess, standing on Nance's porch, one hand tucked into his hip pocket, the other poised to knock again at her kitchen door. Nance knotted the belt of the housecoat at her waist and unlocked the door to admit him.

"Jess," she said. "What on earth . . . ?"

He smiled. It was an odd smile, Nance thought, and telling about it later that summer she would describe it as the kind of smile you'd expect an angel to wear, or a small child who was pleased by everything in the world she saw. Or—and she would never have spoken this to a soul—it was the smile of one of those inmates in a locked ward over at the Mental Health Institute in Independence. Jess looked like that: dazed but happy, looking as if he didn't exactly know where he was, but he was glad to be there. He smiled but said nothing, nor did he make a move to cross the Stones's threshold.

"Come in, Jess," Nance said. "Come sit down and I'll put some coffee on for us."

"Thank you," Jess said, and then he moved forward, into the kitchen, and sat in the chair Nance pointed to. He sat heavily and his sigh filled the hollow of the room; it was as if he were relieved of some difficult weight. He said nothing further. As Nance went from cupboard to pantry shelf to stove, making coffee, getting two cups out of the dishwasher—"We take turns emptying the dishwasher," she told Jess, "but Burton has a bad habit of forgetting his turn"—putting cups, saucers and spoons on the table, she wondered what was the trouble.

"You're up early," she said after a while. Jess looked at her blankly, but, "Yes," he said. "Early."

Nance felt a small jab of fear in the pit of her stomach. "Jess? Is something wrong?"

"No," he said. "Nothing's wrong."

She turned back to the stove, her arms crossed, holding her elbows in the cups of her hands. She decided she could only wait until he was ready to talk, and concentrated on the difficult business of watching the coffee brew. Behind her, Jess shifted in the wooden chair.

"It's the longest day of the year," he announced.

She glanced at the calendar taped to the side of the refrigerator. "That's right," she said. Jess said nothing else, and Nance wondered if the date explained everything.

At about the same time the coffee was ready, Grimmie strolled into the kitchen from the parlor, where he had probably been asleep in Burton's big chair. The cat paused in the middle of the kitchen and began washing its face.

"That's Arlene Tobler's cat," Jess said.

"It is," Nance said. She finished pouring the coffee and set the two cups on the table. Jess was bent over in the chair, wiggling his fingers under the table at Grimmie; the cat stopped for a moment to study the man's fingers, then resumed bathing.

"I surely do miss her and old Paul," Jess said. He sat straight and reached out to draw the sugar bowl nearer. The blankness had left his face—it was as if suddenly recognizing the cat had made something click into place inside his skull—and he shook his head sadly, as if in his mind's eye he was seeing the Toblers as he had last seen them across a game of cards.

Nance relaxed. Jess had a right to his lapses without her or anybody else thinking he was getting senile. Even if he was. She took a sip of the hot coffee while Jess stirred his sugar in.

"Longest day of the year." He said the words without seeming to realize he was repeating himself. "I woke up a little after four o'clock and the dawn was so far along I thought I must have overslept. I got to thinking about people who live in Alaska, or Norway or Finland, way up near the pole, and how they get days when the sun doesn't set at all, and you know?—All at once I felt *deprived*. Can you believe it? Can you imagine the vegetables I'd have if the sun shone twenty-four hours?"

"I can't," Nance said.

"I can't neither," Jess said. "Christ, I'd never be able to keep up."

He chuckled; Nance smiled. Over the rim of her coffee cup she calculated the changes in Jess: he was thinner, balder; even in the years after Carol had died of cancer he had become a different man, she thought, and this bizarre morning was just the latest sign that what was happening was hidden as well as visible. You could see the pain in his eyes, the deeper lines on his cheeks, the looseness of the skin on his throat, the liver spots on the back of his hands. He was what? Past seventy, she thought. *A generation ahead of us.*

"Paul could have kept up," Jess was saying. "Paul Tobler in his prime could have handled a twenty-four-hour sun and as many plantings as God allowed."

He stopped and drank coffee.

"Listen to me," he said, his tone self-deprecating. "Paul's

dead, and Alaska doesn't grow vegetables. No corn; no beans. The growing season's too short." He put the cup down. "And Carol's dead."

Nance didn't know what to say to him. But then, she didn't need to; he just kept on rambling.

"I wake up these mornings, the beginnings of these long days, and I dread 'em. All those hours alone. I get out of bed and climb into the old Dodge, and I drive. It doesn't matter where. I just get in and start 'er up and drive wherever. Marshalltown. Manchester. Charles City. I just point the radiator ornament and follow it."

"Burton says you stood him up, a week or two back," she said.

"Did I? I probably did."

"You were supposed to meet him at the Happy Chef, but you never showed up."

"I forget things," Jess said. "I can remember things Carol and I did together thirty, forty years ago, but I forget to keep appointments in the here and now. I hired a couple of college kids to run the stand and keep my books. I don't hardly trust my head anymore."

"I miss the old days myself," Nance said. "I was telling Burton just the other day."

"It's a terrible life," Jess said. "I remember so clear how long it took Carol to die. I remember the first time the cancer had got so bad that when she stood up from her chair she broke a bone in her leg. *Snap!* I was there, I heard it; I caught her in my arms, else she would've fallen into the damned fireplace. That was the beginning of the end."

Nance bowed her head.

"I remember this old orange cat," Jess said. He held out his hand to Grimmie, who ignored it. "I remember Carol's old pet spaniel. I had the vet put it down the day after Carol was buried."

"It seems an awfully long time ago," Nance said, trying to sound soothing.

"It seems yesterday." The words were angry. Jess stood up

and pushed the cup in from the edge of the table. "I better get going," he said. "Driving over to Grundy Center, doing some errands."

His face was blank again, she saw. She opened the door for him and watched him lumber down the steps and out toward his car— an old, stooped man so thin his trousers bunched under his belt and his blue shirt bloused at his back. She wondered if it was the loneliness that was the worst—loneliness, not age; loneliness, not sickness. The car went down the driveway, out onto the county road, and Nance thought how of all the old crowd she and Burton were the only lucky ones.

June 23

Dear Leenie,

How are you. Burton and I are fine, enjoying the usual wonderful Iowa humidity (ha), but of course hes happy as a man can be, after a loud thunderstorm we had a couple nights ago, and in the 90s and humid since. He said in weather like this the corn will grow 6 inches a day. I believe him. It's up to my arm pits already, and maybe this will be his first decent crop year since he gave up the cattle business. Hes real excited. I dont remember Harvey ever getting silly over a good crop.

Ive been meaning to write you a long time now, but a week ago Monday when we drove over to your old place to do some monkey business of Burtons it got real strong on me to send you a letter. I wonder how your doing, I wonder if you will ever come back this way to see your old friends, even the friends who have done things to hurt you. From outside your place looks the same as ever except its all overgrown with cedar and wild grape between the house and the county road—you can hardly tell theres a house there from the road—Inside tho its different, all bare. I think the spiders have taken over the front parlor where you use to have the big oak china cabinet and the matching Queen Ann chairs, and I think animals must get into the house, maybe down the chimney, because I saw droppings evrywhere and theres a smell. It all looks so sad and forlorn, like the house misses the Tobler families that used to make it bright.

People have been breaking in the house, Burton says, so hes made a trap with a loaded shotgun in the kitchen, a booby trap to catch the boobies. Now if anybody tries to come in the door the gun will go off. It wont kill them, Burton says. It will only hurt them if they come all the way inside. After he set the trap we drove in to the Happy Chef and had pie. Burton let it out that anybody who tryed to break in to the old Tobler place would get a deadly suprise, that was the word he used, deadly, tho he didnt say to anybody what he meant or what the trap is made of. There was a lawyer in the next booth, the same one the judge appointed for Harvey when Harvey said he didnt want a lawyer to spend his money for him. His name is Commoner, Dwight I think or Dwayne, and he said he hoped what Burton did was legal and all. Burton said it was, he said a man has a legal right to protect his property and the lawyer shut up right off. Just the same it scares me, it makes me think of—you know.

I wonder sometimes do you really forgive me? I mean it was my fault evrything happened the way it did, me carrying on with Burton and Harvey finding out, and poor Paul just trying to stop the fight because we were all friends. I go over to Anamosa evry couple months to see Harvey, just because I think I owe him the remembering of him, and I dont believe he is even sorry for what he did. Burton says I should stop going there and says I should put Harvey out of my life for good, but he doesnt stop me going, tho he gets sulky. Harvey is still so mad at me, calls me names to my face, he cant find his conscience yet. Not that I am anyone to talk, I married Burton didnt I and dont feel guilty for loving him tho I was married to Harvey at the time.

Anyway I think alot about you and me and the times we talked. I hope you have forgiven me, you meant alot to me and still do. I think Grimmie remembers you too. You should see how big hes grown, hes the terror of the county. Do you remember we talked about my pap test and how the doctor thought I might have cancer? Well they still dont know for sure and evry month or two I go in and let them test me all over again. Burton doesnt know what to think, I think he thinks hes married to one of those women who always think they have some imaginery sickness or a crazy woman. The doctor says maybe I couldnt have children (not that I want them at this late day!) because of the I.u.d. I used when Harvey and I were first married. Thats real birth control I told her, and she laughed.

I dont know. Sometimes I think its worse to be a woman than any other of Gods creatures. Look at us two, me afraid of the cancer and you a widow for no reason. Somedays Id rather be a cat or a blackbird on a fencepost.

I guess I wouldnt want to be a pheasant. Coming back from your house that day Burton ran into one, it just flew in front of the pickup and he hit it with the left front fender. It scared me, it just appeared and the truck bumped and it flew like a black shadow across the windsheild and over the top. Burton swore. He stopped and got out and sure enough the pheasant had smashed the left headlight. I didnt think we hit it that hard, I half expected it to be alive and walking away from us down the road.

I miss you Leenie. Write me when you can, and please forgive me evrything.

Love to you and to your mother (even though shes never met me,

Nance)

When she finished the letter to Arlene she folded it and put it into the plain envelope she'd borrowed from the pasteboard box in Burton's den. She'd had to look up the address—a rural box number in a town called Chappell, South Dakota—and while she was writing it on the envelope the pen ran dry and she had to finish it with a different pen. Now it looked funny: part of the address in black and part in a sort of wishy-washy lavender blue. She wondered if she should find another black pen and trace over the lavender, but decided that would look even funnier.

Then she stole a stamp from Burton's desk and set the letter on a corner of the kitchen table for mailing.

Out the side window she could see Grimmie making his deliberate way up the green patch of lawn toward the old barn. The grass was still damp with dew; every few steps the cat paused to lick at one of his front paws, as if he was trying to dry them off. What was it about cats? No matter what they were doing, where they were going, they let themselves be distracted. It was as if they didn't care that much—as if they had plenty of time to do whatever it was they wanted to do. Or maybe cats didn't *want*. Maybe they went through their lives moment by moment, never looking ahead, never looking back. But Grimmie was off to hunt; Nance knew that, and you had to believe the cat knew it too. It was what he did every day. It was his occupation, his career. She had seen him sit for a half hour, absolutely still, his whole attention focused on a place among the tall weeds near the half-hinged door of the old barn. Then all at once he would pounce, and later she would find the guts of some small field animal gathering a swarm of green flies at the foot of the porch steps. That was the other side of cats, that made them seem like split personalities: either everything distracted them, or nothing did.

Harvey Riker had been like that. Times he would be so absorbed in the business of the farm that she might as well not have existed—and wasn't that why she'd turned to Burton in the first place?—and other times when he was so restless that his mind and his attention flitted like a dragonfly from this to that to this again. He chose winter hobbies, then discarded them: woodworking, photography, coin collecting—she could scarcely remember them all. He never explained to her why he picked up a new pastime, why he discarded an old; he never explained much of anything. It was good that he had money, so he could afford his changes of mind, his changes of heart. It was good that the farm prospered in the eighties, that he had sold a good-sized parcel of land in the seventies, when prices were high. And now, land prices being down, he was buying—even from prison. That was all the more evidence that when he concentrated his attention on business, no one could beat him.

Burton was not like him. Burton would take her to a movie when he should have been working on his accounts. Sometimes Burton would even lie in bed late into the morning so he could make love to her when he might have been in the fields, minding the corn and beans. Burton watched television with her. She loved Burton; she had feared Harvey. And Harvey had been on her mind ever since the shotgun was aimed, and the trap set, in the empty Tobler kitchen.

B urton was against her visiting Harvey—adamant this time, even angry. "I thought I'd weaned you away from him," he said. "I thought you'd got over him controlling you, trying to run your life to suit himself."

"I *am* over him," Nance said. She sat at the table, not watching Burton while he paced and grumbled. Once he stopped in front of the stove and thumped his fist against the side of a cupboard; she heard cups jump in their thin saucers. "I've been over him for years, the way you mean it."

"Then why do you want to go see the man? It makes no damned sense."

"I think it was being in Arlene's kitchen. It brought everything all back to me—reminded me of that night, the noise, the confusion, the blood and things breaking." But she could not say the truth: *He's haunting me again, Harve is. I have to see him, make the ghost human again.* "It's nothing to do with us, with me and you."

"It's everything to do with us," he said.

"Back then, yes, it was. But not now. This is just me. This is something I need to do, to erase things."

"You still have feelings for him."

"Oh, Burton."

There was nothing to be said. Nothing that she had not said whenever, so thankfully rarely now, the subject came up. She could only deny such feelings. She could only remind him that she had never forgotten Harvey's hitting her, running her down. She could only point to her betrayal of her marriage in favor of Burton. As a last resort she could only say that she had lived more than twenty years with Harvey Riker and, mistake or not, how could she ever deny that?

"I can't stop you," Burton said. "But you know I don't like it."

She stood up from the chair then and went to him. He looked away from her, but she put her arms around his waist anyway and pressed her mouth against his neck.

"Don't soft-soap me," he said. He put his hands on her shoulders as if to push her away, but he didn't push.

"You know he doesn't matter to me any more."

"Then stay home."

"Just this one other thing," she said. "I have to work it out. I have to get him to see what he did, get him to face it for everybody's sake."

"He'll never," Burton said. "After all this time."

"He has to," she said, "or I'll never get that awful night out of my head, ever."

She knew she was saying that she had to give her guilt to Harvey, and Harvey had to accept it or she couldn't forgive herself—and if she couldn't forgive herself, how could she expect Arlene's forgiveness to be genuine? The weight of this realization made her cling harder to Burton, and finally he slid his hands from her shoulders, down to the small of her back, out to the width of her hips, and returned her hug.

"I just think it'll be a cold day in you-know-where before Harvey Riker feels sorry for anything or anybody." He kissed the top of her head lightly and untangled himself from her arms.

"Come on," she said. "Let's go upstairs for a little while."

"You'll be late starting the supper," he said, but he got up, and when she took his hand, which was cool and dry in hers, he let her lead him up the stairs to their bedroom where there was no more talk about Harvey.

It was more than a month later—late July—before Nance visited her ex-husband. Even after she had decided to make the drive to Anamosa—and Burton was still opposed, had argued over breakfast the foolishness of it, "Harve being Harve"—she was uneasy, and blamed herself for imagining she could reach any kind of peace with the man. But in the end it seemed to her that the fact of Harve being Harve was no stronger than the fact of Nance being Nance, and so she had no choice but to follow her heart—and her conscience, wherever that led to.

It was an hour and a half to the prison; she drove her own car, the old Datsun with the rust showing at every seam, even though Burton had in the end offered the newer pickup. The world was deep green now, the corn not yet tasseled but taller than a man in rows that led in every direction, to every horizon. Every couple of miles the corn was interrupted by fields of soybeans, knee-high to a man, their green paler, leaning toward yellow, and their pattern a complexity of thin branches—like tumbleweed. The weather was hot, humid; perfect weather for plants, less perfect for humans. In her face, the passenger window open all the way, the air was hot and almost suffocating, though it was scarcely ten in the morning. The sky was high blue, the sun straight ahead of her scorching. She kept the visor down for its small rectangle of shade, and when she stopped for a traffic light in Manchester she leaned across to roll down the passenger-side window. For the rest of the trip she enjoyed the slightly cooler turbulence of wind surrounding her.

The prison was of brick, dusty red and sprawling behind high chain-link fencing that was topped by an inward lean of barbed wire. It was like an industrial oasis in the midst of the green world, and its appearance put her off as it always did when she visited Harvey. She left the car in the paved lot and signed in at the visitors' desk, letting the reception clerk dump out the contents of her purse, knowing that if the weather had been cold she would have had to take off coat and hat and jacket to prove she was not—what?—bringing raspy files and hacksaws to a man she would hate to see set free? Then she was escorted to the visitors' room, spacious and smelling of cigarette smoke and cleaning materials, the bare wooden tables arranged in classroom rows with folding chairs behind and in front of each one. The room was half-filled with women and children—an infant or two, but mostly the teens considered old enough to withstand the misery of confronting a criminal father—and there was a confusion of conversation amplified by the hard surfaces of walls and uncarpeted floor.

She sat at an unoccupied table, leaned her purse on the floor against one of the legs, waited with her hands folded in her lap for Harvey to arrive. She felt conspicuous by being alone; she almost wished she had listened to Burton.

If Nance had little to say to Harvey, Harvey seemed to have more than enough to say to her.

"What makes you think you have to keep coming to see me?" was what he said first. "What do you think I do all day and all night that makes me need you here?"

"It must be habit," Nance said.

"Stupid habit," he said. His hands were empty, larger than she remembered, and he gripped the side edges of the table with them. It was as if he didn't dare let go, as if he might raise them against her.

"We were married twenty-two years," she said. "You recall?"

"You cheated on me," he said. "Did you forget?" He leaned back in the straight chair on the other side of the surface that separated them. His eyes were not kind on her. But then, they had never been: cold, and gray the color of gunmetal, the expression in them had always wavered between contemplation of her existence in some distant, neutral way and an outright hatred of her—a terrible, wild look that in the past had meant his fists would follow, that had promised the next morning she would have to put on heavier makeup and rehearse stories for whoever asked sympathetic questions.

"I remember how you tried to get even. I remember who you killed."

He took a cigarette from the pack in the breast pocket of his blue denim shirt, lit it with a wooden match he ignited with his thumbnail like a tough guy in a late-night, black-and-white movie, inhaled deeply and noisily, a raw sigh. "Bad luck," he said. "Paul Tobler was always ripe for bad luck."

"He's dead," Nance said. "It was Arlene who had the bad luck."

"Your partner in crime," Harvey said.

"No. She just listened. And she didn't tell; maybe that was her crime."

"It didn't matter whether she told or didn't tell," he said. "I always had my sources."

She felt the chill of unpleasant knowledge. The other voices in the room—the wives and children visiting their men, confiding, weeping, reassuring; girlfriends explaining, coaxing, apologizing or protesting—seemed to have mounted to a clatter of pure noise; a smell of discount-store furniture polish assailed her, the bitterness of smoke from Harvey's cigarette hurt her nostrils.

"You knew?"

"Shit, yes, I knew all along."

"Even before that night?"

Harvey didn't hesitate before he answered. "I'd made up my mind I was going to kill the son of a bitch, sooner or later. What do you think? Yes. Long before that night."

It sank in. "You're saying it was murder," she said. "Plain and simple."

"No."

"Then what else would you call it?"

"The court got it right. It wasn't like I'd planned to do it in somebody's kitchen. Not in front of friends, not when we were drinking beer and playing cards. I might of waylaid him somewhere. Who knows? But it happened the way it happened. It took even me by surprise. You were there. You saw that."

She didn't know what to say. Should she tell Arlene? *He intended all along to kill Burton, just not in your kitchen. He would have done it on a back road, out of sight of civilized people.* "It's long past," was what she said. "I wanted you to help me get over it."

"I thought so," Harvey said. "This is why you keep coming here. For your sake, not mine."

A difficult silence fell between them—because maybe he was right, because she could not contradict him. She watched him smoke, ransacked her brain for something to say. The smoking was a new habit, or the revival of an old habit, for he had smoked cigarettes in the early years of the marriage. She thought now that he wasn't really inhaling—that he held the smoke in his mouth, that sometimes he went so far as to let some of the smoke drift in a curl of yellow-white out through his nostrils. It was a pose, and it made him look cruel, arrogant—the *real* Harvey, she thought.

"I found out why we never had children," she said. "The doctor says most likely it was the birth control contraption—the IUD—I used when we were first married."

He looked baffled, as if not understanding what she was talking about. Then he was irritated. "What the hell do I care about that?" he said.

"I thought you might like to know it wasn't your fault."

"I always knew it wasn't my fault," he said. "Jesus Christ."

She looked away from him. A few feet away a young woman—twenty or twenty-one years old—sat talking to a man no older. She had a child in her lap, barely more than an infant; the child was asleep, one thumb caught in its opened pink mouth, its tousled blond head against the mother's shoulder. The young woman's hair was dirty brown, unwashed; her dress was a flour-sack-floral cotton, her shoes scruffy canvas tennies—the kind high school girls wore nowadays. "He helps me with money sometimes is all," the woman was saying. "There's nothing going on. I swear. We met him at the laundromat and he just took a liking to us."

Dream on, Nance thought. Then: "I think you ought to write a letter to Arlene," she said to Harvey. "At least have the common decency to tell her you're sorry. Tell her you've had a lot of time to think—"

"Are we back to that? Christ, it was more than four years ago. And I told you: as far as she's concerned, it was an accident. There's not one damned thing I should be sorry about."

"Harvey—"

He held his hand up to silence her. "I don't make other people's luck," he said. "Besides," he added. "You shouldn't be worrying so much about Arlene Tobler. You've got problems enough of your own."

"What problems?"

"How should I be sorry for what I did, if you're not sorry for what *you* did? That's why you came, isn't it? Isn't that what you said?" He stood up; a uniformed guard moved toward him from a door at the rear of the room. "Screw it anyway," he said. "Don't visit me again. Keep your goddamned guilty feelings to yourself." He started to walk away, the guard at his side, then stopped to turn back to her. "And don't keep thinking you got yourself any kind of prize package in Burton Stone."

"What's that supposed to mean?"

"You've got a nice memory," he said. "You say you remember that night in Tobler's kitchen, but you don't remember what your precious Burton said. I mean about those Asian whores he had when he was off in Vietnam."

"That was just talk," Nance said. "Men talking fresh."

"Keep telling yourself that." He turned away from her. Over his shoulder he said, "Don't come back here again."

"I will if I want."

He stopped. "God damn it, Nancy," he said. "Please don't waste your time and mine."

Because he hardly ever said *please,* she persuaded herself she had made progress in spite of his meanness.

Now she was in no hurry to get home. It was a little past noon when she got to Cedar Falls, and she decided to treat herself to lunch at the Happy Chef. A salad, a Coke, a small piece of cherry pie. She thought she might bump into Burton, but she didn't know his plans for the day and she wasn't surprised he didn't appear. Some familiar faces passed her, spoke or nodded. When she was almost finished with the pie, Jess came by, saw her, sat down across from her.

"Where's old Burt?" he said.

"I left him home. I just came from Anamosa."

Jess nodded. "Harvey," he said. He looked at the crust of pie on her plate. "Could I have a taste of that leftover pie?"

She slid the plate toward him. "Help yourself," she said. She offered him her fork, but he picked up the crust with his fingers and made two bites of it.

"You remember Carol's piecrust," Jess said with his mouth full. "Better than this bakery stuff."

"I remember." She watched him, wary, not wanting him to slip away into scary reminiscence—but this time he didn't.

"How's Harvey doing?" Jess asked.

"Oh, I can't tell. He's so angry at me, so bitter about everything. You can't talk to him."

"Never could," Jess said.

"But I want to." She thought about that. "I need to. I need to tell him things that are going on in my life—in me. But he won't give me a chance."

"Such as?"

"I want him to write to Arlene—at least tell her he's sorry

for what he did. I want him to care about her. I want him to care about *me*. My feelings."

Jess cocked his head, as if he were trying to see her from a new perspective. "What about you?" he said.

She was on the edge of telling him about the doctor, the tests, the guesses, and then she thought, *Oh no, I can't make him think of Carol dying.* "Nothing much," she said. "Nothing you'd want to hear."

"Anytime you want me to," he said, without finishing the thought.

"I know." She leaned back in the booth and sighed. "I guess it's just that I've made such an unholy mess of things for the people around me."

"You only did your best—like we all try to."

"You're sweet," she said, "but look: all the time I was married to Harvey I wanted somebody—anybody—to come into our lives and say to us both: 'You will be happy; you will really and truly be happy.' But nobody ever did. Nobody said that, and I was never happy. And neither was Harve. You could see that. You could see it long, long before I fell in love with Burton Stone."

"I never condemned you," Jess said. He took her two hands in his; she thought he was going to cry. "Nancy Lynn Carlson," he said, using her maiden name as if she had never grown up, never married anyone, "you are a sweet young person who wouldn't in a thousand years give pain to any man. If any woman has earned her happiness, that woman is you." He bowed his head and kissed the back of both her hands, then released her.

"Jess," she said, choked up. "Oh, Jess . . ."

He gave her an odd smile. "Now where do you suppose Carol has got to?" he said.

Nance put her hand to her mouth as if to hide the fear his words put into her, but it was clear that he wasn't much interested in how she might respond. His eyes were vague now, gazing over her shoulder, as if he saw someone else he knew. "Can't sit here all day," he said. "Got errands to do."

Then he was gone. He was like some skittish animal—a rabbit or a chipmunk crossing a cleared field, darting, stopping, watching out for the redtail. She thought she understood what hawk poor Jess was so skittish about, and it made her sad as well as frightened.

It was one o'clock. Nance took her check to the register, paid it, carried three twenty-five-cent pieces back to the booth and left them neatly stacked for a tip.

Outside, the paved parking lot radiated heat. The air was dead still and heavy, the steering wheel of the Datsun nearly hot enough to burn her hands; she turned the wheel gingerly, holding and letting go and holding again as she steered out of the lot. She had already made up her mind not to go straight home; something about her encounter with Harvey had deeply unsettled her—something more than her unspoken fear that he might still go after Burton when he got out of prison. She had wanted to tell him what else the doctor had said, about the possibility of a cyst, or a tumor, or even cancer in the complex dark of her dead womb. Or nothing at all—a shadow threat. Not that he would have been sympathetic—"Don't try to dump your fucking female troubles on me"—but that telling her fears seemed to diminish them. It was why she wrote to Arlene; it was why she wanted to wake Burton at small hours. It was why she would treasure for the rest of her life Jess's willingness to hear her out; it was the kindness of an old friend, and it was not made any less important by Jess's queer departure.

She drove to the old Illinois Central bridge that Harvey and Paul had once mostly destroyed, leaving the car at the side of the road, making her way down into the ditch and up again to the old railroad bed. The bike-path people had rebuilt the bridge, and railings had been added before the trail was opened so that there was a contrast of weathered and unweathered timbers, the silver-gray against the raw, the new wood against the old charred remnants. She couldn't have said out loud why she needed to walk along the old roadbed, but something nagged at her—perhaps only the day's confirmation that Harvey had *known,* not simply guessed, about her affair with Burton, and probably that meant it really was her own carelessness that had killed Paul Tobler. She wondered who had told. She wondered how they knew.

She thought she had been extraordinarily careful. Even the few times they'd parked in the pickup, they'd gone way across the county line, for heaven's sake. Only once had Harvey seen her car at Burton's, parked behind the tool shed, and that time Burton had been marvelously quick, had invented some reasonable explanation—she couldn't remember what. One other time she had actually been in bed with Burton when the phone rang, and it was Harvey, telling Burton the pickup had a flat and Nance's car wasn't available and could Burton possibly come give him a lift into town to get the flat tire repaired? Burton had put his hand over the mouthpiece and mouthed the word *Harvey.* She had lain as still as a mouse, not daring to rustle the bedclothes or cough or even touch Burton playfully while he talked and listened. Afterward they had laughed and hugged and made crazy, too-fast love, which was all right for her in the wake of so much anxiety; it was satisfactory loving because it was a release, a relaxing—although later still, when Burton had gone to fetch Harvey and the flat, she lay for a long time alone, listening to the too-fast hammer of her heart.

But that was all. She and Burton had never been caught; the only person who *knew* was Arlene, and Arlene might have told Paul but certainly no one else, and Paul was the kind of man who forgot gossip as soon as he heard it—he had no memory for other people's business. Even Arlene never asked the tiny questions, never dug around for the details of Nance's affair. *Then how in the world?*

The bike trail led southeastward, arrow-straight, as far as she

could see. The track had long since been removed—sold for
scrap, she supposed—and the ties hauled away; it looked as if fine
gravel had been put down to replace the crushed rock of the old
roadbed, so the surface was smooth underfoot and under bicycle
wheels. Grass and weeds encroached along the margins of the
trail; wildflowers, remnants of the old prairie, blossomed out of
the weeds. Every so often she saw a rotted railroad tie left behind, pushed off to the side. She imagined homes for snakes,
bugs, small wild animals.

She walked almost two miles—there were wooden mile-
markers driven into the ground beside the trail—under the hot
sun, a kerchief over her head with its triangle of cloth pointed
forward like a visor. By then she was within sight of the empty
Tobler farmhouse, could make out the lines of its roof, the color
of its blue shingles, over the tops of cornstalks—had she come
this far?—and there she turned and retraced her steps. Birds
made their calls around her: the music of meadowlarks, the
squawk of blackbirds. Bees darted and hummed around yellow
and orange blossoms; grasshoppers leaped in her path. She felt
oddly easy. The echo of her unpleasant meeting with Harvey
seemed slowly to melt away; the fret of how he had known what
he did know seemed hardly important at all. Being alone was
good for her, she decided, or entering Nature, or it was only the
refining heat and light of the sun that eased the world. Some
other day she would fret about her informer. As if it could
change outcomes—and anyway, that was the past; this was the
present, and she was with the man she loved. As for what wild
oats Burton might have sown in Vietnam, what did any nameless
woman matter, fifteen or twenty years ago on the other side of
the world?

She'd thought it was true that Arlene hadn't really forgiven her.
Yes, they corresponded, but rarely—two or three months between
letters, some of them scarcely more than postcard messages—and

every time Nance sent a letter to South Dakota, she promised herself she wouldn't be upset if, this time, no answer came back to her. That day would come, she told herself. Arlene's old life, her long marriage, the world that was Iowa—all of it would drift farther and farther into the distance. Arlene would forget their best-friendship; all she'd remember would be what Nancy Riker had done to ruin her happiness.

But when she'd come home from her encounters with Harvey and Jess, and stopped at the end of the drive for the mail, here was a letter. She knew the handwriting right off. *Leenie,* she told herself, and she carried the letter up to the bedroom and propped herself against the pillows. She tore open the letter, excited. They were still friends. If she could have jumped into the envelope, to wrap herself in Arlene's words, that's what she'd have done.

July 14

Dear Nance,

Well, we have the same heat wave in S. Dakota, so don't feel that you're being singled out to be tortured with it—high nineties every day. I look forward to fall and winter, but I know good and well that when the snow is piling up and the temp is down below zero I'll think My gosh, I wish it was last July so I could warm my poor bones. But yes, the corn and beans will benefit, just as Burton says. He sounds a lot like Paul—these men, always concerned with weather and the land and their precious property.

I'm sorry about the damage to the house. Empty houses are so sad. I remember the day I left, ready to drive "home to mother," and how I stopped the car at the foot of the driveway to look back. You know how the driveway is made, so you don't get a straight-on look at the house until you're practically in the yard, and all I could see was the roof and the chimney—and then when I was a quarter-mile down the road to N. Hartford I stopped again and looked back. Paul's house, my house, nobody's house was what went through my mind like a singsong. Well, your shotgun story scares me a little, makes me too think of that awful night I lost Paul. But there's nothing in the house worth stealing, is there?

It's a long time since I wrote you, I know, but you mustn't ever think I blame you for anything. Life goes on. We do what we do the best we know how. You couldn't know how deep Harvey's anger went—and maybe it was that he really loved you but never knew how to show it??? I don't know. People are too deep for me.

Mother passed on. It was right at the beginning of spring, just before the Easter break at my school, and the nursing home called me—said her heart had failed, apologized for not calling me in time to be at her bedside. I almost laughed—I would have if I hadn't been crying—because why would I have wanted to be at her bedside, like some kind of vulture? She hadn't even recognized me in weeks—thought I was one of the nursing attendants, or sometimes her sister, my aunt Lucy Ann who died twenty years ago, or she didn't even know I was there. Well, it was a sad funeral. She'd outlived all her friends. That's what I dread: I don't want to die, but I'd hate to think that the price of a long life is to have nobody left to put flowers on your grave. I'm darned sure Sarah wouldn't take the trouble and who knows what corner of the world Peter will be in?

I'm pleased to hear that Grimmie is still tomcatting around. Paul never much liked him—you know how men are about cats—but he put up with him. I think sometimes I'd like to come back as a cat—to have that beautiful disinterest in the world, just sort of take it as it comes without making a big fat dilemma out of it.

And when are the dizzy doctors going to find out there's nothing wrong with you—because that's what it's beginning to sound like to me. It sounds like there's something about Nancy Riker Stone that resists medical science! If you're feeling okay, and if they can't find anything really negative—just these "inconclusive" results that make you jumpy and cost you money—then I'd tell them to keep their testing to themselves. Paul used to say that if something wasn't broken, you didn't have to fix it.

Anyway, I'm happy to hear from you and Burton. Your letter reminded me of good times and bad, but we need to have nostalgia of all sorts in our lives. I look at my students at the school, and I think how they don't know what life is all about, and I love them and pity them for what's ahead. But then I scold myself for thinking like a grownup!

Well, I do run on, don't I?

Your oldest(!) friend,
Arlene

6

It was late in August when they finally lost the old barn.

If she had known this night was to be filled with such destruction, Nance might have been frightened. As it was, she gave scarcely any thought to the forecast of wind and rain. It had been hot and humid for days—good corn weather—and, as Burton had said, turning off the television after the weather report was finished and before the sports began, "We're due."

The storm began only after midnight, but she had been lying awake for hours in the hot bedroom, a thin sheet over her, wishing for even a slight breeze to spring up, to stir the air and help coax her into sleep. Instead the world was perfectly still, perfectly dark—the moon either not yet risen or hidden behind cloud—and no matter how often she turned her pillow or moved to find a cooler place in bed, she could not let go of the day and be comfortable. Beside her, Burton slept and snored—a betrayal, she thought as she became more and more impatient for her own rest. How could he let her suffer her insomnia alone? "Burton," she would say, in a whisper barely audible, not wanting to wake him but hoping he would hear his name and *be* alert, ready to respond. "Are you awake?" in the same faint whisper. Waiting.

Holding her breath. Nothing answered her except the coarse noise of his sleep.

She turned away from him and pushed the sheet off her hip, letting herself be naked in the blind room. She wished Burton would wake up and make love to her. She wished it were winter, and the fields blank with snow, and Burton in the house with her most of the time attending to his book work. She wished she were not so selfish. She wished Arlene had never moved away to God-forsaken South Dakota and all her bratty schoolkids. She wished she had never married Harvey Riker. She wished and wished. She wished there would be a breeze to come in the open window and brush the damp hair from her forehead and be cool against her skin.

That wish she got. It was announced by light—a far-off flicker of lightning like moments of aurora on the horizon—and then by sound—the faint rolling of thunder to the west, drawing perceptibly closer as she listened. And then the wind; it began as a long sigh through the cornfields, and it made her remember a story Arlene had told her about how the voices of the grain became the words of buried people rising from root to stalk to blossom, accusing their enemies, calling their friends. *Listen to them,* Arlene had written in one of her first letters, *maybe you'll hear Paul saying how much he loved all of us.* But Nance heard no words, only the sigh through the fields and, finally, she saw the curtains billow at the window and felt the brush of air across her nakedness.

You could tell it was going to be a real storm. The lightning got brighter and the thunder louder. The seconds between flash and rumble—she counted them, *a thousand-one, a thousand-two*— got fewer. The noise of the wind grew from sigh to moan to scream; the curtains flapped and one of them flew across the top of Nance's bureau, toppling what must have been a perfume or cologne bottle, and then the draft slammed the bedroom door shut. Burton stirred but refused to wake, and she smiled at the depth of his sleep.

After that the curtains bellied-in less violently. When the rain arrived, softly at first but quickly rising in intensity, Nance got up and closed the window to within a couple of inches of the sill. She went back to bed, drew the sheet up to her chin, and lay on her back, eyes wide open, giving herself to the storm outside. At least this insomnia was justified. The rain swept over the roof of the house as loud as the thunder. The gutters and downspouts ran like waterfalls. The lightning and thunder came almost simultaneously now; the room exploded with light, the house shook with sound. Then there was hail: a drumming on the roof, a clatter against the side of the house, a random sharp *snap!* against the windows. It excited her, the wildness of it all; half she wanted to get up, naked, and be a part of it, imagining herself a white figure dancing outside through rain and hail, hair streaming down her back, wind buffeting her, the wet earth under her feet cold and drawing her down. She saw herself in front of the dilapidated barn, her arms upraised, her body leaning with the weather the way that sorry building had leaned for years.

Then she was sensibly back in bed in the calm and protection of her husband's love, and she heard a new sound. Not hail or wind-driven rain or thunder so near it echoed in the hollow of her stomach like a drum; this was something being torn, something ripped like tree roots out of the ground, a shriek of noise, and Nance knew in an instant it was the old barn collapsing at last. What she was hearing was the creak and clatter of wood giving up its shapes; the few remaining load-bearing timbers, the boards and battens, the rafters and roof supports that had defined the barn in spite of its weakness—she heard them go crashing down. The wind changed key through the broken lumber; pieces of siding slapped against the house; if she had let her crazy imagining take her out to the yard she would have been blown away like any ordinary stick.

Burton slept on. Nance got carefully out of bed and went into the bathroom to look out the window that faced the old barn. In a broad flash of lightning that seemed now to be miles off, she saw the silhouetted ruin of it. It looked as if it had exploded; it was all edges and broken verticals, the pitch of the old roof barely above the level of the earth. By daylight it would be an eyesore; Burton would spend weeks clearing it away.

Burton was out most of the next day surveying storm damage—walking around the wreck of the old barn, weighing the cost of having the shattered lumber trucked away against the time and labor of trimming and stacking a supply of ready firewood for next winter. In the evening he reported to her, called her outside with him to marvel over the details of the barn's collapse, told her how fortunate they were—thank whatever god existed—that the fields of corn that stretched to the horizon seemed to have survived the storm in good shape.

On the second morning Burton was up at five-thirty, pulled on his clothes and went out to tackle the remains of the barn in earnest. He carried a cup of coffee with him. As he descended the porch steps, Nance could see that he was grinning, as if he had decided that the end of the barn was a happy event in their lives, and clearing it away more a game than a chore.

A short time later Nance was upstairs making their bed when she looked out the east window and saw the deputy's car, with its silver shield on the door and its green and white *S* license plate, already stopped in the yard at the side of the house. When the Gish boy—it was so hard for her to believe he was grown up—stepped out of the car, she recognized him immediately and for a moment had to lean against the window frame to steady herself. Seeing him brought back the day after Paul and Harvey's little drunken escapade, when young Gish had taken both husbands to Waterloo for arraignment. And the night Paul died—that was another time she had seen too much of sheriff's cars, although that time it wasn't Deputy Gish who arrived first.

Now she went to the bathroom window, to watch as Burton turned toward the deputy, took a step or two in the younger man's direction. Deputy Gish was hatless, carrying a newspaper, rolled up, in one hand; Burton had on the green Pioneer feed cap, its bill pulled down to shield his eyes from the sun. Behind the two men the barn was a clutter of broken boards and torn walls, the patchy paint, iron-red, glowing in the morning slant of sunlight. She couldn't imagine what they were talking about. It wasn't likely that a sheriff's deputy would be dispatched to the scene of a tumbled-down empty barn.

Now the pair of them turned and walked toward the house, the deputy doing the talking, gesturing, Burton listening and nodding, one hand stroking his chin, the other loose at his side, holding the paper Gish had given him. Then they were out of sight, and then she heard the kitchen door open; she could hear the noise of the rusty spring stretching, the click of the latch. Then an exchange of voices, too faint for her to make out the words, and the door slapping shut. The scrape of a chair, the deputy taking a seat at the table with Burton.

Nance went back to the bed, folding down the top sheet with its hem of blue embroidery, placing the two pillows just so, the decoration of the sheet carefully parallel to the pillows. When she straightened up she felt the familiar ache at the small of her back; was there any other job so unpleasant as bending over to make up a bed? If it hadn't been the bed she shared with Burton, the bed where they acted out the love that made her life so sweet after long bitterness, she could never have tolerated the work. And there was more that waited to be done: Burton's clothes to be put into the laundry hamper and the hamper to be carried down; the water glass and coffee cup on her side of the bed to be returned to the kitchen; slippers to be straightened on the closet floor and her nightgown to be hung on the back of the bathroom door. But curiosity had the better of her; she went downstairs— casually, so it would look as if she wasn't really interested in the deputy's errand—without attending to any of these matters. For a moment or two she listened, and then she made her entrance.

"You're out early," she said to the deputy. She tried to make her voice light, even though she saw the moment she came into the kitchen, saw by the expression on Burton's face and the serious look on the young deputy's, that something bad had happened. She realized she was carrying over one arm the nightgown she'd meant to hang up in the bathroom. Flustered—but by what?

"There's been an accident," Burton said.

Nance turned toward Deputy Gish.

"A man's been shot," the deputy said. "Out at your other place."

"At Arlene's?" she said. "Dear God. Who?" She looked at Burton. "What happened?"

Burton shook his head. She didn't know if he was saying he didn't know what had happened, or if he was warning her not to ask questions.

"It's Peter Tobler," Gish said. "Driving west to visit his ma in South Dakota."

"Peter." She caught her breath and covered her mouth with the fingers of her right hand. But the deputy was mistaken. Peter Tobler was out of the country, a million miles from here. Arlene had said so. "It couldn't be Peter."

"I'm afraid it is."

"Is he dead?"

"He broke in at the house," Burton said. "No, he's not dead."

Oh, God, she thought. *Leenie will have a fit.* "Was it the trap?"

Gish nodded.

Nance turned away. She pictured Peter breaking in, forcing the front door; she imagined the gun going off. Did he think his mother still lived there? "In his own house," she said.

"Well, you can't say it didn't work." Burton laid the newspaper on the table in front of him. "Just like I said."

"How bad is he?"

"Broken leg, flesh wounds, shock," Gish said. "Doctor in the emergency room says probably the kneecap has to be rebuilt."

She looked at Burton, who shrugged and opened the newspaper as if he was going to read the front page. "He came too far in," he said.

"Somebody has to call Arlene," Nance said. *That will be me.* "She'll be sick about this."

"It served him right," Burton said. He folded his arms, the cap bill hiding his eyes. "Trespassing."

"She won't see it that way, Arlene won't." She sat down across from Burton, heavily, as if her legs couldn't support her any longer. "Peter and Sarah both, they grew up in that house."

"Looking to steal stuff," Burton said, though of course they both knew the house held nothing of value.

"He told me he was just looking for a place to get out of the rain, a dry place to sleep," Gish said.

"Christ, why didn't he go to a motel?" Burton said.

"He says he'd run out of money. Says he knew the house had been sold, but he didn't think anybody'd mind, it being unoccupied."

"I mind," Burton said. He looked at Nancy. "I damn well mind. And there's nothing wrong with a man protecting his own property, is there?"

"Not as far as I know," the deputy said, "but I'm no lawyer."

"Who cares about lawyers?" Burton said, and the deputy smiled and nodded as if he didn't care about lawyers either.

"What do we have to do now?" Nance said.

"Oh, I'm not here to ask you to *do* anything," Gish said. "I'm just a messenger, just telling you what transpired."

"But we *know* Peter," she said. "I haven't seen him since he was just a teenager, but still—he's my best friend's boy."

"And never was any good," Burton said. "Never quite right in the head."

"No, Burton, no. You mustn't talk like that." She would have to tell Arlene today—as soon as the deputy was gone. She saw that clearly. It didn't matter what the news might do to the friendship between them.

Burton looked away.

"Officially," he said to Gish, "is this the end of it?"

"I doubt that."

"What more?" Nance wanted to know. She remembered what things had been like after Paul died. Questions for Arlene, questions for herself, questions for Burton and poor old Jess. Witnesses.

"There'll be an investigation—because of the gun. The BCI poking around. I expect the newspapers will stick their nose in."

"But we weren't there," Nance said. "We don't even know as much as you do."

Gish looked apologetic. "Like I said," he told her, "I'm only a messenger." He stood up as if the action were an effort. "Sorry to start your day this way."

"It's all right," Nance said. "It's terrible, but it's not your fault. You have to do your job."

Burton stood too. "Thanks for bringing up the morning paper," he said.

Telling Arlene about Peter was the hardest thing Nancy had ever had to do—harder than daring to fall in love with Burton, or finding the courage to divorce Harvey, or trying not to think about the cancer that might or might not be growing inside her, and it overshadowed even her fretting about what the law could do to Burton for setting up the trap gun in the first place. It was so awful that what had begun as a favor to Arlene, to keep the Tobler farm in the hands of friends, had turned full circle and become an echo, an ugly mirror picture, of Paul's death. *In that same kitchen.*

She had to wait until the afternoon. It was late August, probably schools were back in session and Arlene wouldn't be through teaching until—when? Probably four or five o'clock, Nance figured. She would try the number at five, and keep trying in case she might be going out somewhere for supper. Arlene would never again be her friend after she'd delivered her news.

Arlene answered on the third ring, her "Hello" sounding a little breathless. "I just walked in the door," she told Nancy. "School starts next week, and we've had teachers' meetings all day long. What a nice surprise to hear your voice."

"You may not think it's so nice after you hear what I have to tell."

"Oh, dear," Arlene said. "Oh, dear Nance, what's wrong? What's happened?"

"Something terrible," Nance said. She had decided simply to blurt it out, not beat around the bush, but Arlene interrupted.

"You're all right?"

"Yes, I'm fine."

"It's not your Burton—not some accident?"

"Leenie, no. Not that at all."

"Not poor old Grimmie?"

"Leenie, you've got to let me tell it. It's about Peter."

There was a silence at Arlene's end, but only for a moment or two, and then she said, "How can that be? Peter's in China. He's teaching farmers about hybrid corn."

"No," Nancy said, "no, he's not. He's right here. They took him to Waterloo. He's been hurt." *There. I've told it.* But now the worst was to be revealed.

"Hurt how?" Arlene said. "Is it bad?"

"He got shot."

"My God. Who did such a thing?"

Nance moved the phone to her left hand; her right had got so sweaty she could hardly keep a grip on the receiver.

"Nobody did it," she told Arlene.

Another silence. "That makes no sense," Arlene said. "What are you talking about? Is Peter dead?"

"Oh, Leenie," Nance said, "do you remember me writing you about how Burton was trying to keep trespassers out of your old house?"

And then she broke down. She wept and stammered, but she got the words out as best she could, blubbering apology, begging to be forgiven—yet again—trying not to be a woman who brought nothing but pain to the only woman friend she had.

"He was on his way to you," she managed. "He'd been given a new job by the government, and he had three weeks off, and he was driving to surprise you. He didn't have much money. He didn't see any harm in looking to spend the night in an empty old house he'd used to live in." She shifted the phone again and tried to find something to blow her nose with. "It was raining and blowing," she said. "He didn't know about the shotgun."

"How bad?" Arlene said. "Calm down, Nance; calm down and tell me how badly he's hurt."

"I don't know. They took him to Covenant, in Waterloo."

"Is he dying? Is he conscious?"

"Yes. Yes, he's conscious. He's not dying. It's just his leg. But I don't know how bad it is."

"Can he call me?" Arlene said. "Will you tell him to phone me?"

"I will," she said. "If he hasn't already, it's because he's at the hospital, getting fixed up." Nance blew her nose. "They say they're going to put him in jail."

"Jail? What on earth for?"

"Trespassing. That's what the deputy said."

Arlene snorted. "Have him call," she said. "Or have the doctor call. I can't get there until tomorrow, or maybe the day after. I have to get in touch with the principal, so he can find a substitute."

"Oh, Leenie, I'm so sorry."

"Nance—" Arlene said, and then stopped. "Nancy, I always appreciate that you're sorry." And then she hung up.

Nancy set the phone in its cradle. She had to admit: you couldn't blame Arlene for being angry.

You didn't have to be there at the house to see in your mind's eye exactly what happened that night in late August. It was dark, the moon covered by clouds, a warm wind gusting from the west that would eventually bring in its wake the sharp, violent thunderstorm that finished off Burton's hollowed-out barn—lightning striking so near the Tobler house it actually brought down half the landmark cottonwood, and torrents of rain that half-filled the roadside ditches for two days, and hail big enough to crack the glass in a couple of upstairs windows. Windows that in fact had once looked out of Arlene and Paul's bedroom.

You could imagine Peter parking his car at the top of the drive to the Tobler place—where the next day the sheriff's people would find it—and walking, fast so as not to get wetter than he had to, up onto the front porch of the dark house, the cedars and scrub tall enough to dwarf him, dense enough to hide him. And when you came down to it, what did it matter if he was hidden or not? This was the house he'd grown up in, the place he'd called home more than half his life. Whatever country he was posted to by his bosses in Washington, it must have been this Iowa farmhouse he pictured when he felt the brush of nostalgia coloring his thoughts. He'd have known the rooms were probably bare, that there wouldn't be a bed to lie down on, but he'd be dry and safe from the storm when it broke. When morning came, he could look around—go from room to room, rehearse whatever his memories might be. He'd look at the damaged kitchen wall, a proof Peter had never seen of how his father had died. He'd have had no idea about the shotgun whose muzzle was aimed at the door he'd be obliged to force. He'd been in the States less than a day, had landed at O'Hare only five hours before—Beijing to Hong Kong to Honolulu to Seattle to Chicago; twenty-five hours of broken sleep—and by the time he paid for the rental car, he was down to his last ten dollars. But that was enough, if he drove straight through: a couple of meals on the road, and then he'd be at his mother's. But he was more tired than he thought, almost nodding off more than once between Dubuque and Waterloo. The old homestead would be a godsend.

So here he came, onto the porch, in one hand carrying a tiny flashlight, the kind you hang on a keychain, its brightness barely enough to illuminate the keyhole on a car door; the other hand holding a plastic credit card he hoped would be stiff enough to slip the lock. And so it had done. The beveled brass tongue slid away from the striker plate, the door was unlocked, Peter was free to enter the kitchen.

The screen door had opened outward, but the door Peter had just forced was inward-opening. If it had been daylight, he might have seen the way the trap gun was set up—how the nylon fishing line was strung so that when someone opened the door he put tension on the triggers of the shotgun pointed toward him, and how the farther in the door was pushed, the farther the nylon drew the triggers back until eventually the hammers would give way and the gun would fire. He might have noticed that the triggers of the double-barreled gun were staggered, so that the first shell would explode when the door was opened a foot or so, the second when it was opened the distance of a farther foot. Approximately. Burton hadn't done the mathematics; he hadn't attended to the details of the geometry. All Burton cared was that he had contrived the trap so that the deeper into the house the intruder came, the worse he would be hurt.

After the first explosion, in fact, if Peter's leg hadn't given out under him—for the first blast of buckshot caught him in the right calf—he would never have sustained the second, more serious wound. But there was luck again. When his right leg buckled, he fell forward so the door opened wider. The nylon line went taut, and as Peter was falling to the kitchen floor, the second burst from the gun shattered his kneecap.

For almost a day and a half he lay in the empty kitchen, not able to walk, half unconscious with pain and shock and loss of blood. After the first hour, the storm broke in earnest, rain and hail lashing the isolated house and its outbuildings, beating down the cornstalks that stretched north and west away from the place, stripping leaves from the creaking cottonwood, sending sheets of water across the porch and spilling it into the kitchen through the opened door so that Peter was half-drenched after all, his discomfort made so much the worse by the cold and damp. The thunder was deafening, the lightning strikes nearer and nearer; Peter must have believed that he would die of electrocution if not of his wounds, and when the stressed cottonwood split open he may have thought from the sound of it that the roof was blown off. That night must have seemed endless, and the next, calmer night, and the empty day between them. Probably the irony of *where* he was suffering was not lost on him.

It wasn't until six-fifteen on the morning of the second day that Deputy Gish, on routine patrol duty, caught out of the corner of his eye a flicker of light off glass. He pulled in behind the car, noted its Illinois license tags and the rental-company sticker on the windshield, then went to take a closer look at the house. He could see that the front door was open. It was reasonable to assume that whoever had opened the door was still inside, so Gish approached the porch warily, his service revolver drawn, his eyes and ears tuned for movement or sound. You never knew. When he set his weight against the door to open it the rest of the way, something held it; when he slipped through what opening there was, he stumbled over the useless left leg of Peter Tobler.

A̲ll these facts came out in testimony at the trial, which under ordinary circumstances would have been scarcely more than a formality. In truth, there was considerable informal discussion about the connection between the defendant and the place where the trespass occurred—whether it was legally possible for a Tobler to be charged for entering a property still known in that part of the county as "the Tobler place." In the end, Peter Tobler was charged with unlawful entry and trespassing; he pled no contest. He appeared before Judge Floyd Andersen, at the Black Hawk County Courthouse in Waterloo, the first Tuesday in September—on crutches—to hear a sentence the judge said he regretted but felt "honor-bound" to pronounce: three months in jail, payment of actual damages to the property owned by Burton Stone, and a fine and court costs amounting to something less than a hundred dollars. Arlene had sat behind her son, in the courtroom's first spectator row. When Judge Andersen passed sentence, she compressed her lips and said nothing, and then she turned to look hard at Nancy Stone.

If looks could kill. The phrase crossed Nance's mind and then vanished. That wasn't Arlene's message; it was more complicated than that. It conveyed years of schoolgirl-like closeness, secrets shared with no one else in the world, an equality that paid no attention to differences of sophistication or intelligence, and it recorded yet another casual betrayal Arlene hadn't deserved.

In the week since Arlene had come back to Iowa, she had hardly spoken with Nance. She had turned down an invitation to stay with the Stones, and she had refused, politely, to eat dinner with them. She had taken a room at the Ramada in Waterloo "to be nearer Peter," and spent most of her time traveling with him between Covenant Hospital and the county jail. "He'll always have a limp," one of the doctors told her. Peter had laughed it off. "I'll carry an ivory-handled cane," he said, "and look distinguished." This was what one of the doctors told Nance and Burton, long afterward.

Peter was different from the schoolboy Nance remembered. He seemed smaller—hardly bigger than a twelve-year-old, Nance thought—and she wondered if the way he'd had of intimidating people by his manner and his big talk was what had made him seem larger in her eyes. His sandy hair had begun to thin at the front, and he had grown—or was trying to grow—a scraggly little mustache. He showed no particular emotion as he stood before the judge, and Nance supposed he was "on" something, some sort of drug the doctors might have given him for the pain in his leg. She wished she could ask Arlene about that.

Peter didn't testify in his own behalf; even when he was asked, he had nothing to say before the sentencing by way of complaint or explanation or any expressed desire for leniency. His court-appointed lawyer stood beside him and shook his hand when the bailiff arrived to take him away. Arlene followed, as if she were going to share his sentence.

Nance could see that for Burton the day was a triumphant one. He had defended himself against an enemy and he had prevailed by being practical and by refusing to be taken advantage of. If he felt any regret for Peter's injuries—and she knew he did, after his initial anger had subsided—the verdict had all but erased it. The outcome of the trial had vindicated him; it justified his use of force.

But for herself the day in court was an ordeal, made so much the worse when Dwight Commoner—the same lawyer the court had appointed to defend Harvey in the murder of Paul Tobler and who had plea-bargained the charge against his client down to manslaughter—stopped Burton and her on the front steps of the courthouse as they were walking to Burton's pickup. Commoner came up behind them and clapped his hand on Burton's shoulder.

"Justice done," he said. "A season at the county's expense to meditate on his sins." The lawyer nodded in Nance's direction. "You folks must be pleased."

"Not pleased," Burton said. "But satisfied."

Commoner fell into step beside Burton.

"You may remember," he said, "that I was having lunch at the Happy Chef the day you set up that trap of yours and came in bragging on it—getting the word out, as it were."

"I do remember."

"And you'll recall I said at the time that I hoped you knew what you were doing."

"I do recall," Burton said. "And this case proves I did know. What I thought might happen *did* happen. I was right to defend my property."

"No question," the lawyer said. "Trespass was made, damage admitted, and retribution exacted. But trespass is dealt with in the Bible, as well as in the Criminal Code. Precedents. We lawyers always look to the precedents."

"What's your point?" Burton asked. By now they were at the truck. Nance had gone around to the passenger side and got in. Burton stood holding the driver's side door handle.

"No particular point," Commoner said. "Only I sat there during the sentencing and got to wondering about punishment— about the fit between the crime and the come-uppance. Not that I imagined it mattered that you knew the victim. A little abstract meditation, was all."

Commoner held out his hand; Burton ignored it.

"The fact is: I didn't know the so-called victim," Burton said. "He was a child the last time I saw him."

"Well," the lawyer said. "We'll probably meet each other again. We seem to like the same eating establishments."

Burton watched him retrace his steps into the courthouse. Nance looked at Burton, trying to read his face as he climbed into the cab. He shook his head—perplexed, she thought.

"I suppose we'll soon know what *that* was all about," he said.

7

I should get over there," Burton said—*there* meaning the Tobler place—"and cut up that old cottonwood."

He had been restless since the court proceedings and the encounter on the courthouse steps a couple of days before. Nance didn't know how she ought to respond, how to try and settle him down—whether anything she could do or say would make a difference to him.

"There's no hurry," was what she said. "You've still got the barn to clean up."

"That too," he said, "but if I put off either job, the harvest'll be on us before we know it, and then if there's an early snowstorm . . ."

And then, and then. He'd find an excuse, some downright necessity, to get at that fallen limb, that lightning-struck reminder of a time before damage. Imagine conjuring snow, she marveled, when it was barely September.

"I could use your help," Burton said.

"All right," and she followed him outside, though while she waited for him to lock up the house she wondered what sort of help she could be—remembering how she had "helped" the last time they went to the Tobler place together. "Moral support," this time, or only someone to keep him company.

"You're not going to ask me to run that chainsaw, are you? I'll have to go back in and change clothes." She meant it as a joke; and of course Burton took it that way.

"Let the woman I love dirty her lily-white hands?" he said. "What kind of man do you think I am?" He opened the truck door for her, closed it after her and got in on the driver's side.

"But I wish Paul was alive," Burton said. "He and I'd make short work of tree and barn both. We'd have ourselves a nice lot of firewood. If not for this winter, then next."

"I'd guess the tree's pretty dry already," she said.

"Or the storm wouldn't have split it off so clean," Burton said. "That's what I think, too."

All the way to Toblers' he was quiet. Nance could imagine what he was thinking: how Peter Tobler had come out of no-where to complicate his life—*their* lives; how nothing could be done about it; how it was all well and good that the boy was in jail, but no one could say if that was the end of it, what with the furor that was starting up in the newspapers.

"It's a shame," Nance said. "Arlene told me once how the county had put that old tree on its official map."

"*X* marks the spot," Burton said. "You got to wonder how long the rest of it will stand. It's only half a tree left. One more strong wind, and the county'll have to look for a new landmark."

"It's a shame," Nance said again.

The stricken cottonwood had been split—by wind or light-ning, one or the other—leaving one of its trunks still standing, the other fallen toward the driveway, but not across it. Burton stopped the truck just beyond the fallen tree's topmost branches, shut off the ignition, and pulled on the hand brake. Nance sat in the truck while he went around to the back and dragged out the chainsaw. When he pulled the saw into life, she covered her ears against the scream of it, the insult of its noise.

In the end, of course it was Burton who did all the work, and

Nance truly along merely for her company—a companionship more imaginary than real, for most of the while he reduced the limbs of the fallen tree to firewood, Nance stayed put inside the cab. What did it matter? she asked herself, for how ever could they have talked to each other over the chainsaw's deafening engine? Inside the pickup's glove compartment she found a dog-eared paperback with its cover torn off—an old Perry Mason mystery, probably left over from a trip to the Suds & Duds when the washing machine broke down last year—so at least she could make the time go faster.

After a half hour or so she closed the book and put it back where she'd found it. For a while she watched the wind ripple the tops of the cedars, then she had the pleasure of seeing two pheasants—male and female—strut across the drive ahead of the truck, and finally she stepped down from the pickup and, with a wave back at Burton, trudged up the hill to the farmhouse. The door was locked again, but looking through the front window into the empty kitchen, she could see that the woodblocks nailed to the floor were still in place and a tangle of fishline lay nearby. The shotgun had been "seized as evidence" and impounded by the sheriff's people.

She sat down on the top step of the porch, listening to the terrible chainsaw and the brief, high whine of each cut log. She couldn't see her husband for the cedars, and for the first time since Paul Tobler's death, she found herself wondering why no one had ever thought to tame this overgrown front yard. Here was a good two, two and a half acres that might have been planted with something and, knowing Paul, that should have been worth his trouble. But Burton had owned the same land for more than two years now, and neither had he tried to reclaim this acreage.

By the time Burton finished his work, the day was more than half gone and Nance was famished. When he drove the truck up to the house to turn around, she went down the steps to meet him.

"I hope we can go home now and have lunch," she said. "You must be as starved as I am."

"I've got an appetite," he said. "And I've done all I'm going to do today. Tomorrow I'll see if I can't round up old Jess, and maybe that fellow, what's-his-name, who's renting the Riker place. That was a lot of tree; the three of us can divvy it up."

He walked her to the pickup and opened the door for her. "I looked at those old two-by-fours and one-by-sixes rotting away out there," he said. "Nothing useful."

"That's from the tree house the Tobler children were building, years and years ago. Peter and Sarah, and I don't know who-all else from around here in those days."

"Kids," Burton said. "They never finish what they start." He headed the pickup down the hill.

"Did you ever think you might figure a way to plant this couple of acres between the house and the road?"

Burton waited at the foot of the drive for a school bus to go by, dust billowing in its wake.

"It wouldn't be easy," he said. "You see how it slopes down to here. It's pretty low, and it holds the wet—that's why these cedars flourish like they do. Then, higher up, toward the house— that's where they laid in the septic field."

"I guess it wouldn't be worth it," Nance said.

Burton pulled out onto the gravel road and headed homeward. "Not hardly," he said. "Not unless we got super desperate."

As Burton turned into their own driveway, Nance caught the glint of sunlight off the windshield of another pickup, drawn up alongside the tool shed. It was the same shed she had once tried to hide her Datsun behind, back in the days when she began to be brazen about seeing Burton, and, for a split second, the idea that Harvey was out of jail and was waiting to kill them both set her stomach churning.

"Who's this?" Burton said.

And now Nance recognized the old pickup. "It's Arlene," she said.

"Sweet Jesus," he said, "what's she up to? She bringing another kid to screw up our lives?"

"I doubt she wants anything." But Nance thought she knew her husband's anger, and at the same time she imagined she'd have shared it, if not for her closeness to Arlene.

"I've got nothing to say to her," he said. "You can be as friendly as you care to, but don't speak for me. You might remember that there was no sign of her when you and I got married."

He slammed the door of the cab and strode toward the house. There was no time to say, *But she has a job; she's not her own boss.* Nance got slowly down and waited as Arlene approached.

"I'm driving back," Arlene said. "I wanted to tell you good-bye."

"I'm glad." She wondered if she was genuinely glad, or was this just something you pretended—something automatic, because you were a generous person? Burton couldn't bring himself anywhere near that kind of generosity, as if Arlene was as much to blame for what had happened as Peter was. Probably Nance was being disloyal by not snubbing Arlene, but how could she turn on her oldest friend?

This was new, this divided loyalty. It was a thing she hadn't experienced before, and now she wasn't sure how she ought to confront it. She hadn't been torn between Harvey and Burton; that was ridiculous, no contest. If she had made a list of the good on one side, the bad on the other, Harve was all bad, Burton was all good. And there had never used to be any competition where Arlene was concerned: she was Leenie, dearest friend and secret sharer, and there was no more important person in her life. But now. . . .

"It's an interference, isn't it?" Arlene said—as if she had read Nance's mind. "What Peter has done. What Burton did. The trial." She stood a few feet away, her eyes averted as if she wasn't able to look squarely at Nance. "The world is changed. The world is corrupted."

"I know what you're saying," Nance agreed, though in fact "corrupted" put her off for a moment. She knew the word. Some-

times it meant a thing was spoiled, rotted, like what happened to
the dead under the earth, a word you heard at funerals. Or it
meant what men in politics did, who took money for favors or
lied out of selfishness and for their own profit. But Leenie was
using it a different way. Nance could see that. It was their friendship that was spoiled, friendship that neither woman could trust
anymore—at least not with whole hearts.

"Peter has a claim on me," Arlene said. "I can't help that.
He's my firstborn, the male child to carry forward Paul's name,
Paul's lineage. If Paul hadn't died, if we hadn't lost the farm, it
would have come down to Peter. As it is, if it weren't for him, the
Tobler family tree would stop short."

Nance couldn't think of anything to say. Arlene was turned
away from her, and what she could see were bowed shoulders,
broad hips that said strength and womanness and middling age,
a gaze—though she could only imagine it—set across the landscape of Iowa-autumn browns and yellows.

"And *you* have a claim," Arlene said. "I always thought—
excepting only Paul—that you were the strongest connection I
could have to another person. I'm not sure you aren't even now,
never mind Peter. But," and here she turned her face to Nance.
Tears, Nance told herself. *She's crying.* "It's been pulling me
apart," Arlene finished.

"Oh, Leenie," Nance said. They hugged each other. *And now
we're both blubbering,* Nance thought. *Just what women are supposed
to do, and Burton had better not come outside at this minute to witness.*

Then they subsided.

"They took Peter to Anamosa," Arlene said, the strength
back in her voice, "but I'm sure that's a mistake. I talked to that
lawyer, Commoner, and he says that for Peter's particular crime,
the sentence is supposed to be served in a county facility. Not a
state prison."

"I'd heard that," Nance said.

"So I guess, for now, I've done all a mother could be expected
to do for her black sheep, and I'm heading back to my job.

I talked to the principal on the phone this morning. He's covering my classes for me, and it's perfectly plain he hasn't got a clue about middle schoolers."

"I wish you could stay longer." She meant it—as if with more time together, the two of them could solve the world and all.

"I don't want an administrator's nervous breakdown on my conscience," Arlene said, and then she almost smiled. "You can tell yourself I'm leaving Iowa for humanitarian reasons."

They hugged again, this time without tears.

"You drive safely," Nance said.

"This old truck won't go fast enough to be dangerous."

"You be sure to call me when you get there."

Arlene climbed into the truck. "Peter wouldn't like me to tell you this," she said, pausing on the running board, "but he's hired Commoner—that lawyer—to represent him."

"Whatever for?"

"He didn't say—or he wouldn't."

"It seems kind of late in the day for that," Nance said. "The trial is over and done with."

"That's what I told him."

"What's he up to?"

Arlene shook her head. "I'd be the last person to know. But it was always that way. Sarah was the one who told me everything. Peter was his father's son, everything bottled up inside. It's why the two of them fought so."

And why Paul never visited Peter in the hospital, Nance remembered.

"But as I always tell my classes: The world is a strange place, and it's full of people. You never know what will happen next." Arlene drew the driver's door closed and leaned over the window sill. "Good-bye, Nancy," she said. She put out her hand, as if to shake Nance's.

Instead, Nance took the hand and pressed it to her lips before letting go. "Call me," she said. "Write me your wonderful letters."

The engine clattered into life. Arlene waved once as the pickup headed down the drive, and once again just before it disappeared in the dust of the road to New Hartford.

*D*ear Leenie,

Im sorry we didnt have more chance to talk while you were here, but I could see how stressed you were and how worried for Peter. I know you blame me, and Burton too, but you know niether one of us would want to see you or yours hurt, even a little bit. Peters time at Anamosa or wherever will pass real quick, and hell be with you befor you know it.

I hope your okay and that the kiddies are being nice to you and the principle didn't have his breakdown. Im hanging in as they say. Burton didnt reset his trap—and he wont—on the advice of the sherrifs people. Besides they still havent given back his shotgun. Youll say its locking the barn door after the horse was already stolen, but be glad at least nobody else can get hurt.

We didn't get much chance to talk, so you probly don't know this. That same night your boy got shot was the night Burtons old barn fell in. Burton says it turns out there was only 3 posts strong enough to hold up that whole hugh barn—and the wind that nite just caved it in. Burton has most of the old boards and 2by4s cut up and stacked alongside the shed.

I dont know if I told you this or not but Harvey said (I went to see him in July) that hed heard from way back all about me and Burton from somebody, and that hed planned right along to shoot Burton one way or another, just not in your kitchen. And you and me were so privat about it! It makes me feel awful. I worry what will happen when they let Harvey out of jail. If he'll come after Burton and finish what he planned.

She thought she might feel more like finishing the letter later on, so she pushed it aside and set on top of it the crystal paperweight Burton had given her on their first anniversary, the little frog with bulging eyes she'd seen and exclaimed over one afternoon in the Crossroads Mall. She felt a little better now; in spite of everything, it was a relief to have Leenie to confide in, but it was also good that she was a couple of hundred miles away and not nearby. This way Nance could choose what and when. She didn't have to worry about Arlene taking her by surprise; she didn't run the risk of blurting out something she hadn't come to terms with, wouldn't get flustered by a response she wasn't ready for. It was bad enough that the lawyer Burton didn't like, Commoner, would likely be nosing around asking questions, talking to the sheriff's people, maybe even visiting Peter, who was still in Anamosa. She was sure Arlene would have something to say about that, but it was just as well she wasn't here in person. Letters were a safer way to talk. In a letter, you constructed your reasons as you wrote. In a letter, you couldn't be ambushed, and you wouldn't start crying like the day Leenie went home to her schoolhouse.

She went downstairs, humming, thinking she ought to start supper. She could hear the sound of television coming from the parlor—Burton watching the news?—and went toward it to ask Burton what he'd like her to make.

The room was empty, the television screen bright with the colors of a war somewhere, refugees bundled into muddy camps, no one watching the horror. *You know how you expect a person to be there,* she would add to the letter awaiting her upstairs, *how when you walk into the room your mouth is already open for the words but theres nobody to say them to and they dont come out.*

"Burton?" she said. By then she had turned away from the parlor and gone to the living room. Here was Burton, sitting at the bay window in the half-dark, seeming to be gazing out over his fields, watching the line of light from the vanished sun spread along the horizon like something poured, something flattening out against the far-off ground. "Is there anything special you'd like for supper?"

"Whatever you'd like," he said. He didn't turn his head. Closer, she saw now that his hands were up at each side of his face, as if he was leaning into them, a man deep in thought, or dreaming.

"Thinking about all the wood you've got to stack tomorrow?"

"Not really. Haven't called Jess yet."

"Is something wrong?"

"Long day," he said. He sighed. "Long week. What a mess it all is."

She sat herself on one arm of his chair and brushed the hair back from his forehead. "It's all worked out," she said. "Peter's going to be all right except for a little limp. And Arlene understands; she'll forgive us."

"Not *us*," Burton said. "Me."

"You can't blame yourself. He broke in. He knew his mother didn't own it anymore."

"It's not how I planned it." He rubbed his face between his hands and swore softly. "How the hell could I know that my burglar would turn out to be runty little Peter Tobler? If he'd been a halfway normal person, the shot wouldn't have touched him."

"It was bad luck," Nancy said. "They've even sent him to jail."

"I know." He took her hand and kissed her fingers. "Now I wish I'd never set the trap. I swore to God when I came home from Nam that I'd never again give pain to a living soul."

"You didn't intend to."

"It was a gamble," he said. "In my heart I knew damned good and well somebody might get hurt."

"What happened since the trial?" she said. "You seemed pleased with yourself at the time."

"That lawyer," Burton said. "He took the wind out of my sails a little."

She bent over to kiss him, twisting a little to reach his mouth with hers, wishing he might kiss her back. "So," she said when he kept his gaze straight ahead, still absorbed in the diminishing twilight, "what about your supper?"

"The worst thing," he said. "I was expecting a bad guy, but what I got was only a guy looking for a place to lie down out of the weather."

Peter just wasn't lucky, she would write. *You know he hasn't had much good luck ever since he almost killed the Jensen boy all those years ago. I felt sorry for him in the courtroom, coming in on crutches, having to be helped by some lawyer not near as smart as the one the judge appointed for Harvey. And I could see how you hurt for him, too.*

"How about pork chops?" she said. "And string beans and applesauce."

"Sure." He pushed himself forward, forcing Nance off the arm of the chair. "I think I'll get myself a beer," he said, "watch what's left of the news."

She was lighting the burner under the string beans when the phone rang. It was a woman who said her name was Samantha, she was from the college, and she was one of the people who'd been helping Jess Eriksen with the running of his roadside produce business—bookkeeping, clerking—and did Mrs. Stone have any idea where Jess might be?

"I haven't seen him in a while," Nance told her. "Are you worried? Do you think he's in trouble?"

Samantha didn't know, but yes, she and Terry—Terry was the other college person helping Jess with the stand—were beginning to worry. Jess had driven off early yesterday morning, not telling anybody where he was going, and she and Terry hadn't seen him since. It was true that this wasn't the first time he'd climbed into the old Dodge and taken off without a word to anybody, but usually he was back the same day. Even when he took a longer trip—sometimes he went to Des Moines or Davenport, Samantha said, and once he'd gone all the way to the Twin Cities because he said he needed something for the car that nobody in Iowa seemed to have in stock—he'd be back by the afternoon of the second day. Did Mrs. Stone think Mr. Stone might have seen him yesterday?

"I'll ask him," Nance said. She laid the phone on the counter next to the coffeemaker and went to get Burton.

"Who is it?"

"It's one of the young people working for Jess. She's worried about him—says he's been gone two days."

"Oh, that's just Jess." Burton set his beer on the window seat and got up from the chair. "He's always going off to be by himself so he can talk to Carol's ghost without people thinking he's crazy."

Nance followed to the kitchen, thinking *poor Jess* and remembering the last time he'd visited, the time seeing Arlene's cat had turned him into his old clear-minded self.

"Hello," Burton said into the phone. He listened, looked at Nance and winked. It gave her a little thrill, that wink. It said there was still something special between them; it said he wasn't worried about Jess. "Well, I wouldn't sound the alarm just yet. I've known Jess for a number of years, and I can tell you he's able to take care of himself. Probably he just knows I want him to help me load some cordwood tomorrow, so he's making himself scarce."

He listened to what Samantha had to say to that, and then he covered the mouthpiece with his free hand.

"Would you fetch my beer for me?" he said to Nance. "That's a good girl."

When she brought the beer to him, he was saying to Samantha, "I know, I know, but we all get a little addled with time. You young pups will find that out as you get older."

He took a swallow of beer and shrugged in Nance's direction. Would Samantha ever get off the phone?

"Seriously," Burton said, "wait till tomorrow morning. If he doesn't show up by then, give me a call." He hung up. "Kids," he said. "They've got no patience nowadays."

"Jess does act strange sometimes," Nance said. "Maybe it's Alzheimer's. You hear more and more talk about that kind of thing."

"He's old and he's lonely and he's forgetful. That doesn't make him a case. He can go where he pleases for as long as he pleases. Anyway, we've got enough troubles of our own without looking for new ones." He gestured toward the stove. "And your beans are about to boil over," he said.

After supper—Burton had already climbed the stairs to bed—Nance went back to her letter to Arlene, avoiding harder subjects by describing the wreckage of the old barn before Burton had gone to work on it with a chainsaw, and then she closed with a postscript:

> P. S.   Jess E. hasnt come home for two nights and the young people who work for him are upset. They called Burton asking if wed seen him and we said no. I told you Jess is getting 'funny' in his old age didnt I? Im going to say a little prayer for him. Maybe you could add Jess's name to your prayers for Peter.

Peter Tobler was out of the hospital, still sitting in jail in Anamosa; Burton had finished explaining—first to the sheriff's people and then to a man from the state, who'd driven up especially from Des Moines—how he'd come to be setting traps with a loaded shotgun; and Nance and Burton's life, except for old Jess and his adventuring, seemed on the verge of returning to normal.

Nance was in the parlor, dusting, when she happened to glance out the bay window to see Todd Clausson's green sedan moving up the driveway with its flashers working, and that meant official government business. It was Todd's own car, but he used it to deliver the mail—a white rectangle of cardboard with U S MAIL printed on it in big block letters showed in the lower corner of the windshield on the passenger side. She'd overheard him talking to Burton out by the mailbox one afternoon: "They'd wanted me to drive one of those little milk-crate post office trucks, the ones with the steering wheel on the right hand side and painted all red, white, and blue. But I said no. Turns out I get paid the same, using my own vehicle, plus I get the mileage reimbursement besides."

She looked at the china clock on the mantelpiece. It was just after one-fifteen, about the right time for the mail delivery. She wondered what Todd was bringing that he couldn't have left in the box; even if it was a package, he usually managed to figure a way to hang it from the flag. She laid the dust cloth and the can of polish on the coffee table and went out through the kitchen to the side porch, pushing a wisp of hair off her damp forehead— they were in the middle of Iowa's usual late-September heat wave—and waited at the top of the steps to see what Todd was delivering.

The sedan came to a stop in front of the ruin that had been the old barn, then backed and filled until it was facing down the driveway. Todd slid out of the front seat with a packet of envelopes in one hand. The motor was running; the flashers kept flashing.

"Afternoon, Todd," she said. "Something important?"

He stood beside the front steps and handed the mail up to her. "Registered," he said. "Got to get your signature on that yellow slip."

"Come inside for a minute," Nance said. "Cool off a little."

"Don't mind if I do." He climbed the steps and trailed her into the kitchen. "It's so damned hot I can't use the air-conditioning. All the stopping and starting overheats that old Chevy on a day like this."

"I've got some lemonade," she said, "if Burton didn't drink it all."

"Lemonade would go good."

Nance put the mail on the kitchen table and opened the

refrigerator. The lemonade pitcher was two-thirds empty; she decided to pour two glasses and make some more before Burton got home.

"Saw Burton's pickup at the Happy Chef this morning when I started out here," Todd said. He pulled out a chair and sat at the table. Nance set a glass of lemonade in front of him.

"He might have been swapping stories with Jess Eriksen," she said, "or it might not have been Burton's truck," she said. She sat opposite Todd, sipped her own drink, pulled the yellow receipt in front of her to sign it.

"Oh, I'd know Burton's from a mile off," Todd said. "When you two were first carrying on, I'd see it on my way home, parked at that little picnic turnoff up near Janesville."

Nance put her glass down. "Really?" she said.

"Or sometimes after lunch at The Shed I'd see it pulled off into the weeds on the old Hildebrand place outside Dike." He drained his glass. "Hell, I know that truck all right."

"I didn't realize we were so public," Nance said.

She felt sick to her stomach. Now she wondered if everybody in the county had known all along that she was carrying on with Burton. Harvey said he had known for a fact—she realized it had to have been Todd Clausson who told him—and why wouldn't the rest of the county have known? But if anyone was going to be the bearer of gossip, naturally it should be the postman, who probably read all the postcards before he delivered them, and who could study the return addresses on every letter he carried.

"That was before the two of you started getting together here at the house," Todd went on. "When the cold weather set in." He smiled and winked. "No secrets amongst good neighbors."

"Apparently not," she agreed. And why talk about it now, after she and Burton had been legally married close on to two years?

"Anyway," Todd said, "I guess you haven't heard about old Jess. He's a missing person."

"No, he isn't. He's away for a few days. Burton thinks he's on a business trip." Minneapolis, she wanted to say; the Cities. That was what Burton thought.

"That's not the latest," Todd said. "I was by Eriksen's an hour ago. The sheriff was there. The two kids who work for Jess found his address book, and they're calling around to find out if anybody's seen him in the last three days. The sheriff's organizing a search party."

"That's a lot of foolishness," Nance said. "He'll come home when he feels like it—when his errands are done." She remembered his abrupt departure from the restaurant, the day she'd confided in him. *My errands,* he'd said. She'd watched him through the front window, hurrying to his car, wheeling into traffic.

"I'm only giving you the facts," Todd said. He consulted his wristwatch. "Got to get moving," he said.

Nance signed the receipt for the letter and slid it across the oilcloth toward him. "Here's the slip," she said. "Thanks for delivering to the door."

"Just following the rules." He stood. "I'm grateful for the cold drink."

"Just being neighborly," Nance said.

She watched him get into the car, watched the car go blinking down the drive. *Damn busybody,* she thought. The next time she visited Harvey she would know exactly where she stood. But what should she think about Jess Eriksen?

The envelope was oversized, manila-brown with a window that showed both Burton's name and her name—their last name first—and address. The envelope was fat. It carried more than two dollars worth of postage and was stamped *"REGISTERED"* in red; a long number was handwritten under the word.

Nance wanted to open it, but thought she shouldn't because it was only half addressed to her. She wondered if she should even have signed for it with Burton not home. She put it on the kitchen table, next to the sugar bowl and the salt and pepper shakers, and sat at the table to think about it. From the way she watched it, it was as if she expected it to move by itself, or open itself, or that at the very least she was trying to read its contents through the brown paper. At the same time, she was half afraid to find out those contents. She could not have said how she knew the envelope held something bad, but she did; whatever the reason, it was a knowledge—an uneasy intuition—that she felt in her bowels, and she was almost happy when she heard Burton pull into the yard. She heard the truck door slam, then her husband's footsteps crossing the porch, and here he was in the kitchen, bending over to give her a quick kiss on the cheek.

He picked up the envelope as soon as he saw it. Nance watched him tear it open, held her breath as he unfolded the thickness of several pages and began reading. His lips moved silently.

"Todd Clausson says Jess is missing," she said.

"That damned gossip," Burton said. His tone was distracted, and he didn't look up.

"Todd says they're starting a search for him. They're calling up everybody who knows him."

"Mm." He scowled and shook his head, shuffling the pages in his hand.

"What is it?"

"You won't believe," he said.

"Maybe I would."

"Peter Tobler," he said. "He's suing us."

Nance shivered. The uneasiness in her stomach turned cold and she could feel goose bumps on her bare arms. She'd been right: the letter was bad for them.

"I don't believe it," she said. "Arlene wouldn't let him do such a thing."

"Believe it," Burton said. "What's his mother got to do with it?"

"Anyway, how can he sue us? He's in jail for trespassing on our property."

"Violation of his civil rights. Pain and suffering. Loss of income." Burton shook the paper in her direction. "There's a whole list of stuff we're supposed to have done to him. He's asking for a bushel of money."

"He's in jail," Nance repeated, as much for herself as for Burton. Neighbor or no neighbor, jail meant you'd done wrong; jail was punishment; jail was justice done; jail was the be-all and end-all of this matter, wasn't it?

"Guess who's his lawyer," Burton said. "Commoner. The guy who jawed with us after Peter was sentenced." He sat down opposite Nance. "He's been laying for me," he said, "ever since that day in the Happy Chef."

"Why would he do such a thing? He doesn't even know you."

"Ambulance chaser," Burton said.

"What's that mean?"

"He sees a chance to make a buck, and he steps in with a trumped-up lawsuit."

"But he can't win," Nance said.

"You're damned right he can't win," Burton said. "I'll make him sorry he ever pulled a trick like this."

"I'm going to call Arlene," she said. She watched her husband sit at the table, the paper unfolded between his elbows. *At least it wasn't from my doctor.*

I wondered what it was," Arlene said. "Ever since he told me about the lawyer."

"And you're going to let him do this?"

Arlene sighed, a small brushing of sound over the miles of distance between the two women. "I can tell him he shouldn't. I can tell him he should forgive and forget—that it was an accident and that you two are as sorry about it as can be. He'll never listen to me."

"What does he want from us? We can't turn back the clock."
If only we could.

"I know he needs help to pay his medical expenses. Heaven knows I can't afford to. And Peter's not a saver. He doesn't have anything in the bank, and his government insurance won't cover him because he got hurt while he was committing a crime. And now he doesn't even know if he'll get a new assignment, what with his bad leg."

"So now he'll have the lawyer expenses on top of all that," Nance said. "What kind of sense does that make?"

"I'm sure he's thought of that," Arlene said. "He's a grown man, Nance. He's not stupid. Anyway, I can't tell him what to do. He's always been stubborn. He's never been the kind of person who'd listen to reason."

"He should be ashamed of himself. That's what I think."

"Nancy—"

"And you should be ashamed you can't talk some sense into his head."

Nance waited. She heard the intake of Arlene's breath at the other end of the line, and when her friend spoke, the tone of her voice was different.

"Nancy," she said, "I don't want to fight with you, but you've got hold of the wrong end of things. Peter's crippled, and you two bear some of the responsibility whether you'll admit it or not. God Himself knows I hate to see my only son dragging my closest friends into a court of law, but I won't pretend there isn't some justice to it."

"He won't win," Nance said.

"That's between his lawyer and yours. I've said all I'm going to say on the subject." And she hung up, leaving Nance listening to the dial tone.

Dwight Commoner was in his office across the street from the county courthouse. The office was a long, narrow room with bookcases along two walls and a high Tudor-style window at the far end. Commoner's desk was in front of the window, which had horizontal blinds that were open so the light streamed in from behind him, silhouetting him. Nance imagined that was so you couldn't read the expressions on his face when you talked with him, but he could read yours clearly. He stood when she and Burton came into the office, and the light followed him as he came forward to shake Burton's hand, to give a nod in Nance's direction.

Burton ignored the offered hand, just as he had at the courthouse. "I'll come straight to the nub, Mr. Commoner," he said. He waved the brown envelope at the lawyer. "What's this monkey business of suing the *victim* of a crime?"

"Why don't you call me D. C.," Commoner said. He went back to his desk, sat down, leaned back in the chair; the chair spring creaked loudly. "Everybody does."

"I'll stick with 'mister,'" Burton said. Nance hugged herself. She'd never seen Burton so riled, so plain angry, much angrier than she had been when Arlene hung up on her.

"Suit yourself." Commoner tipped his head to one side as if he were studying the couple before him. He was going to try to lord it over Burton, Nance saw, and it was at that moment that she realized they'd probably wasted their time by coming here. What had they expected? What had *she* expected? This plump little man in his three-piece suit, the gold chain across his vest— as if people even carried pocket watches anymore—his whole attitude superior and off-putting. What did he care about them?

"Well?" Burton said.

"Why don't the two of you sit down, be comfortable," Commoner said. "Don't make this into something personal and unfriendly. It's all in the family, so to speak."

"How can it not be unfriendly?" Burton said. But he sat in a vinyl-covered chair to the left of the lawyer's desk. Nance settled herself into a leather couch, far away at the back of the room, just inside the door. "I'm being sued by a goddamned burglar. Calling him 'friend' doesn't change that."

Commoner sat forward. "Now hold on," he said, "let's get something straight. Breaking into your place is one thing. That's a criminal act pure and simple, and the man who did it paid his fine and court costs and did time in prison for it. Not being a stranger didn't give him any advantage whatsoever."

"He asked for it," Burton said.

"But what *you* did to Peter Tobler—that's another thing entirely. You may be an innocent man under the criminal statutes—I say *may* be. Defending your property, protecting your rights, all that—but under the civil code you're on the other side of the fence." He leaned back; the chair screeched. "Now there's no point in you blaming *me* for what's presently going to take place. I'm not the aggrieved party; I'm simply representing him because he isn't competent to represent himself—doesn't know the finer points of law, doesn't have any experience in front of a judge and jury—"

"Except when he was found guilty of breaking and entering," Nance put in. "And once before, when the court sent him to the MHI in Independence." *He tried to murder somebody,* was what she wanted to say.

Commoner ignored her—didn't even do her the courtesy of looking in her direction. "So I'm simply standing in for him in this matter. He asked me to; I agreed. It's a civil rights case, plain as plain can be, and our intention is to win it."

"This paper—" Burton flourished it. "This fancy paper says he wants damages. For what?"

Commoner sat forward again. "Burt Stone," he said—pompously, Nance thought—"you set a trap that injured a fellow human being. This chap is going to go through the rest of his life with a limp, and probably with bad nerves, and his government service has probably gone by the wayside because he now has a criminal record. All because of you and the extreme way you chose to guard your real estate. Do you have no conscience, man?"

"Of course I've got a conscience. Maybe your man should have thought about the consequences of his crime."

"He faced the music," the lawyer said. "He's paying *that* price. But if it were you, would you expect to be paying for the rest of your life?"

"I'm no crook," Burton said. "I wouldn't break the law. And anyway, look at what you're asking. A half-million dollars?"

"We broke it down—and remember, that's only a ballpark figure; a judge, a jury, who knows what they'll say? Maybe more, maybe less. But think about it: loss of income. Tobler is twenty-nine years old, so suppose he was able—before your shotgun went off—to work till he was sixty-five. That's thirty-six years of useful job life taken away from him. Figure he could've earned twenty thousand dollars a year—no, he's a skilled white-collar person, sophisticated, world-traveled, so figure more than that. Figure thirty thousand—which is what he was earning on his last assignment for the Agriculture people. Times thirty-six years." Commoner worked the keypad of a desk calculator. "What do you think?" he said. "That's more than a million right there. Medical costs? Doctors and hospitals don't come cheap; he's already got bills over two thousand dollars. And never mind the *unconscionable* delay in treating his injuries. Pain and suffering—what do you figure that's worth? How do you measure pain in dollars and cents? Can't be done; you have to look at precedent. The man's a cripple. A half million is a cheap price; thank your stars the man's not a professional athlete—football, basketball—think what *that*'d be worth in court. Denial of civil rights? You can't put a price tag on it. And we're not even specifying punitive damages; we could have asked for a whole lot more—on grounds I haven't even got around to researching. The humiliation of being locked up—illegally—in a state facility for committing a county offense, for one."

"You haven't got a leg to stand on," Burton said.

Commoner smiled, just a trace of change to the shape of his mouth in the shadow cast over his face by the outdoor light.

"No," he said, "it's Tobler who doesn't have the leg to stand on. And that's the whole damned point, isn't it?"

Nance winced. She didn't like Commoner, didn't like his looks or the high and mighty way he talked, but she wished Burton hadn't said what he'd said.

"That isn't funny," she told Commoner.

Commoner turned his head to look at her; the change in light over his shoulder made her blink. "No," he said, "it isn't, is it?" He turned back to Burton. "Ask your own attorney if we have a case."

"I don't have any attorney, and I don't plan on getting one."

Commoner showed his shadowy smile. "This is a straightforward argument, and if it's decided on its merits the outcome is a foregone conclusion," he said, "so I'd advise you—seriously, man to man—not to try and represent yourself. Get legal help."

"Peter Tobler wouldn't have known to do this legal stuff if you hadn't gone to him and egged him on," Burton said. "Isn't that true?"

"I didn't approach the man," Commoner said. "Didn't make a move in his direction, in spite of the fact that I was in county court on the occasion of his sentencing—as you may remember. The case was brought to my attention by an acquaintance of his."

"My understanding was that Peter doesn't have any friends around here anymore."

"As a matter of fact, it was someone he got reacquainted with when he was moved to the Anamosa facility." Commoner turned over a sheaf of papers on his desk. "What some might call *serendipity,*" he said. "Your former husband, Mrs. Stone. Harvey Riker."

Nance braced herself for Burton's reaction. "That's just like Harvey," she said, "sticking his fingers in every pie."

"My free advice," Commoner said, "is to get yourself a decent lawyer. I can't stress this too strongly. Cut your losses; don't try to defend yourself."

"We'll see about my losses," Burton said. He glared at Nance as if she were responsible for what Harvey had done now. "Let's go," he told her.

He stalked out of the office; Nance followed without another glance at Commoner.

And now Jess Eriksen was a genuine *missing person*—it was official. He had been gone, no one knew where, for nearly two weeks. There was no sign of him: nobody had seen him, heard from him, caught sight of his old Dodge. The police had sent out bulletins to surrounding states; they had scoured the county roads within a radius of ten miles, then twenty, then fifty; they had borrowed a helicopter from the Polk County sheriff's department and flown back and forth over the ripe Iowa fields for days. No Jess.

Burton was beside himself, Nance could see. She knew how he felt—*as if I didn't have problems enough.* The letter from Commoner, suing them on behalf of Peter Tobler, had thrown across their lives a shadow such as they had never known. Their affair years earlier—the stress of that secrecy, the sneaking around that had made them both feel ashamed—was nothing compared to this. Burton was especially *crazy*—there was no better word for it. He had done nothing illegal. He had defended his own property, private property, against a stranger breaking in; the trespasser had been brought to justice. As for Nance, she would never forget Arlene's abruptness, or get over Commoner's scorn.

"Why won't they just let the damned thing drop?" Burton said. "Why can't they ask me to pay the guy's medical bills, and call it square?"

"You sound like me," Nance said. "Wanting the world to be simple and commonsensical."

"God forbid the world should show a grain of sense," he said.

They were upstairs, getting ready for bed. Nance was already under the covers, a pillow doubled behind her head, waiting for

Burton. She wondered where Jess had gone. She wondered how good a lawyer they could afford, and whether whoever it was could stand up to terrible D. C. Commoner. She wondered when, if ever again, Burton would turn out the lamp and whisper love words to her; when, if ever again, he would come inside her to heal the fear in her heart and the constant cramping deep in her belly. But all she could do was watch his shadow dance over the walls while he undressed, admiring the stark whiteness of his sweet body against the deep tan of his arms and neck, wishing from the center of her soul for everything lost to be restored and made whole.

"Harvey said something real mean to me," she said—not certain why she was bringing it up at this moment in her life with Burton.

"When was this?"

"Last time I saw him. Last time I visited Anamosa."

He pulled back the thin bed sheet and slid under it. "And what was it he said, this 'mean thing'?"

"Something about all your Asian women," Nance said.

Burton sat up. "My what?"

"You recall the night Paul got shot? You were trying to pretend you didn't have a girlfriend hereabouts? You said how you'd got your fill of sex off all the Asian girls you'd known in Vietnam."

"Maybe I said something like that. That doesn't make it true."

"I know," she said.

"Harvey was giving out all that crap about me parking in the boonies. I didn't want to give us away."

"I know." She nestled against him; he lay against the pillow, put his arm over her. "Does that mean there weren't any women in Vietnam?" she said. "Not any prostitutes?"

Burton was silent for what seemed a long time, as if he were framing his answer—making it soft enough for her to bear.

"You don't have to tell," she said.

"There's not much *to* tell," he said. "I'm not going to pretend there wasn't any women at all. But I was young then, not very experienced, so you can't blame me for giving it a try."

"How many?"

"Two, maybe three." He raised up on one elbow and put out his hand to touch her bare shoulder. "Nance—"

"No," she said. "It's all right." And then she said, "That Harvey Riker. He surely knows what he's doing when it comes to making people hurt."

H ow could you do this?" Nance said. "What business is it of yours what happens or doesn't happen to poor Peter?" She was sitting across from Harvey in the public glare of the visitors' room—Harvey half smiling, smoking a cigarette, squinting at her through the gray haze between them. "Whatever connected you and me is legally done with. I came to you that last time to see if you'd finally tell Arlene you were sorry for what you'd done to her life. All right; you wouldn't lower yourself. But now what on God's earth makes you think you need to mess up me and Burton?" She didn't add the part about the women in Vietnam—how for a while that had come to be part of the mess.

Riker shook his head. "Old Burton must have been pretty fucking mad," he said, "to send you flying over to Anamosa to bitch at me."

"I came on my own," she said. "But of course he was upset." That was putting it mildly; Burton had raged, not *at* her—he loved her too much, he was too gentle a man for punishment— but *around* her, talking to himself in the pickup on the way home from Commoner's office, muttering in the living room over a can of Old Milwaukee, cursing Harvey, lawyers, the court system. "Who wouldn't be?"

"What's crazy Peter suing you for? How much?"

"Half a million dollars."

Harvey laughed, half choking on cigarette smoke. "Christ," he said. "Not bad."

"I thought you knew all about it," Nance said. "I thought you put him up to it."

"All I did was, I told him about the lawyer who'd got me off on manslaughter instead of the murder of his daddy. I told him that what Burton did to him sounded to me like he wanted to kill him. Hell, yes, I was the one telephoned Commoner and asked him if he'd be willing to talk to Peter. He sounded interested—said he'd think about it. That's all I did."

As if that wasn't more than enough. "How did you even know about Peter in the first place?"

"They put him right across the corridor from me. And even if I hadn't seen him, I'd read about him. If you wondered how I pass the time when they don't have me working in the laundry or digging in those damned vegetable gardens they call a 'farm' or stamping out license tags in the machine shop, I go to the library." Harvey stubbed out the cigarette in a cardboard ashtray. "I bet that surprises you. I was never a reader, was I?"

"So you already knew about it from the newspapers?"

"Page one," he said. "The famous trap-gun business, the poor kid wounded in old Paul's kitchen by your wonderful, gentle Burton and his loaded shotgun. Big black headlines." He crushed out the cigarette and folded his hands across his belt buckle. "I asked myself: If you weren't there, did you pull the trigger? If the kid had died, would Burton be a murderer by remote control?"

"I don't think so."

"Then you'd best think again," Harvey said. "Because that's the question Peter was going to ask D. C." He laughed. "Talk about 'love thy neighbor.' "

Nance turned away from him. She was beginning to understand she'd never be free of Harvey and his anger at her—that one way or another, directly or indirectly, he was going to get even with her for falling in love with Burton Stone.

"I wish I'd never got married to you," she said.

"That makes the two of us," Harvey said.

"And you *know* how kind Burton is. Always has been. You never liked him from the beginning—long before he paid any attention to me—because he shamed you."

"Pantywaist," Harvey said.

"He shamed you by being nice. He doesn't have your temper. He doesn't have your filthy mouth."

"And he doesn't have sense, business or common," Harvey said. "Here's a man who wouldn't be a farmer because he didn't want to be like his old man. No, he couldn't bring himself to take on a successful—well, reasonably successful—operation. Didn't want to give his father the satisfaction. Has to try raising beef cattle. Then he turns around and gets out of the cattle business because he won't—*can't*—compete with the big boys: companies that opened the feedlots so they could be efficient and make more profit."

"It's cruel," Nance said. "Hundreds and hundreds of animals in too small a space. All they do is eat and stand and lie in their own shit and stink, day in and day out. That's cruelty. Burton won't make a living off cruelty."

"Burton won't make a living," Harvey said.

"We get by."

Harvey lit a fresh cigarette. "Sure you do: just barely. I wonder what'll be left after Tobler gets through with you. Fucking zip—that's what."

Nance stood up. She hated his mouth. "We'll see," she said.

But he'd scared her. Driving home from the prison she passed a trio of Black Angus steers tethered by the side of the road near an iron gate, each with a red tag stapled into its left ear, the three of them waiting to be loaded into a trailer and taken to slaughter. She thought she knew how they felt.

After supper Burton stayed at the table and asked Nance to bring him a second can of beer—an unusual excess for him.

He drank it slowly, meditating on each sip, each swallow. She didn't know what to say, sitting opposite him, nursing a cup of decaf coffee, so she waited for him to break the silence.

"I feel—you know—vulnerable as hell," Burton said, as if she had asked him and he had been all this while thinking about his answer. "I called a lawyer while you were over to Anamosa— that Sandstrom fellow Todd Clausson's sister married."

"Jimmy Sandstrom," Nance said. "He used to do odd jobs for Harvey and me when he was in high school. He always wanted to grow up to be a lawyer."

"I didn't know that," Burton said. "I only knew he'd done some work for Jess when Jess wanted to arrange his business affairs after Carol passed on. I thought he might know something about this—might advise me what my chances are."

He paused, drank. Now was he thinking Jimmy Sandstrom was too young to handle this?

"Well?" Nance prompted.

Burton set the beer glass down. "That's why I'm feeling vulnerable."

"Did he say we'd lose?"

"I didn't ask him that, nor he didn't come right out and say it, neither. What I said to him was that I didn't see how I could be hurt, seeing as how I don't have any money in the bank to speak of, and land values are down—so how could Tobler and his sneaky lawyer get any settlement from me? You can't get blood out of a stone, I said. Ha–ha."

"Not funny," she said.

" 'I'm not worth anything,' I said. 'Peter Tobler can't touch me.' "

"But he must have told you otherwise."

" 'It's not like bankruptcy,' is what he said. It's not like paying your debts a nickel on the dollar, and keeping your house and car and the necessities. It's like you have to convert everything into cash and give it all to the person suing you. If they win, that is. So if you figure this farm and the land I bought when Peter's father got killed, and the value of both houses and the barn and all the machinery—and even the value of this year's corn crop—then it adds up to maybe a quarter-million dollars minus a hundred thousand left on the second mortgage and the equipment payments." He shook his head. "If I lose," he said, "Peter and your friend Arlene get their farm back. They get everything I own."

"Everything *we* own," Nance said.

"Same thing," he said. "Me or us, it'll be gone."

"I don't see how Peter can win."

"Sandstrom says it's possible. Sandstrom says a jury might be against me because of the trap—that it would look better if I'd actually been there protecting my property in person, that then they wouldn't think I was so cold-blooded. He said the way it happened made me look indifferent to human life. Those were the words: 'indifferent to human life.' "

"I should think they'd understand," Nance said, "if they own property themselves."

"If they're farmers, Sandstrom says. Maybe. But he says Iowa's changing—there's not so much farm mentality in the state anymore. No rural sympathies anymore. Not like it was in my dad's day.

"And then there's the fact Peter's not a stranger, which complicates the case, Sandstrom says."

Nance shook her head. It wasn't vulnerability she saw in her husband's face, but despair—the sort of expression she'd seen in Arlene after Paul was killed, in Jess after Carol died, in her own mother when her father didn't come home from the Pacific. And in herself Nance felt helpless—as if love was useless under these circumstances, and the strength of all her feelings for Burton was a private strength that had no public effect in the world.

"I keep wishing that old Lab of mine hadn't took off and got himself run down in the road. I could've let him loose over there at night. He'd've taken care of old Peter, and it wouldn't be half so bad for us if the man was chewed up by a pure and simple watchdog."

"If wishes were horses," she said. *Arlene would still have blamed us.*

Burton drained his can of beer. "I think about what Dad owed when he was farming this place. His debts were next to nil. When I took over from him, all he had in the way of machinery was an old John Deere tractor and a bunch of attachments he'd made himself. He sowed corn out of an old oil drum he'd cut in half lengthwise and welded end to end. He'd set this thing on bicycle wheels and punched two holes in the bottom of it, as wide apart as the distance between rows; then he'd rigged a seat above and behind it that a person could sit on and keep that trough level with seed. That was my job when I was a kid: keep loading the seed and be sure it kept level so the rows would plant evenly, two rows at a time.

"When I decided I wanted to be in the cattle business, it was mainly because I'd've had to spend a ton of money on new machinery if I expected to do any good with corn and beans. Anyway, I'd just got out of the army; I was impatient to be myself, and I didn't want to end up like my dad—dried up and still barely scraping by. I got rid of all Dad's crazy inventions—sold the John Deere, scrapped most of what was left over. You remember; those were the days when everybody was making fun of me for going a different way. Paul was leasing more and more land. Harvey was buying and buying, some to plant and some to get rich off of—buying low and selling high to the real estate developers. The seventies, crazy times. Then by the time I finally decided to come back into the fold and raise the same corn and soybeans as everybody else around here, land was up again and I had to borrow to the hilt for the new equipment. You know."

"But that was a decision we made together."

"The point is: we need time to catch up, and this damned lawsuit is going to set us back."

"We'll come out of it just fine," Nance said. "I know we will."

Burton gave her the sharpest of *you're crazy* looks. "That's pure prayer," he said. "The absolute purest fairy tale of prayer."

Well, why not? Nance thought. *If you think something's hopeless, what harm can it do to pray?*

Late Sunday night, Jim Sandstrom came by unannounced. Burton was in the kitchen, catching up on the parts of the *Register* he'd missed at breakfast; Nance was already in bed, trying to read a romance novel she'd borrowed from the rental section of the Cedar Falls library—but not having much luck at it. Her mind was full of too much else: Peter and the lawsuit, the week's mail, Burton's mood, what might happen next. When she heard the voices from downstairs, she was relieved. She put the book aside, got her robe out of the closet, and went down to the kitchen.

"We've got a trial date," Sandstrom was saying. "Seventh of October in Waterloo." He looked up when Nance came into the kitchen. "How-do, Mrs. Stone."

"Hello, Jimmy."

Burton sighed. "Smack in the middle of harvest," he said. "Wouldn't you know."

"I could ask for a postponement."

"No," Nance said. "Let's get it over with."

Burton started to protest. "Nance—"

She interrupted. "Did you show him the letter?"

"No."

"What letter?" Sandstrom said. "Something about the lawsuit?"

"I'll get it," Burton said.

He left the room. Nance could hear him opening a desk drawer, rattling papers. What had he done? Tried to hide it?

"It was addressed to me," she told Sandstrom. "It's from some woman who read about us being sued."

"On our side, I hope."

Burton reappeared. "Fat chance," he said. He held the letter out to Sandstrom. It was written in blue ink on peach-colored stationery:

Dear Mrs. Stone,
I cannot help but wonder if, when you and your husband set your "death trap," you didn't think about the "adventures" of child-hood. My late father, Carl B. Weatherly, was the soul of integrity itself. He grew up in Fort Dodge, one of five children. He had some really great stories about his early days. One favorite story concerned the time that he and two of his brothers spotted some pigeons around the barn of an old abandoned "haunted" farm near Fort Dodge. They returned to the barn at night hoping to catch some of the pigeons, as they roosted, since my dad was al-ways a pigeon lover. The point is that, to my dad, as a child, the farm was "abandoned." Yet it had to belong to somebody. How many adventurous "Tom Sawyers" or "Huck Finns" would never have grown to adulthood if death traps were permitted on all such properties?
You and your husband should "count your blessings" that you have only an injured grown man on your conscience, and not a dead child.

Yours truly,
Mrs. Harold W. Carlsen

"You see?" Nance said. "This is just one letter. I bet there'll be more, and I don't think I can bear it—the blame, as if we *wanted* to kill somebody. If the trial started tomorrow, it wouldn't be too soon for me."

She looked at Burton.

"Okay," he said. "Okay by me."

—
8
—

In the first week of October, three days before the trial was to begin, Jess Eriksen turned up; it had been almost exactly a month since the two young people who worked for him called Nance and Burton to say they had not seen him in two days. Nance heard about it from Evelyn Sandstrom, who was Jimmy's wife and Todd Clausson's sister. Todd had heard about Jess's reappearance from Harlan Taylor, who was renting the Riker farmland and had actually found Jess—which meant that Todd had got it firsthand.

It seemed—and this is pretty much the way Nance told it to Arlene Tobler when she next wrote—that Harlan had been out in the fields with his corn picker, trying to get his harvest done before a predicted rainstorm, when he discovered Jess. It was about ten at night; Harlan was working with the picker lights turned on, his older son, Harold, driving the truck alongside to catch the shelled corn as it poured out of the chute, and his younger son, Jeffrey, waiting with a second—borrowed—truck to take his brother's place when he had a load. They'd done about half the section, working from south to north toward the county road that led to New Hartford, when Harlan saw his lights reflected back at him. He was surprised, startled, and stopped the picker inches before one of its blades would have punched a hole in the radiator of Jess's old Dodge.

Harlan and Harold got down from their respective cabs and walked over to the station wagon; Jeffrey came running up from behind, wondering why they'd stopped work. The three men opened all four doors and the tailgate, but the car was empty. There was no sign of a driver, and Harlan got into the driver's seat, intending to start the car and drive it out to the roadway. What he found was that the ignition key was already turned way over to the right, and when he tried the starter he got no spark at all. Later, when they tried to jump-start the car, they found the gas tank was bone dry; everybody, including the highway patrol and the sheriff's department, theorized that Jess had left the engine running and it had eventually run itself out of gas. It made sense. After the gas tank ran dry, the ignition being on had worn the battery down to nothing.

Not that the Taylor men knew at the time that it was Jess's car. They were new to Black Hawk County, renting Harvey Riker's farm a couple of years earlier when Harvey was sent to jail, and while they might have known Jess's name from hearsay or from driving past the sign in front of his produce stand, they weren't familiar with his possessions. All they knew in that first half hour or so was that someone, somehow, had driven an old Dodge station wagon into their fields and left it there. They hadn't brought flashlights, and it didn't make sense to drive the corn picker or the trucks all over a half-harvested field looking for God-knew-who, if anybody. Harlan decided to call it a night and telephone the sheriff in the morning. They could look for the car's driver—if he wasn't actually home and long since safely tucked up in bed—in the useful daylight hours. They left the car and the picker and Harold's partly-filled truck sitting in the field, and rode home together in the truck Jeffrey was driving. Harlan hoped that the predicted rainstorm wouldn't materialize, and it didn't.

Early the next morning, a crisp one with a touch of frost lingering on the roadside grasses, cold enough so you could see your breath, the Taylors met a pair of sheriff's deputies and a sergeant from the highway patrol headquarters in Cedar Falls and the six of them fanned out from the dead station wagon to see if they could find a driver. It didn't take long. The younger Taylor boy hadn't gone twenty feet into the tall, dry-stalked corn when he found Jess curled up like a child, knees under his chin and hands folded under his cheek, between two furrows. "That's Jess Eriksen," one of the deputies said. "I know him by those clothes." Probably a good friend would have known Jess's features, even despite the changes death had already made in him, but it wouldn't have been a pleasant recognition. The medical examiner said later that Jess had been dead for weeks, and when he was told the last time Jess had been seen, said he thought it likely Jess was already dead by the time he was missed.

Now that it was light, the searchers could see that the station wagon was mired up to its hubs, and they could also see the path the car had followed into the field. It had come in from the driveway leading to the Riker farm and had followed a straight line from northwest to southeast; then it had moved in a kind of spiral, making a pair of connected circles, one wider than the other, until it stopped where Harlan had found it. The highway patrol sergeant suggested that Jess had gotten confused and driven into the field, then had tried to find his way out—first by driving in circles, hoping to reach an open space, and then by leaving the car to look for an opening on foot. "Poor bugger," Harlan said.

No one was surprised that the earlier searches had failed to discover the Dodge. The cornfields had already begun to dry to yellow when Jess first vanished; the color of the car was like the color of the dried leaves; at ground level the height of the surrounding ripened corn hid the car entirely. "You'd have thought the tracks

would show," one of the deputies said. "But just the same, most of
the stalks would've stood back up in a day or two," Jeffrey said.
"I'd like to know what blind man was flying that helicopter," Burton said to Nance. "Some hotshot, I'll bet. Some young kid thinking he was out for a joyride."

It had to be Alzheimers, Nance wrote to Arlene. *There isnt any
other way to explain it. The poor dear man, at least hes with Carol now,
and happy dont you think.*

She was devastated by Jess's death. She sat at the kitchen table
and heard herself all over again pouring out her heart to him in
the humidity and careless bustle of the Happy Chef. She saw all
over again his concern for her, his sympathy; it was written on his
face, it gave light and focus to his vision—as if the suffering, the
difficulty of others, called him back to here-and-now reality
from his own overpowering despair. Widower, failure, timeworn
old man, he was still human, with the gift of compassion. Compassion was rare in the world; you hated to see the small store of
it diminished, even by a single death.

The trial, *Tobler v. Stone,* commenced on a Monday morning
with the selection of the jury. Everyone was in the courtroom,
up on the third floor of the county courthouse. Peter and his
lawyer, D. C. Commoner, were at a table to the right of the
bench where the judge was supposed to sit; Burton and Nance
were with their lawyer, James Sandstrom—though Nance could
not think of him as anything but "Jimmy"—at a second table to
the left of the bench. A smaller table in front of the bench was
where the court reporter sat, taking down whatever anybody
said. The jury box was to the right, facing inward, and a bank of
tall windows to the left overlooked the courthouse parking lot.
A railing separated the trial participants from the spectators, only
this morning the "spectators" were only the people who had
been called as prospective jurors; there were twenty or thirty of

them, more women than men, and they were scattered about the room in seats that didn't look all that comfortable, waiting to hear their names called.

It was just like on television—Nance imagined Perry Mason or Ben Matlock or anyone from *L. A. Law* would have been right at home here—except everybody was waiting for something to happen. There was a kind of impatient buzz and whisper in the room that sounded hollow up to the high ceiling and back again. Men in uniforms with American flags sewn over the breast pocket scurried back and forth, coming in and out of a door at the right front of the courtroom; bringing in pads of paper, it looked like, and pencils they were laying out on the tables and the judge's high desk. Peter and Commoner were having a conversation, their heads close together so they could talk without being listened to. Burton, close beside her, sat with his shoulders hunched and his hands clasped between his knees. He looked miserable—partly, Nance knew, because he despised these proceedings, so unfair, so *legal* and inhuman, and partly because of the work waiting to be done in the fields. She reached out and put her hand over the two of his.

"This is just so much bullcrap," he said—rather too loud, she thought.

She squeezed his hands. "Hush," she said softly.

She'd noticed Peter Tobler the moment he came into the courtroom, making his difficult way on two wooden crutches, his left leg in a cast that went from ankle to above the knee. She'd nudged Burton.

"Grandstanding," Burton said. "He didn't have that cast on, a month ago."

Sandstrom had leaned forward so she could see his face. "He's had a lot of surgery since then," he told her. "You'll hear all the details once the judge gets things under way."

Now, studying this young man who threatened to make them poor, Nance noticed he looked much more respectable

than he had on the day he was sentenced to a jail term for breaking into his old homestead. Arlene would have approved. He was
better dressed, with a dark gray suit and a plain dark red necktie;
he was clean-shaven—the sparse little mustache was gone—and he
looked like he'd got himself a fresh haircut. Looking at the heavy
cast—the left leg awkwardly straight out in front of him—
Nance felt a qualm of sadness, a small shiver of fear. If *she* could
feel sympathetic toward Peter, what would a jury feel?

Arlene hadn't made a second trip to watch the civil trial. She
felt obligated to the school where she taught. Nance imagined
that she wouldn't want her son to lose his case, but she hoped
Arlene wouldn't take much pleasure from his winning.

Jury selection took all morning. The judge came in, everybody
stood up and sat down again, the court clerk read out the partic-
ulars of *Tobler v. Stone,* and then the men and women in the spectator section stirred and resettled themselves in the hard chairs to
wait for their names to be called.

They were called twelve at a time, came forward and sat in
the jury box—smiling, some of them, looking nervous, others.
Commoner and Sandstrom took turns asking them questions.
Were they employed? What did they do to earn a living? Had
they ever worked on a farm? Had they read about the original
break-in, seen newspaper stories, formed an opinion about the
incident? How did they feel about the use of force? Had they
ever had to defend their own property against an outsider? Had
they ever been arrested? Had they ever been in jail? Had they
ever had surgery or spent time in a hospital? Had they been on a
jury before?

Not every man and woman was asked the same questions,
but the same questions were asked time and time again. After
the two lawyers finished talking with each set of twelve, then
they decided which ones they wanted to reject, which ones they
wanted to keep.

"D. C. and I each have a bunch of peremptory challenges," Sandstrom had told Burton and Nance in the corridor outside the courtroom. "We can knock somebody off the jury without having to give a reason."

"How do you decide?" Nance had asked.

"I want to get rid of anybody who seems to be too liberal, too humanistic. I want sympathetic types, but sympathetic to the property owner, not to the party who got injured. It's no easy call, I'll tell you. We need Republicans, but at the same time I want to excuse these folks who don't know anything about farming, who don't have any experience with rural life. Also I'm leaning toward the women who've been called. Women have more *heart* than men, and I think we're going to need heart. Agreed?"

Burton shrugged. "I don't see it matters that much. Right is right. If people can't see that, then I don't care if they're male or female or Martians."

"We trust you," Nance told Sandstrom. "You do what's best."

When all was said and done, the two lawyers had put together a jury of twelve women—three of them black. The only men selected, two of them, were among the six alternates, who would probably never take part in the final decision.

I think that was the first time I felt like something good might happen for Burton and me, she would write to Arlene. *All those women, all those good hearts, as Jimmy Sandstrom said, and I couldnt imagine theyd vote against us when they heard the truth. Even the colored would understand, and maybe especialy them.*

Even you might understand, she wanted to add, but didn't.

From the transcript:

> COMMONER: Mr. Tobler, would you please tell the court what happened on the 16th of August last.
>
> TOBLER: Where should I begin?

COMMONER: Begin wherever you think has relevancy to your case against the Stones.

TOBLER: Well, I'll begin that afternoon.

COMMONER: That's fine.

TOBLER: I'd flown into Chicago in the afternoon— around three-thirty. I was pretty tired. I hadn't managed to get much sleep between Hong Kong and Seattle, and got even less between Seattle and O'Hare. By the time I'd come through Customs, I'd really rather have booked a hotel room and caught up on my sleep.

SANDSTROM: Your honor?

THE COURT: An objection, Mr. Sandstrom?

SANDSTROM: A question of relevance.

COMMONER: We intend to establish Mr. Tobler's physical state, your honor, prior to the incident at issue here.

SANDSTROM: I'm sure I should be grateful Mr. Commoner chose not to commence his questions with Mr. Tobler's graduation from high school, or even with the date and place of his birth, but it does seem—

THE COURT: Overruled, Mr. Sandstrom.

COMMONER: Continue, Mr. Tobler.

TOBLER: The fact was, I had very little money in my pocket. Enough to rent a car to drive to my mother's, in South Dakota, and not much more. I figured that once I was out of the city, I could pull off somewhere and catch forty winks if I needed to.

COMMONER: Go on.

TOBLER: I held up pretty well until I got to Waterloo, and then it occurred to me that if I could keep my eyes open until I got past Cedar Falls, I could stop at the house where I grew up.

COMMONER: But you knew that place had been sold— that it no longer belonged to your mother or anyone else in the Tobler family.

TOBLER: Oh yes, I knew it. I knew Burt Stone had bought it, not too long after my dad was killed.

COMMONER: Then what made you think you could stop there?

TOBLER: Well, I also knew the house was empty. Nobody was living there, so who would care if I took advantage? It was pretty stormy by then—wind and rain, a lot of lightning ahead of me. Anyway, my mother was good friends with the Stones. I didn't think they'd mind if I slipped the lock and got in out of the wet.

COMMONER: Your honor, before Mr. Sandstrom rises to tell us he is confused, may we stipulate that the vacant house Mr. Tobler is telling us about is identified in the suit pending as "the former Tobler home on West Creek Road, five miles to the west of Union Highway"?

THE COURT: Mr. Sandstrom?

SANDSTROM: Agreed, your honor.

COMMONER: Continue, Mr. Tobler.

TOBLER: I was kind of sad when I got up to the old house. One of the front windows was boarded up, there were weeds growing in the driveway. I remember thinking it was a shame nobody lived there, and I wondered why the Stones didn't just tear the place down if they didn't have any plans to use it or rent it out.

COMMONER: Where was your car?

TOBLER: I left it in the driveway. It's a long, curving driveway, a slalom my dad designed—so that if a stranger pulled into it down by the county road, he wouldn't be able to see the house. Kind of a security precaution, I guess.

COMMONER: Then what?

TOBLER: Well, I went up on the porch and looked in through the window that wasn't boarded up.

COMMONER: And what did you see?

TOBLER: Not much of anything. I got a lightning flash

for just a second or two, and I could see there wasn't any furniture inside.

COMMONER: Continue.

TOBLER: I tried the door. The screen door was open. The inside door was locked. I actually tried using my old house key, but the lock had obviously been changed.

COMMONER: So how did you get in?

TOBLER: I used a credit card. Just like in the movies. Stuck it in between the door and the frame, and slipped the latch tongue.

COMMONER: Simple as that?

TOBLER: Probably it wasn't a very expensive lock.

COMMONER: And then?

TOBLER: After I'd slipped the latch, I started to push the door open.

COMMONER: The door opened inward?

TOBLER: Yes. I pushed it open about eight, ten inches, and I'd just started to step into the house, when bam, there was this explosion inside the house and I felt something hit my left leg.

COMMONER: Where, exactly?

TOBLER: Just below my left knee. It took me by surprise, and my leg sort of buckled. By then the door was open wider, so when my leg gave way I was falling into the house.

COMMONER: Then what happened?

TOBLER: And then, that was when I heard the second explosion, and this time I saw a flash from the floor in front of me. This time it was my knee got hit, squarely. It didn't hurt much, believe it or not. I guess I was already numb or in shock. And I kept on falling.

COMMONER: What did you do?

TOBLER: What could I do? At first I just lay there, trying to figure out what all the noise was, why I was flat on my

face. I reached down and felt my leg all wet, and then I just
blacked out.

COMMONER: How long were you unconscious?

TOBLER: Who knows? I'd come to and then pass out, and
come to and pass out again. Once when I was awake I could
hear the wind whistling like a banshee and the rain was
blowing in the open door, soaking me good. I guess I lay
there all night and all the next day and the next night too.

COMMONER: Did you know you'd been shot?

TOBLER: I thought it must have been some kind of gun
that knocked me down. In daylight I could see it was a
shotgun.

COMMONER: But when you'd looked in the window,
from outside on the porch, you hadn't seen any indication
there was a gun inside?

TOBLER: No. None.

COMMONER: And was there any kind of warning? Like
a sign posted near the house or along the driveway that
said the property was protected with a trap gun? Anything
like that?

TOBLER: I didn't see any sign. I didn't have any warning.
I just pushed open a door and bam, my leg was wrecked.

COMMONER: I think you're lucky to be alive.

SANDSTROM: Objection, your honor.

From the Des Moines *Register*—

To the Editor:

With regard to the case of Tobler versus Stone now
being tried in Black Hawk County District Court, it
seems that everyone is trying to get into the act as to
what is right or wrong with so-called "shoot-thy-
neighbor" laws. As a representative of the people of
Iowa, I would like to express my opinion.

To those who are opposed to such a law I would refer them to the Iowa Constitution, Article I of the Bill of Rights: "Section 1. All men are, by nature, free and equal, and have certain inalienable rights—among which are those of enjoying and defending life and liberty, acquiring, possessing and protecting property, and pursuing and obtaining safety and happiness."

This gives one the right to protect his property but does not say how. I think when a person finds someone destroying his property or stealing it, he should be able to use any method that is necessary to stop it, without the fear of having some jury or courts say he was liable for any damages which might occur. If we do not do something to protect the property owner, rather than the criminal, it might come to a point where some of these property owners will take the law into their own hands.

—*Eben Forrester*
State Senator, Carroll

On Wednesday afternoon Judge Kelly declared a recess so the Stones could attend the memorial service for Jess Eriksen. The service was held in the Episcopal Church in Cedar Falls, which surprised Nance. She knew Jess hadn't gone to church since Carol died; she knew too that he was down on the Episcopalians because the lady minister who conducted Carol's funeral had made her sound like a drudge and a house slave—not the cheerful, intelligent woman who kept Jess's books and filled his life with love, and who didn't complain when he misunderstood the etiquette of the game of bridge. "I swear," Carol used to say, "Jess doesn't know a club convention from a Farm Bureau convention." The lady minister was new and hadn't really known Carol, and she made things worse by trying to pretend she had.

Remembering how things had been when Carol was alive made the service for Jess a little more bearable. The church was too bright and too big. There was no casket, nothing of Jess to see and think on. He'd already been cremated; apparently he'd made a will that specified fire—which was another surprise, Nance thought. You'd think a farmer would want to spend eternity in the earth that had given him his livelihood.

The crowd was a small one: the Stones, the Raymond Claussons, Jimmy Sandstrom and his wife, the two young people who'd been helping Jess in his produce business. There was a scattering of people Nance didn't know—younger, most of them, perhaps people who knew Jess from being customers of his. One surprise: Peter Tobler attended, sitting in the back row with his lawyer beside him. *Filling in for Arlene,* Nance thought, recalling how close she had been to Carol. A further surprise: Harvey Riker came in just after the service had started. He was with a deputy in uniform, the two of them handcuffed together. They sat up front; not once during or after the service did Harvey even so much as look in Nance's direction. She wondered if maybe he was genuinely sorry Jess was gone.

From the transcript:

> COMMONER: Please state your name and occupation.
> HARTLEY: Abraham Hartley. I'm an orthopedic surgeon.
> COMMONER: You are on staff at the University
> Hospitals in Iowa City?
> HARTLEY: I am. I also maintain a private practice in
> Coralville.
> COMMONER: And is the plaintiff, Peter Tobler, a patient
> of yours?
> HARTLEY: He has been a patient.
> COMMONER: But not a private patient.
> HARTLEY: No. That's correct.

COMMONER: Would you tell the court how you first came to treat Mr. Tobler?

HARTLEY: He was brought to the emergency room of the University Hospital on August 19th, this year. Brought down from Waterloo by ambulance. I was on call at the time.

COMMONER: What was his condition?

HARTLEY: He was on crutches. His left leg was broken below the knee and the kneecap itself was damaged. It was apparent that an attempt had been made to set the broken femur, but it was clearly a stopgap.

COMMONER: Which means?

HARTLEY: I'm told that a paramedic made a temporary fix of the leg so Mr. Tobler could be tried on a breaking and entering charge.

COMMONER: Did this "temporary fix" in the name of rough justice complicate Mr. Tobler's condition?

HARTLEY: I don't suppose it did him any good, but no—I don't think it measurably added to his medical difficulties.

COMMONER: Which were already considerable and sufficient?

HARTLEY: Indeed.

COMMONER: What did you do for Mr. Tobler?

HARTLEY: We set the broken femur and secured it with stainless steel pins—to ensure proper healing, inasmuch as the fracture was complex. My team and I rebuilt the patella, the kneecap, by borrowing material from the pelvic bone to replace bone that had been shot away.

COMMONER: A difficult operation?

HARTLEY: Moderately. Time-consuming.

COMMONER: The leg will be in a cast how long?

HARTLEY: At least another four months.

COMMONER: And what's your prognosis? I mean, how fully will Mr. Tobler recover from the effects of the gunshot?

HARTLEY: Hard to tell. He'll never have complete

articulation of that knee joint, but what percentage of movement will return after therapy? No, I simply can't say.

COMMONER: But that left leg will never be the same.

HARTLEY: Never.

COMMONER: He'll always walk with a limp?

HARTLEY: Always. Quite a pronounced limp, I should guess.

COMMONER: And feel changes in the weather in that knee?

HARTLEY: Possibly.

COMMONER: And the steel pins?

HARTLEY: Not sure. Probably they'll stay. Probably he'll always be a nuisance to airport security people.

[Laughter]

THE COURT: Order, if you please.

Dear Leenie,

You cant imagine how we feel, me and Burton. When Jimmy Sandstrom finally got Burton up in the witness chair, evrybody knew it was really all over. Poor Peter sitting there with one leg straight out and in that hugh cast. That Iowa city doctor talking about how bad the knee was damaged and showing pictures, ex rays of before-and-after. People in the court room laughing about how the screws in the mans leg would set off airport alarms. It was no joke to us I can tell you. When Jimmy asked Burton why hed set up the shotgun all he could say was that he was sick and tired of all the vandalism.

The morning after the verdict we both got our pictures on page 1 of the Register, but I didnt testify because a wife doesn't have to testify if its her husband on trial. What wd I have said anyway? That there wasnt anything in the house to steal except maybe some old mason jars youd left in the basement, so what was the point of lethal force. And then if theyd asked me about the shot-gun Id have had to say Burton knew it would hurt anybody who tried to come in that door—so just as well I was quiet.

*I dont know what to make of that jury. All of them women
so all of them must have felt for Burton and for me, must have
understood how hard itd be for us to pay the judgement against
us. Not the whole half a million he sued for, thank god for that,
but a hundred and 30 thousand dollars! The 30 thousand for
medical and costs whatever that means, and the rest what they
call* punitive damages. *Where did they think wed get money
like that????? Well, Burton says we have to sell maybe not evrything, but alot of what land we own. He thinks we'll have to
sell your old farm. But still that might not bring enough money
to pay your Peter. What do you think Peter wants to do with so
much money?*

*Sandstrom says we should appeal—to the supreme court in
Des Moines. He says the judge in Waterloo gave instructions to
the jury that predjudiced them and practically forced them to vote
against us. Like he told the ladies on the jury that history showed
that trap guns couldnt be used unless human life was in danger
and when Peter broke into your old house he wasnt endangering
my life or Burtons or anybodys. He also told them that it didnt
matter that Peter was breaking the law when he was shot. I mean,
how could the jury say anything else??*

*So I think we will appeal and Jimmy Sandstrom is pretty
confident we will win this time—he says he is working with a
partner of his whose argued cases as high as the US supreme
court. But meanwhile we have to pay up. Jimmy says he is willing
to wait for his legal fees (he gets fifty dollars an hour! can you
imagine) but Peter has to get his judgement.*

*The Episcopal service for Jess was alright but I doubt Jess
would of liked it, seeing as it was that lady minister he wouldnt
talk to after Carols funeral. Jess had himself cremated, I dont know
what was done with the ashes and dont care, I guess. I'm sorry you
couldn't of been there. It was strange to see Peter at the service. I
didn't think he cared about Jess, except then I remembered one
summer he worked at Jess's produce stand—but just a couple of
weeks wasn't it? And Harvey was there if you can believe, hand*

cuffed to a guard from the prison. He didn't look my way, just
stared at the floor. It was strange to see him out in public. It set me
to thinking. I hate to say it, but I believe what I will do is talk to
Harvey and see if he will buy the land from us and hold it for us
until we get the supreme court to undo what the court here has
done to us. Then we can buy it back and get our life moving ahead
again. Harveys got the money alright. Dont you think he owes
something to us all?

Hope your well and happy,
Nance

She wasn't sure how she should talk to Burton about her in-
tentions. She knew it would upset him—at least at first—and
that she'd better have all her arguments lined up and ready to go
if she expected to persuade him. And he was depressed about the
verdict—she could see that by the way he acted. The first night
after the verdict he went to bed early and slept late the next
morning; he picked at his food; he drank whiskey and water instead of Old Milwaukee. It was all he could do to drag himself
out of the house and see to the harvest. And he blamed her.

"You could've testified," he said. "Sandstrom ought to have
put you up there. You could've said I've never meant harm to anybody in my life. You could've said how I was in the army in Nam
and I learned my lesson about killing. I'd seen it and I'd hated
it."

"But if Mr. Commoner asked me about the gun," she said,
"I'd've had to say you knew what you were doing. I asked you if
it would kill a man, and you said no, but it would give him a permanent limp. Those were exactly your words: *a permanent limp.*
And that's what happened, and that's what I'd've had to answer
to Mr. Commoner."

"If you told the truth."

"Of course I'd tell the truth," Nance said. "Would you want
me to lie?"

He was silent then. He was too good to say that he wanted

her to lie, but something between them was changed. She couldn't say what—not yet. Just *something*, and she knew the change had begun the day she helped to set the trap that caught Peter.

Nance Dear,

I don't know what to say about your verdict. There's no fairness possible here—at least from my side of it. If Jimmy Sandstrom (so hard to believe he's all grown up and graduated law school!) wins your appeal for you, then I don't know how Peter'll pay his lawyer. And if you don't win, then I'll be watching old friends suffer. It's awful, no matter how you look at it.

I can't say what our old farm would be worth nowadays. I don't recall how much Burton paid for it—that was almost five years ago. Are land values up or down? They don't seem to have changed much here in S. Dakota, from what I read in the Sioux Falls paper. The worst thing for you is that people know you're desperate, and so they'll try to get your land cheap. Back when we auctioned off the machinery—look at me still writing "we"!— nobody bid top dollar. What was I going to do, keep Paul's tractor and picker and all that just because the bids weren't high enough? If you need, you need.

Poor Jess. Maybe his ashes got scattered on his fields where he put in his labor and sweat. And what's going to happen to his land? Harvey Riker does have the money—that's true. He's shrewd, and maybe he'd help you out—but you'd better go slow with him. He's got that grudge against Burton because of you, and don't you ever forget it—Harve surely won't. If you can think of anybody else who might be well-off enough to help, you should go to them instead of Harve.

Your letters bring Iowa back to me—the good times as well as the bad. It's all changed now, nobody's the way they were, we're all worse off or dead. I look at the youngsters in my English classes and I think how they just don't know what *life is. They all want to get away from here, away from the farm, away from the*

Midwest, and they think somehow that will solve the boredom and
uncertainty of being a teenager. Well, my kids moved away when
they were old enough, and I can't say as they're so darned happy.
You see what Peter's like, and all Sarah ever did was call me up
and weep over her boring marriage.

   I don't think I ever sent you the poem(?) I made about Paul
dying. I wrote it last winter, on sort of the anniversary of the
shooting, because it was a gloomy day that had put the gloom inside me, and because when I was in college I'd written poetry to
make me forget the humdrum of going to class and having no social life to speak of. That was before Paul, of course, and now I
get in the same moods after Paul. I'll write it out for you (the
poem):

FOR PAUL

Mostly it is in the skies
our seasons live—in a gray
march of weather's frontiers
over the fields, low clouds
heavy as hog dugs and plump,
swollen by rain and wind.
Imagine the dirt has mouths
needing to be fed something.
Let it be sun or cyclone,
that thing, hail or yellow
dust; let it be murderous
or kind, just so it nourish
the land. We are the land,
lying here in our hard beds,
trying to drink the clouds
as they blow, saying: Make us
into grain, weeds, any green
flourishing of the spirit
winter has taken out of us;

make us whatever can grow
from this earth new-opened.

    I haven't fiddled with it to make it scan better, but I tried to
make it a hopeful poem. Paul would have laughed at me. "Hog
dugs?" he'd say. "You never in your whole life saw any clouds
like that!"
    My thoughts are with you on the one side, and with Peter on
the other.

Arlene

Jimmy Sandstrom came by almost every day after the end of the trial, and Burton acted differently toward him, too. *Disappointment,* Nance thought. He'd done something perfectly natural, defended what was rightfully his, and the world had let him down by saying no, it wasn't natural after all. Everybody had failed him: the court, the jury, his lawyer, his former neighbor, even his wife.

"We'll win the appeal," Sandstrom insisted. "I swear it: we'll get the reversal."

"So you say." It didn't sound as if Burton believed the lawyer. Partly it was that Jimmy was young, and so she thought Burton could not respect him. "I never saw a man act so helpless in a court of law," Burton had said to her. "Like he'd never gone to law school at all." Partly it was that Jimmy had believed in the virtue of an all-woman jury, and he had been mistaken in his optimism. Partly—the biggest part of all—it was that the money judgment had to be met, and there was no money.

"We were lucky the jury rejected most of the claims," Sandstrom told them, "or we'd be in a pickle. No compensation for lost wages; a reduced award for pain and suffering. That's the good of it." He had his briefcase open, was sorting through papers. "The bad of it is that the settlement's due sooner than we might prefer."

"We can't hold back until the appeal's decided?"

"No. We have to pay something. Good faith. The court's looking over our shoulder."

"*My* shoulder, you mean," Burton said.

Nance ached for him. Now every time Jimmy Sandstrom drove away, Burton went to the cupboard and got the whiskey down. Then he sat in his recliner, staring out the window whether it was day or night, shaking his head.

But land had to be sold; there was no getting around it. Burton's plan was to sell eighty acres of Paul Tobler's one-hundred-sixty and maybe add the old house into the deal as incentive, perhaps, for some young couple just starting out.

"That way we're doing good for somebody else, while we're doing what we have to do for ourselves," he said.

In the back of her mind Nance continued to hold the hope that Harvey could partway make up for the bad he had done by buying some of their land, holding it, then selling it back when she and Burton were able to afford it. She had absolute faith that Burton would "bounce back" and, with a couple of good years, make enough to rebuild their old lives. Harvey had the money; Harvey could afford to wait awhile for a return; Harvey *owed* her.

"Why not keep all the Tobler land?" she said. "At least for the time being. We've got two hundred forty acres here, all told. Why not sell the south eighty? You have to cross the road to get to them anyway. It's always felt to me as if they weren't even part of our farm, cut off the way they are."

Her logic was that the Tobler farm was right next to Harvey's, which would make it that much easier to persuade him to buy.

"Since when have you paid any attention to land matters?" Burton wanted to know. "You can barely raise a flower garden."

"I'm just trying to be sensible," she said, and she saw, from the way he gave her an approving smile, that she'd won—though probably he figured that eighty acres was eighty acres, never mind which farm they came from.

The land brought four hundred an acre, the auction conducted on a Sunday morning in the parking lot of the courthouse with thirty or forty people on hand. Nance drove into town with Burton, the two of them solemn and silent the whole twelve miles, and they watched the sale from a window of city hall, across the street. The next day in the Waterloo *Courier* there was a photograph—taken from a hallway behind them without their even knowing it—that showed them in silhouette at that window, and beyond them, so washed out by distance as to look unreal, the heads and hands of bidders.

"Who bought it?" Burton wanted to know when he met Sandstrom afterward.

"Coronet Seed Corp, up near Elkader. Going to turn it into a demonstration plot."

Nance watched Burton's shoulders slump, and she knew how to read him. He had hoped—against hope, she knew—that some neighbor, some friend, would have won the bid. Then, after the high court said the Black Hawk jury was wrong, maybe he could have bought back the land. But why did it have to be a friend? Nance wondered. Why not an enemy who owed you something?

"It's worth a whole lot more than thirty-odd thousand," Burton said. "That's not even a quarter of the judgment."

"What could we do?" Sandstrom said. "You can't set a reserve price when the county's handling the sale."

"Harvey would have offered that much," Nance said. It was too bad if Burton didn't like the idea; she'd said it out loud for the first time, and she'd keep saying it.

"Riker bought Eriksen's," Jimmy Sandstrom said. "Got it real cheap—three fifty an acre."

"That son of a bitch," Burton said. "And how's he going to farm it from jail?"

"He could be let out in less than a year," Sandstrom said.

"Some damned 'justice,'" Burton said.

Nance shivered. What if she went to Harvey now without even letting on? Yes, Arlene was right about him, but really, who else was there?

After Sandstrom had gone, Burton poured his whiskey—it was a habit now—and settled into the recliner. Brooding, Nance thought, but how could she coax him out of it?

"I hate even to see that kid lawyer," he said. "That 'sympathetic' jury of his—you know what? Did you know that one of those negro women has been called for jury duty five times just this year? She's the Black Hawk County token minority; it's her goddamned career."

"I can't believe that," Nance said. "That can't be true."

"Believe it," Burton said. "Plus, every time Jimmy Sandstrom comes to call, every time he opens his mouth, it costs us more money. You notice?"

Nance saw this as her opening. "Speaking of money," she said. Then she couldn't think what to say next that wouldn't hurt him or make him all the more angry.

"What about it?" he said.

"I hate to see you so upset about it," she said. "But if Jimmy is so sure he can get the judgment against us reversed by appealing—"

"He's whistling past the graveyard," Burton said. "He's got no more idea than Arlene's tomcat what the Supreme Court will do."

"I thought he sounded optimistic."

"He's a lawyer. It's his job to sound optimistic. It's how he makes his living—being optimistic to the right people." He sipped his whiskey, then held the glass against the lamplight. The light through the glass laid orange shadows across his face, as if he was standing in front of a church window—and that made her think of Jess and Paul and how fragile strong men could get if the world grew too hard for them. "It's a sham profession," Burton said. "Lawyering."

"He's doing his best," Nance said.

"And you. You're getting to be a sham wife."

The words came out of nowhere. She thought then—as she also thought later—that she'd rather he'd struck her across the face than say such a thing to her. That would have been Harvey's way: the back of his hand, hard, painful, but over when it was over. Not this hateful blow that went straight down to her heart, that took the starch right out of her so she had to sit down and try to catch her tears before they drowned her.

"Burton," she said, and her voice broke. Then she blurted it out: "Harvey's got money and plenty of it. He could buy our land and keep it until we're able to buy it back."

He set his glass on the windowsill and stood up. "I suppose you think that's funny," he said.

Later on it occurred to Nance that she'd said it, just at that moment and just in those words, to get away from the hurt of his calling her a sham wife—the way an animal tries to walk away from his pain because he doesn't realize it's inside him.

"He could," she said. Now she was weeping. "He *could*," she said again, almost in a whimper.

When Burton stalked out of the room he did it with a word she had never heard him use in all their time together. "Fuck it all," he said.

After that she did a curious thing: went over to the window, picked up Burton's glass and drank the whiskey that was left in it. There wasn't much. It tasted sweet, and that surprised her, because the smell of it was always so sharp in her nostrils when he poured it from the bottle in the kitchen. When the glass was empty she sat in Burton's recliner and stared out the window, wishing she could be tired enough to sleep, but not knowing if she dared go up to bed in case Burton might ask her to lie down somewhere else—on the downstairs sofa or in the spare room. He'd never done that to her, but he'd never before said the *f* word either.

She sat for more than an hour, holding the whiskey glass until the joints of her fingers ached. Way off, along the distant ridge the land sloped up to, she watched a combine move back and forth through an invisible cornfield, its bright lights—six of them, some mounted high, some low—like a relentless traffic denying sleep.

$$9$$

At first Nance wasn't sure what had waked her up, and then when she'd rubbed her eyes and propped herself up on one elbow and tried to think what day it was, she heard what sounded like someone knocking at the outside door—except it wasn't that. The knocking was irregular, and went on and on; it certainly sounded like knuckles on wood, like somebody insisting she or Burton open up, if you please, but she knew it couldn't be that—or hoped it anyway, remembering all the awful visitors of the past few months. Was it some animal? But what animal could it be? She'd seen raccoons, possums, woodchucks; Grimmie brought home mice, chipmunks, a squirrel (for which she scolded him), and once a rat with a fat tail and terrible long teeth. When she tried to imagine how any of those animals could make a noise like this, she was baffled.

She shifted herself in the bed to prod Burton, but he wasn't beside her. That brought her wide awake: she knew where she was, what day it was, what had been said and done the night before— how she had put the whiskey glass in the sink and come softly up the stairs into the bedroom, how she had undressed in the dark and put on her nightgown, how she had brushed her teeth also in the dark and come back to the room and slipped into her side of the bed as gingerly and quietly as could be. She remembered thinking that if Burton didn't wake up, he couldn't deny her, and so he hadn't. She'd drifted off then into a dreamless sleep, comforted by the warmth of the man close beside her. But now she was alone, and something was knocking against the house.

She got up. The time was just past dawn. She wrapped her white bathrobe around herself against the early-morning chill. On her way to the bathroom she stopped at the head of the stairs to listen. No, the knocking was not from the back door, nor could she hear any sound of Burton—no spoon against a coffee cup, no rattle of newspaper, no creak of floorboards under his boots. He'd be in the fields, of course, bringing in the last of the corn against the threat of a hard freeze.

The knocking went on, irregular, knuckle-loud. Nance tried to make a pattern out of the noise, but there was no pattern. When she went to the window and looked out, there was Grimmie, a motionless orange shape against the yellowed grass, looking up at her. Then the cat's head moved as a shadow crossed surprisingly and swiftly through Nance's field of vision; a woodpecker—of course—red-crested and ladder-backed and not much bigger than a sparrow, had flown to the silver maple near the house. There it clung to the trunk, a sharp outline of life in the midst of black branches and the tatter of brown leaves.

Because Burton was out of the house, she wouldn't need to account for her comings and goings this morning—it felt like conspiracy, what she was doing without telling him. It was a feeling she hadn't had since that frenzied time when she was carrying on with Burton behind Harvey's back. What she was doing seemed outside time, or it was the end of a sequence of events that had run faster and faster until now they made her breathless, running to keep up. That was it: she had to talk with Harvey before she was worn out, before she dropped in her tracks and saw everything slip away.

She dressed quickly, made herself a cup of instant coffee and washed down a slice of wheat toast with it. She left Burton a note on the kitchen table, propped against the sugar bowl. *Back in time to make your lunch,* it said. The note was just in case; it wasn't likely Burton would stop for lunch, and she wasn't really sure she could be home by noon.

The world had changed since her last visit to Harvey. The green had gone gold and brown, the tall corn and the misty pale green of the beans had for the most part vanished, cut down in harvest, bundled and shelled and flayed and carted off to storage. Some places, some fields, some combine was still at work, leveling the crop, leaving in its wake the fine dust Nance knew could be explosive if confined—you read about men dying from a single spark inside a silo. The early sun was bronze gauze in the dust; if she had stopped the car and stepped out she would have smelled—what? The earth, or the earth's perfume. Arlene would have had words for it, or a whole poem.

She parked where she had parked before, across the asphalted lot from the prison entrance. The maple at the edge of the lot was stripped now, its leaves heaped—probably by a convict gardener—at the corner of the paved area, waiting to be disposed of. Mulch, Nance thought. But not—not ever—some wonderful larger mound a child might plunge into. That was for a world unlike this one; that was for freedom.

Harvey was not happy to see her.

"What's this about?" he said. "I don't need to listen to any more of your whining."

"I came on an impulse," she said.

He put a cigarette in the center of his mouth and lit it.

"It's okay," he said. "I was in the laundry. Hotter than hell."

"I've wondered sometimes," she said. "Do they pay you for the work you do in prison?"

He scowled. "Just tell me what you want."

"I just wanted to know how you are." She squirmed in the plastic chair across the table from him. How to bring up the subject of land, money, helping out Burton? "I haven't visited for a while."

"I haven't missed them—our little chats." He breathed out smoke; didn't try to direct it away from her.

"I need a favor," Nance said. As soon as she had said it, she wondered if she should really have said *need,* if she ought to have said *want.*

Harvey smiled.

"It's to do with the farm," she said.

Harvey's smiled broadened. "I've been reading about you two," he said. "I never thought me talking to old Commoner would have such an effect. How those Toblers do mess up us Rikers."

"I hope you're proud of yourself," she said.

"I hope you're satisfied," Harvey said. "That this is where your fucking lust has finally got you."

She was silent. What could she say? She thought she could understand how Harve's mind worked—how one thing had led to another, like dominoes set on end by a smart schoolboy to make a pattern—except that Harve didn't see that there was a fork in the pattern when you applied it to life. There was a place where the fall of dominoes went in two directions; it wasn't her lust, it was Harvey's cruelty, and then it was his jealousy. Everything had proceeded from the night in Leenie's kitchen.

"You know what's happening?" she said. "How we have to raise money."

"I read the papers. I told you that."

"Then—"

"Christ," Harvey said, "what do you want me to do? Be the savior of the man who wrecked my marriage?"

"You've still got money in the bank—a lot of it. Money drawing interest. Compared to most folks, you're rich."

"So what?"

"And everybody knows you bought Jess's place."

"It's an investment," Harvey said. "It's a gamble."

"I never knew you to gamble," she said.

He stubbed out the cigarette. Looked at her—appraising not her but the whole situation, she knew. Leaned back in his chair.

"So what is it you want from me?"

"Buy Burton's Tobler land."

He snorted. "That's crazy," he said.

"At a fair price," she said.

"Is that all?"

"No." She shifted her position again, cleared her throat, took a breath. "When this is over—when we get back on our feet— sell the land back to us. At the price you paid for it."

Harvey didn't smile. She wondered what he was thinking.

"How is old Burton supposed to get back on his feet?" he said.

"Crops," she said. "You'll let him work the land and sell his corn, his beans, whatever he decides to grow."

"Why don't you ask crazy Peter Tobler? He's the one's got the money. And it's your money. That's icing on the cake."

"Don't joke about this."

"What about me? What am I supposed to get out of doing you this 'favor'?"

"You'll take a percentage of what we earn."

He scowled. "What percentage?"

"Ten."

"Thirty."

"Twenty."

He shook his head, looking disgusted, and reached for another cigarette. "What if you *don't* get back on your feet?" he said. "I won't wait forever."

She thought. "Five years," she said.

"Three."

"Five. No bargain here."

He smirked. "I'll let you win," he said. "Say it's for old times' sake."

"You won't be sorry," she said.

"*You* might be," he said. "Because you can bet I'm going to be on your damned doorstep."

"How will you do that?"

"Because I'll be out of here in a couple of months," Harvey said. "Less. Six weeks."

"How can you be?"

"Good behavior," he said. "I'll have paid more than four years of my life for the death of old Paul. Don't you think that's about enough?"

Nance couldn't say. The idea of Harvey Riker linked to *good behavior!*

"It's what they call 'ironic,'" he went on. "If it turns out Burton can't pay his debts, we'll be like ships that pass in the night—me going out, and him coming in."

"No," she said. "That won't happen."

"I'll do what I can for you," Harvey said. He winked at her and put the cigarette to his lips. "Twenty-odd years of you and me might as well count for something. So long as I don't ever have to talk personally to Burton Stone."

"You've promised."

"I've got to look out for myself, too." He touched a match to the tip of the cigarette; she could smell the match, the sulphur, the lit tobacco, for a moment the acid smell of Harvey's breath as he blew out the small flame. The smoke made blue layers between them.

"Please," she said.

He laughed, then looked around for one of the guards. "You stay right where you are," he said. "This is business, and I want it put down in writing."

She found Burton in the parlor, sunk into the recliner. The sun was low and threw long, slender shadows across the fields toward the northeast; a redtail had taken up a position on one of the nearest fence posts, watching. But what was there to be seen? The

fields were stripped now, only the stunted remnant stalks of
the corn plants, yellow and dry on the black earth, looking like the
aftermath of a battle. No sign of life, Nance thought—but of
course that was what the redtail was looking for: life. At this time
of the afternoon, any animal trying to cross the bare earth would
be easy to see, casting a shadow yards long. The hawk would rise
up in one instant, strike in the next, and the animal—field mouse
or ground squirrel or rabbit—would be airborne, its cries small
and lost before you knew what happened.

"We have to talk," Nance said.

"Not now." He shifted in his chair, folded his arms. He
smelled like the fields, the earth, his own sweaty labor, smells familiar and pungent. It all made her slightly dizzy; how could she
want him so much, and he be indifferent to her?

"We have to."

"I'm worn out," he said. "The Taylor boy's a good worker,
but the work's just about as much as the two of us could handle."

"I had a long talk with Harvey," she said. "He's willing to
help us out—if he doesn't ever have to deal with you directly."

Burton got up out of the recliner and sat on the window seat
facing her. If it had been morning, he'd have been in shadow and
she wouldn't have been able to make out his features, but at this
hour the waning light behind him made almost no difference.

"Help us out *how?*" he said. "What have you gone and done?"

"He'll buy the Tobler farm."

"And?"

"He'll hold it. We work it and pay him a percentage of the
income. When we can afford it, he'll sell the farm back to us. For
what he paid."

Burton squinted at her. "Why's he doing this?"

"He's doing it for *me.*"

"Why? Did you promise him something?"

"He's doing it for a lot of reasons," Nance said. "For the
blame Arlene put on me for Paul's death. For the way he treated
me when we were married. For things he's said to me since you

and I got married. For taking Peter's side against you and me."
All these reasons, she thought. They were the ones Harvey ought
to have had, though probably he didn't.

"And what else?"

"Nobody promised him anything," she said. What did Burton
think? That she would want anything to do with Harvey Riker
that way? It simply showed how frantic he was, between the lawsuit and the guiltiness, between giving up the land and working it.

"How much?" Burton said.

"Sixty-seven thousand dollars. That's almost four hundred
twenty dollars an acre."

"And buying it back? How long do I have?"

"Five years. Harvey says the law gives us only a year to re-
deem the land, but he won't hold us to it. We can keep on working the land. We can keep most of the profits."

"How much is 'most'?"

"We give him twenty percent."

"Jesus."

Burton stood up and turned to the window. Nance moved to
be just behind him, looking out over his shoulder. The hawk was
gone; so were the endless shadows. She put out her arms and embraced him around the waist, her cheek against his back and the
damp of his shirt, hearing his heartbeat.

"You got all this in writing?" he said.

"Just the land-sale part and the percentage. He didn't offer
anything else in writing."

She went on holding him as hard as she could, and for almost
another minute he allowed her to. Then he took each of her hands,
separated them and pushed them to his sides. He turned to face her.

"I guess we have to do it," he said. "But I don't trust that son
of a bitch."

He put his hands behind her shoulders and kissed her forehead. It was a soft kiss, not repeated, and his hands didn't draw
her body against his. She understood: he was not thinking of
making love to her.

The fifth anniversary of Paul Tobler's death came and went, the weather as much like that night as Nance could have imagined—a thaw after deep cold, the back roads churned into mud by school buses and farm traffic, the prospect remote of the county grading equipment arriving to smooth travel, because what was the point? A week later snow fell, the graders became plows—and winter, the harshest part of it, held no surprises.

From their kitchen window Nance watched the big car pull into the driveway, the back end sliding on a veneer of ice—"fishtailing," Burton would have said. Its headlights were on high beam; on the uneven drive the twin rays pulsed across the grim twilight.

Burton came up behind her, slid his arms around under her breasts. *What a wrong time to arouse me.* He wore a slight whiskey smell, but it was not unpleasant. She was used to it now, a sweetish heaviness that whenever she was close to him was like a drug, an addiction.

"Who do you suppose it is?" she said.

"Don't know."

It was midafternoon, the sky gunmetal gray, the landscape almost its mirror with ice and old snow left over from the storm a few days past. With the daylight as weak as it was, Nance couldn't decide on the car's color; it was dark, it might have been black or deep blue or even green. All she could tell was its size—a Cadillac or Lincoln, she thought. She was certain she hadn't seen it before.

"It's a Lincoln," Burton said. "The big town car—but not a new one."

"Who do we know drives one of those?"

"Nobody," he said.

The car stopped in the yard. The driver's door opened and a man emerged. In one hand was a briefcase; the other hand held his collar closed at the throat. He was halfway to the house before the car's headlights blinked out.

"Sandstrom," Nancy said.

"Where'd he get a fancy machine like that?" Burton said. He let go of her and went to the door, opening it while Sandstrom was still coming up the porch steps.

"Bitter day," Sandstrom said. He brushed past Burton into the kitchen, rubbing his hands. "Your roads out this way are a real challenge."

"Let me take your coat," Nance said.

"Much obliged." He slid out of a plaid mackinaw and let her take it from him. "I can't stay. I just brought some news from Des Moines."

"Good or bad?" Burton said. He eyed Sandstrom warily—as he always did when the lawyer visited. *Write me a check and I'll give you some news: that's Jimmy.*

"Well . . ." Sandstrom looked around the room, set the briefcase on the kitchen table, and settled himself in a chair beside it. "No real surprises. I'd say the news was pretty much neutral."

She saw the disgust on Burton's face.

"What does that mean?" she asked. She was holding the lawyer's coat against her chest, the collar against her chin. The coat radiated cold, even though he'd only walked from the car.

"They turned down the appeal."

Burton looked at Nance. "That's *neutral?*" he said.

Sandstrom sighed the sigh that Nance had learned meant the lawyer was doing his best to be patient with their ignorance. "This is procedural stuff. The State Supreme Court can only rule on whether or not the district court made mistakes in the way they ran the trial, and that's what they did. We argued that the instructions from the judge to the jury were improper. The court said everything was kosher. We argued that protecting one's private property was justified, they cited quite a number of cases that limited the level of protection."

"That sounds to me like we lost," Burton said.

"You'd be amazed—I sure was—how many cases like yours have come up in the courts." Sandstrom opened his case and took out a sheaf of papers. "And not just guns. There's folks who set dynamite to go off if somebody broke in. An actual bomb."

"This was our appeal," Burton said. "It seems like this whole thing is dragging on forever. You told us this would resolve it. End it."

"Think of it as a temporary setback," Sandstrom said.

"Sounds permanent to me."

"We still have recourse," the lawyer said, "if you'll permit."

"Which is?"

"To enjoin execution of judgment. In so many words, we argue that the court can't *enforce* its decision to hit you guys for all that money."

"Can we win?" Nance draped Sandstrom's mackinaw over the ironing board set up in the kitchen corner.

"It's possible." Sandstrom leaned back. "It's a reasonable chance."

"I don't want *possible*," Burton said. "I want *for damned certain.*"

"I can't promise that."

"Then the hell with it." He went to the cupboard, took down the bourbon bottle. Nance understood that he knew he was solving nothing, that he drank only to put a space between himself and a judgment that seemed more and more final. In the mornings, sober, he always said, "I know it's pure weakness. I know the one thing that'll end it is to pay and be done with it."

Never mind that there was no money to pay with; you could not take nothing from nothing. They'd sold two hundred forty acres' worth of two farms, paid more than eighty thousand to Peter Tobler, and still owed fifty thousand plus to the lawyers. The two of them could only go on watching their lives shrink and shrink, closing off one room after another in this house to cut down the cost of staying warm.

We're living in the kitchen and the parlor [she wrote Arlene].
We brought the bed downstairs and moved the sofa and one of the
big chairs out to the shed, so now evry day we go to bed when its
dark under the table and pull the guilts up to our chins and watch
the tv. When we go upstairs to the toilet we bundle up like we
were going to the outhouse just like in my grandpas day and we
dont flush unless its number 2.

"I think we should do it," Nance said. "Do whatever you call
it to stop Peter collecting any more money."

"Enjoin," Sandstrom said.

Burton raised his hand toward her. "Nance—" he said.

"We can't *not*," she said. *We do all our heating with the kitchen*
stove, she'd written, *burning whatevers left of that old barn the wind*
blew down.

She watched Sandstrom. The lawyer was watching Burton.
Burton rubbed his hand up his forehead and over the top of his
head, as if he was smoothing his hair. He couldn't smooth his
forehead, Nance thought.

"All right," he said. "They can't make it any worse for us."

"That's my take on it," Sandstrom said. "We'll argue that
there's no precedent for the kind of punishment the district
court jury dumped on you, and that the punitive damages should
be set aside."

"I pray we win," Nance said. "Just for a change."

"No prayer about it." Sandstrom said. "It's a good sensible
argument."

Burton said nothing. Nance knew what he was thinking:
Another goddamned lawyer's bill. Another goddamned wait for some-
thing to happen.

"How do you like my new car?" Sandstrom said. "New to
me, I mean. It's four years old, but it's absolutely immaculate inside and out."

F rom the Des Moines *Register*—

JUNGLE MENTALITY: AN EDITORIAL

The reactions of people to the Stone case are discouraging. Overwhelmingly our mail is from people who disagree with the Iowa Supreme Court. These people argue that the Stones were in the right to set a spring shotgun which fired at a trespasser, Peter Tobler, maiming him for life. They are angry at the jury which awarded Tobler $130,000 damages and at the Supreme Court for upholding this award in a unanimous ruling.

We are discouraged to find that so many people in this civilized society place property rights above human life. We wonder how many of these people have digested all the facts of the Stone-Tobler case and really understand the principles, which makes us wonder whether we have done a good job of making them clear.

Many of our correspondents seem to think Tobler was a desperate, armed criminal seeking entrance to kill the Stones. The Stones weren't there. Tobler entered the abandoned house to get out of the rain. Worst of all, it was a house his parents used to own, the place where he was born and raised.

We have mail from all over the country from "law and order" types who see the Stone case as one where the courts favored the criminal against the law-abiding citizen. Actually, the courts favored law and order over the jungle. The Stones were the ones who committed the violence.

We cannot believe that these people writing us

think trespassing in a search for shelter is a worse crime than an attempt to kill. If the courts decided it was legal and proper for owners of abandoned buildings to put in lethal booby traps to keep people out, who would be safe?

To keep our faith in mankind, we can only believe these people didn't get all the facts and jumped to hasty conclusions.

Dear Leenie,

Well you probly read about it in the papers or saw it on the tv that we lost our appeal to the Supreme court, it was unanimous which was a surprise to Jimmy S too. He thot hed made a strong argument but told Burton how all the precedents were against us. Burton read the opinion, but I couldnt make sense of it so gave up trying. I dont know what were going to do. Even with Harvey buying the rest of your old place—I told you that, didnt I? Even with that we still owe Peter nearly 50 thousand dollars. Therell be the crop money, Burton says we averaged 137 bushels last year, but that wont cover. Burton is going to go to work for John Deere starting next week, on the midnite shift which means when Im ready for bed hes just leaving and when I get up hes just going to bed. No great loss I guess, because he doesnt much put his hands on me lately—mores the pity. I miss his affection.

I try to think back how we got in all this mess with guns and stuff, and I wonder if its because of children? I think how Harvey and I didnt have children and of course Burton and I dont and wont. I think not having kids makes property seem really important, that's why Harvey was (is) so posessive of land and once upon a time me, and why Burton rigged up the shotgun to protect the house. Property is all theyve got, these men of mine. If wed had children, the children would be important, not unhuman things, houses and land. You and Paul had your kids and that made you more people people, not property people. You were al-

*ways happier than me and I think your kids were a big part of it.
Harvey and I just had each other and you know what familiarty
does!*

    *But that doesnt explain your boy Peter. It amazes me how
you seem to have no control over him. Id of thought a person as
smart as you and as good a friend to me as you have always been,
could have stepped in and spared us the terrible time weve had
which has ruined us. I know he was hurt, and I know it was Burtons fault but it wasn't done on purpose. You knew that. You were
so close to both of us and already to take our side.*

    *As if I didn't have troubles enough, now Ive made my last
visit to the ob/gyn woman. I said to her I was sick and tired of
tests that showed something and nothing at the same time, and I
said to her that yes more and more I get these pains deep down in
my plumbing, sort of like the cramps that come with your period,
but I wasnt about to have surgery. They just want to* explore, *she
said and I said go tell Columbus. I did say that. I know Im getting older, I can live with a little discomfort. The truth is I dont
know why a woman my age needs to keep having the monthlys
anyway. Whats the point?*

    *Leenie, I looked at the kitchen calender this morning and re-
alize it was just 5 years ago this month that Paul got shot.
When I close my eyes I still see the gun in Harveys hand, I still
hear it going off. I know Paul is alive for you, you not remarry-
ing tho I know you could. I know from the beautiful poem you
wrote for him and sent to me. I know because if I lost Burton Id
feel the same and keep him alive in my heart forever. Im not
saying happy anniversary, you mustnt think that, but I am saying I sat right down and said one little prayer for Paul and then
started this letter to you. Sometimes I think what happened with
Peter is God getting even with me and Burton because we were
sinners.*

               Your friend (I hope) in spite of evrything,
                     Nance

*PS—Harveys out of jail. Hes letting the Taylors stay on at
the farm and hes renting a place in town. I dont know his plans, I
hope he decides to move somewhere else.*

*PSS—I heard from Todd Clausson that Harveys thinking
about cutting down the rest of that big cotton wood tree of yours that
got lightening struck. He says hell maybe put in some kind of feedlot there but that's talk to needle Burton.*

It had seemed to Nance that the threat of the feedlot was just
Harvey being Harvey, yet barely a week after she'd mailed the
letter to Arlene, a muddy flatbed truck—SAMSON BROTHERS,
INDEPENDENCE IA, in orange lettering on its doors—pulled into
the Tobler driveway and unloaded two men and a bright yellow
bulldozer. It was Sandstrom who brought the news, stopping by
that evening in his new-to-him Lincoln to pick up another in-
stallment check against the Stones's total debt to him.

"Didn't even bother to put a saw to it," he said. "The tree
was that brittle—what was left of it. The bulldozer man took it
down, roots and all, on his third run at it."

"Arlene will be sick about it," Nance said.

"Then don't tell her," Burton said. "It's nothing to either
one of you at this late date."

"You don't know the half of it," Sandstrom said. "I know
you think you had an agreement with Riker, but he's already
gone back on his end. He's sold the Tobler land, and his own
farm besides, to a packing company from Kansas City. That's
more than three hundred acres all told—"

"Three hundred forty," Burton said. "Christ, they'll fatten
enough cattle and hogs to feed the Chinese army."

"How could he?" Nance said. "We should sue him."

The men were silent.

"Well, we *should*." But she knew why Burton wasn't saying
anything, and why Sandstrom cleared his throat and stood up to
say his good-byes to both of them.

Afterward, remembering what Harvey had said about "business" the last time she'd seen him and asked for the favor, Nance realized she was angry, and hurt, but not shocked. That was how the world was nowadays: it pulled the carpet out from under you. At least now the world would slow down and she could catch her breath; perhaps it wasn't too late for her and Burton to start their lives all over again from scratch. What sort of life might it be?

It was no use now to ask Leenie. Paul was gone, Peter and Sarah were gone, and now, whatever it had meant to her, the cottonwood was gone too. *Harvey started it all,* she could tell Arlene, *and now he's finished it.*

March 10

Dear Nancy,

I can't speak for the men of this world. I can't say why one good man is dead, another good man is ruined, and an evil man has grown wealthy off the land he stole from both of them. I can't say why we two patient women share the penalties of solitude and shame only because our privacies were turned inside out and shown to the world. As the poet says: "Lord, what a way to inherit the earth!" Worst of all, I can't say it was children made the difference, when a child who was raised on love and respect for the rights of others turned on a classmate, and then when he was grown turned on a neighbor. Even though Paul and I had much happiness from ours while they lived at home. You know firsthand how they brought pain as well. No blessings are unmixed, are they?

I used to believe that Paul was a true innocent—that unlike most other men I have met in my life, he was not selfish, not ambitious, but only self-possessed and assumed other men were the same.

Now, these five years after his dying for the sake of keeping peace, I understand that he wasn't so innocent as I thought—that his love of the land he farmed was more than love, but a kind of covetousness the Bible condemns, a particular sort of greed for a particular kind of wealth. He'd been land-rich and wanted to stay

that way. He was no different from Harvey then or Burton now;
he only softened the greed with love—love of family, love of me,
a desire to express his love by giving us the crops we all profited
from. I never met a man so inward in love, so outward in the offering of it.

And Burton too. He was at the center of Paul's murder and
your sin—yes, Nancy, that's what it was—as if you and my husband were satellites around Burton's star and you and Paul were
more 'involved' with each other than you with Burton or Paul with
me. I marvel at that. After the funeral, after the terrible auction and
the farm's sale, while I was driving to South Dakota like a woman
going back to her girlhood, I turned over and over in my mind the
way we were all related—oh, the blue sky of that spring after
weeks of rain, the roadside ditches brimful of bright water, the fields
black and plowed but not yet planted, even in May!—the conspiracy of you and me, Paul's annoyance, Burton's clumsiness, the
idea, now we both know, that it was the mailman spilled the beans
to Jess and Jess who set it all off that evening over cards. I thought
how hard it was to blame Harvey—I mean really blame him, to
be surprised by the violence that exploded out of him that sorry
night. How humiliated he must have felt in front of other men.

But I decided I couldn't blame you either, that if anyone was
going to be blamed it had to be Paul, because he tried to step into
the middle of two sorts of passion—as if he didn't know squat
about either kind himself. Paul wasn't an innocent; he was an
ignoramus.

I worked this all out driving west, driving backward into a former life, and I've lain awake night after night going over it in my
mind until it spills over into my dreams. I say to myself: now I understand it all, now I don't blame anyone, now I forgive everyone
except Paul—because he needn't have taken himself away from
me, he cared more about you and Burton than he did about himself and me. My God, Nance—that's what I said to myself then,
out loud, somewhere just the other side of Sioux City, My God!
Paul didn't know how to focus his love; it just overflowed onto

*everybody, willy-nilly, and I had to stop the car on the shoulder
and turn off the ignition and rest my head against the steering
wheel and I cried and cried until I was cried out and looked
around and realized I didn't even have a hanky to blow my nose
with—I'd packed everything away that well.*

*Well, Nance, you confided in me so I'll return the favor. You
won't believe it, and it happened just the way I'll tell it, but I'll
make it short because I know you think me better than I am and
don't need to be hit over the head with being wrong.*

*My first afternoon in Chappell more than 4 1/2 years ago, after
I'd seen Mother I took a turn out of town to the school where I
was going to teach in the fall. It wasn't quite the hometown place
I remembered from forty-odd years ago, but at least it was in the
same location. It was bigger now; the original school looked like it
was still in use—I could see Easter drawings taped to the windows inside—but there was a big new building next door to it and
the words Chappell Middle School—that's what they call them*
now, Middle Schools—*over the front entrance. It looked like a
small factory, maybe a place where they made electronic stuff for
some bigger corporation, and it didn't have a lot of windows, but I
thought to myself that probably it was comfortable inside with good
fluorescent lighting easy on the children's eyes. I told myself it
wouldn't be so bad, going back to the classroom. God knows I'd
be a lot smarter than I was in those old days just out of ISU!
And maybe a little wiser.*

*Anyway, I drove back into the center of town feeling not so
down, just maybe a little tired from yesterday's driving and emot-
ing, and I was looking for a permanent place to stay. I stopped at
Chappell's only gas station—I decided to ask one of the locals,
and besides, I needed gas—and got out to serve myself at one of
the pumps. This man came out and stopped me.* No self-service
here, *he said.* Full service only. *And he sort of grinned at me
and told me it wouldn't raise the price of the gas and he wouldn't*

charge me anything to check my oil. He made checking my oil sound like doing a pelvic, and I wondered if I should say never mind and skip my questions.

But there was something familiar about the man, and wouldn't you know that after the innuendo—the idea that he was flirting with me—and the gas-pumping, and a little conversational give-and-take, he turned out to be a classmate of mine from high school—a boy named Davey Meyers.

What he did was close up the station and invite me over to his place for dinner. I assumed his wife would do the cooking—that she'd be generous and welcome an old school chum of her husband's, and in fact she might even be another classmate herself—I couldn't recall who Davey'd dated in school, but I knew there was somebody and it wouldn't be a surprise if they'd made it permanent.

But there was no wife. He told me she'd died five years earlier—cancer, of course—and he'd been 'batching' it ever since. Said he'd gotten to be a pretty good cook, simply because he couldn't afford eating out every day and over time got so sick of hamburgers and meatloaf and grilled cheese sandwiches that he'd just naturally had to learn some fancier menus. And in fact he served up a chicken casserole that was as good as you or I could have made, and served a nice Paul Masson white wine with it, and even had ice cream ready for dessert. It was wonderful and we talked a lot and laughed even more about our school days, and we got a little serious about our lives since high school—he'd gone to a community college in Sioux Falls and got an A.A. in auto mechanics, but neither one of his grownup boys had wanted to dirty their hands (he said they were 'far-flung' now, and he laughed about how he must have been the one that flung them)—and then we just sat at the table, staring into our wineglasses and thinking deep thoughts.

I'd told Davey before dinner that I'd checked in at a local motel—there was only the one—but the subject hadn't come up again and I hadn't thought about it, I was enjoying myself so. The two of us cleared the table, and then we did up the dishes—I

washed, he wiped—and then we sat down to finish the second bot-
tle of wine he'd opened. I was drifting—happy, mellow in the way
Paul and I used to get when we were young and the kids were
asleep—and Davey stood up and yawned and said Well I guess
it's bedtime. *I can't even say* one thing led to another. *He*
took my hand, and I stood up and followed him into his bedroom,
and we undressed and got into bed. Simple as that. No words, no
will-you or won't-you. Just kisses and touches and before you knew
it we were making love as if we'd been lovers all our lives. I can't
explain it. It was only wonderful and easy.

I'd never been with any man but Paul, and I'd not really
wanted to be. Yes, I'd missed it the way you miss old pleasures, but
I'd never considered finding a man to take Paul's place. Yet this,
with Davey—I can't explain it. But it showed me a capacity in
myself I hadn't realized I had. You can't condone adultery,
Paul would say, and I couldn't argue with him. But it's clear my
body could have. I'd never have been unfaithful to Paul, but I
could sure be unfaithful to his memory! I ought to be ashamed of
myself—but I'm not. And thinking back to our conspiracy days, I
think it showed me why I was tolerant of your carrying on with
Burton without knowing why.

That was the only time, as if the two of us needed some kind
of push, out of the connections we'd had with the dead into atten-
tions to the living. We'd both given, and taken, all we'd needed of
each other that one night. I buy gas from him; we're friends in a
neighborly sense. It's enough.

So many things have come clear to me over the years since Paul
died. I used to be baffled by Paul in those weeks before that night
in our kitchen—his feelings about the poor bikers, who only wanted
a place to ride, away from the awful traffic the cities generate nowa-
days. I used to say to myself This is not like Paul, *who had al-*
ways been live-and-let-live, who had a kindness that it seemed to
me came from a genuine core of humanity that drew me to him and
made love so strong between us. I couldn't understand what had
changed in him, why the strip of farmland that had been the old rail

right-of-way was so important to him that he would deny his own
nature. I couldn't have put that into words then—*only* now, *think-*
ing and thinking about it. He was not land-greedy by nature; what
could be the matter?

I think now—*I* believe *now*—*it had everything to do with his*
father—*his father's death. When his father died, it stopped Paul's*
life in its tracks. Teaching, marrying me, having a family that would
be the first generation not to farm, not to live or die by sweat and
dirt and weather—*we were going to be the first white-collar Toblers!*
And then Karl died—*he'd never quite got over Betty's, his wife's,*
passing away—*and it changed Paul's life and mine right out of the*
blue. He had to decide whether to carry on the farm, be a farmer in-
stead of a schoolteacher—*he knew he couldn't do both*—*or sell the*
farm, land and all, to some stranger and say goodbye to tradition,
continuity, that wonderful land grant signed by President Franklin
Pierce himself.

Which, in hindsight, is what he should've done. We can both
see, now, how the kind of idealism that makes small farmers stay
on the land is a lost cause. In the end they're all going to be swal-
lowed up by the big agricompanies because that's what this country
is: money and size. Nothing else matters. Instead, Paul chose the
farm, kissed the white-collar good-bye the way a priest might leave
his church. He gave himself heart and soul to that farm—*I can*
swear to it—*and he was good at it until the economics caught up*
with him. He wasn't smart enough to see how the big companies
did it—*how you had to keep getting bigger or you'd go under. He*
was friends with Harvey, but he didn't have Harve's talent for
wheeling and dealing, or Harve's knack for double-dealing. Paul had
too much conscience.

But I was talking about what changed in him. It wasn't only
the economics and his ignorant innocence. It was his father. What's
amazing to me, and I'll never completely understand it, is how his
anger at his father (Why did the old man have to die, and
why did he have to do it while you and I were just starting
out? *he'd said once) could turn into a dedication to the land, and*

how that dedication when it was pushed turned into something very much like greed and selfishness—a land hunger, you might call it. I know you're not much of a reader, but Paul got to be like the man in an old story by Tolstoi— "How Much Land Does a Man Need?" And the answer is, there is no answer. God knows we couldn't afford to buy more land, but if we could get even that narrow right-of-way for nothing. . . . That's how he must have had it worked out. That's why he was so stubborn against the bike trail, so crazy for land he was willing to be a criminal. And then, of course, after he realized what he'd done, then he was the old Paul, taking his punishment, serving his time, as a matter of principle. God forgive him. God forgive me for not understanding what had happened in his head, his heart. I stood by him, but it was blind of me—my husband right or wrong. I could have done better for him.

Don't ask me even now what it is that turns rage against a man's father into a defense of what the father held dear. Some psychiatrist could tell me, I'm sure, but I'm not asking one of them.

This is a pent-up letter, I know. What I'm saying is that for years and years, especially after the children left home for good, I couldn't imagine a different life—and now I have it. I don't have a man, and I don't own property, and I don't carry the burdens of motherhood. What I have is a self-sufficiency, and my teaching, which keeps the self-sufficiency from turning into complacency. I mean I can't let myself be smug or I would lose my contact with the boys and girls in my classrooms. God knows they're selfish and cruel enough without my behaving as if it's okay for them to be that way.

Nance, don't be beaten. It's horrible to be stolen from, to have your lives pushed and pinched into a smaller and smaller space as if the world is shrinking around you, but it doesn't have to beat you, or tear you apart from Burton. This is all I'm saying. I'm not trying to offer my own coming to terms as a model for you to follow, or to make you envy me, or anything like that. I'm only saying that you mustn't believe that the way things are for you and Burton today is the way they will be for you tomorrow. Burton can rebound, and he will, even if he has to start out by taking that job in the tractor works.

Maybe it's true that what Peter set in motion by trying to go home in the perverse way he did was God's way of punishing you for loving outside the boundaries, or maybe it really started longer ago in the kitchen of the same house—but how can I understand God's timing when I have never been able to understand how capricious men apply Justice to their own actions. You have to believe— please, Nance—that even if the law has been unjust to you, even if somehow I've been unjust to you, that doesn't mean life is unjust. In the end, Peter came here to see me for one day only, and then he was gone without giving me an inkling of his plans. Shame? I hope so, for it would mean that somewhere deep down he learned some-thing from us after all.

I'm sorry for the failure of your appeal, and sorrier still for meanness Harvey's done to you on top of everything else. It's the worst kind of revenge. I won't burden you with a bunch of stupid phrases like Never trust a man, *or* The first thing you do when you fall off a horse is get back on. *I don't even talk that way to the kids in my classes. But I do look at them hard, and wonder what the world will bring them. I tell them,* In a dozen more years we reach the millennium, a special, rare moment in the history of our world. *I leave it at that, let them ponder it. What it will mean for them, I can't guess. What it will mean for me, it doesn't matter. What it will mean for you and Burton—that's something you two have to talk about together. If there's any one thing you should learn from me, it's that you don't dare let the violence that comes from a gun destroy the whole rest of your life.*

My love from the heart,
Arlene

I'm sorry about the old cottonwood. Paul would have said Let it go; as firewood at least it's useful. *But I loved it all the time I lived with Paul, and the Lord knows how many hours I spent looking at that tree like it held the secret of our lives!*

The night the letter came, Nance read it over and over, as if she were trying to make a prayer out of Leenie's advice—as if repetition might make it true. Why had she raised the question of children? Not only because of Peter, but because one night in the middle of last summer, when Burton had come in late from the fields and sat exhausted at the head of the bed with a glass of Jim Beam sweating in his hand, she'd asked him what was the matter, that he was looking so distant. "I was thinking how we never had children, you and me." That was what he'd said. "I was thinking how different we'd have been." "Do you regret not having them?" Nance had said. "I don't know," he'd said. Then he took a long swallow of his whiskey and looked into the bottom of the nearly empty glass. "Maybe I did have them," he said, "and just don't know it."

It was only the third time—and it was the last time—that she'd been made to think about the two years he'd spent in the war, and about the women he might have made love to. Just for a short while she'd felt sorry for herself and for not knowing exactly what happened in Vietnam twenty years ago. But then she looked at it from Burton's point of view, and felt terribly sorry for *him*.

This night, Burton had already gone to work in Waterloo when the bright light of the moon on the snowfields woke her up. For a while she lay quiet, thinking she might doze off if she didn't face toward the window. Finally she gave in and got up to sit on the window seat, looking out across the white glow of land like the redtail watching for living shadows at day's end—except the moon was high up and all the shadows were short ones. The leftover ruins of the collapsed barn were like children's pick-up sticks, thin and black, edged in icy white. *It could be the picture of our lives,* she thought. *What we used to be, what we are now, what we will be when the last woodstove fire burns itself out and the last bidder drives out of our farmyard. It's like Arlene's cottonwood, that waited and waited for its appointed time.*

Then she went to sit at the kitchen table, to wish for Burton to finish his shift at the tractor works, to come straight home, to lie with her forever no matter where they might have to make their bed.